C000103345

Seduced
BY YOU

K

Seduced BY YOU

Fake dating isn't supposed to be this hot.

When my ex-fiancé has the gall to invite me to his wedding, my gut reaction is "Hell, no."

Until my best friend, Kadon Kingcaid, proposes another idea; he'll accompany me as my richer, better-looking boyfriend.

Crazy, right?

I'm a former catwalk model, not an actress.
Still, it's three days. I can pretend I'm in love for a weekend if it means exacting the revenge I'm owed.

It's all going so well. Then Kadon kisses me right in front of my ex.

Suddenly, it doesn't feel so fake anymore.
But whatever has ignited between us isn't real.

We're not playing for keeps...Or are we?

A note from Tracie

Dear Reader,

I wrote this book during a really difficult time in my life, and there were moments when I thought I wasn't going to be able to finish it. When I write, I immerse myself in the world, but when there's chaos in my personal life, the voices stop talking and the words don't come. And that's what happened with Seduced By You.

But Kadon and Leesa pushed through the fog and wouldn't let go until I'd written their story. And you know what? This is my longest book to date. It's also one that I will look back on and think, see, you're resilient. You can push through the dark times and produce something pretty dang wonderful.

I hope beyond hope that you agree with me.

A note from Tracie

I also had help along the way in the form of my amazing author friend, Lasairiona McMaster, who listened, cajoled, and coaxed me and, sometimes, even gave me a much needed dose of tough love. I'm really not sure what I would have done without her unlimited friendship. I do know that if she hadn't read an early copy of Seduced and waxed lyrical about my damaged surfer-loving billionaire, this book probably wouldn't have seen the light of day. So if you love Kadon and Leesa as much as she does, you know who to thank!

Enjoy reading Seduced By You. I'd love to hear what you thought once you've finished reading. Why not join my Facebook reader group Tracie's Racy Aces, and take part in the discussion over there.

In the meantime, turn the page and dive in to the fifth installment of the Kingcaid Billionaires. Enjoy every page.

Happy reading.

Love,
Tracie

Chapter 1

Leesa

**When the apocalypse comes,
cats will rule the world.**

FIFTEEN MINUTES HAD PASSED SINCE I'D TOSSED THE stupid pink wedding invitation with its scalloped edges and handwritten calligraphy onto the coffee table. Bewildered and angry—like a snorting-bull-ready-to-gore-the-matador angry—I paced, wearing out a strip of my living room carpet.

How dare he? *How dare he!* The sheer arrogance of the man. What on earth had possessed my former fiancé to send to me, of all people, an invitation to his wedding? Was Benedict so narcissistic that he thought, for a single second, I'd *want* to attend? Or was he just rubbing my nose in it, squeezing the last drops of humiliation out of me? Knowing him, both things were probably true.

Although, why he'd left it so late to invite me was something of a mystery. I bet there'd been a cancellation and his bride's stinking-rich parents didn't want any spare seats ruining the aesthetics for *Hello!* magazine. And as they'd invited half of England, suitable replacements must have been in short supply. Except I was the furthest from a *suitable replacement* as you could get. No one invited their ex-fiancée to their wedding. No one except *my* ex-fiancé, it seemed.

As if I'd give him the satisfaction of attending his shitty wedding to his shitty fiancée, someone I'd once thought of as a friend, albeit not a close one. They could stick their invitation to the grandly named Grange Manor, owned by Benedict's soon-to-be father-in-law, up their arse. Twat.

In spite of the rage spreading like a wildfire through my bloodstream, I chuckled. My English mother had taught my French father that word when they'd first met, and he loved it.

My smile fell. I hadn't spoken to my parents in nine months. My mother's outrage when I'd informed her I'd decided to quit modeling for good, at twenty-six, still stung. The life of a catwalk model was short enough without wrecking one's own career, Maman had said. We'd exchanged bitter words, and I hadn't seen either of them since. I refused to make the first move. They owed me the apology, not the other way around.

Screw Benedict. Screw my parents. Screw the shallow world of modeling, where girls' biggest concerns were that they'd eaten two lettuce leaves for lunch instead of one. I had a new life now, thanks to Kadon Kingcaid. I'd met him shortly after Benedict had broken off our engagement. He'd given me a job and a chance to show the world I wasn't the airhead the media made me out to be, or Benedict's ex-fiancée, whom he'd publicly dumped. I was me. Annaleesa Sabine Alarie, half French, half English, all fucking woman.

I read the card once more, but instead of throwing it into the trash, I slipped it inside my purse. I should burn it, but with my luck, I'd set fire to the house. Perhaps I wanted to hold on to my anger for a little while longer. It was a heck of a lot better than hurting. That sucker of an emotion weakened me. Rage and indignation fueled me.

Leaving Dash, my once-stray cat whom I'd adopted six months ago and who now ruled my life soaking up the sun, I unlocked the cat flap, filled his water bowl, and gave his ears a final scratch. "Be good, you little shit. No bringing friends over while I'm gone."

He answered by licking his paws, his startling blue-gray eyes narrowing as if to say, "I'll do whatever I want, and there isn't a thing you can do about it." The worst thing was I couldn't argue with his logic.

Kingcaid Beach Club Saint Tropez, where I worked as the VIP Operations Manager, was located right on the seafront. It took up a considerable amount of real estate. If I hazarded a guess as to the value of the land alone, I'd put it in the high tens of millions. Possibly even the hundreds of millions. Everyone who was anyone came here from the moment the club opened in March to the day it closed for the winter on October 31.

Hence the requirement for someone to look after our

3

most important guests. My role was to ensure that those guests had their every wish catered to. Sometimes, it was a pain in the rear, but most of the time, I enjoyed my job. It wasn't easy. Because of the shorter season down here in the South of France, we worked seven days a week, with only an occasional day off here and there. As this was my first season, I was exhausted. Even my bones hurt. I couldn't wait for the next four weeks to pass. I planned to head off somewhere warm, work out a plan for my long-term goals, and relax.

I did *not* plan to attend McJerky's stupid November wedding in the cold and damp English countryside. Not a chance.

The guard stopped me and checked my credentials, then lifted the barrier and let me through. The infamy of some of our guests meant that security was, by necessity, tight. We couldn't allow a single unapproved visitor inside the beach club. Our clientele paid enormous sums of money each year for a membership to Kingcaid's worldwide beach club resorts. It would only take one so-called fan to approach a star in their executive bungalow, and the hard-won reputation of Kadon's business would disappear faster than Dash chasing a mouse.

Kadon prided himself on ensuring privacy and delivering top-class service, and as a member of his senior management team, I'd make damned sure I upheld the values of this organization.

I maneuvered my car into my allotted space and got out. A cool breeze blew strands of hair across my face. I tucked them behind my ears and fastened my jacket. The temperatures would reach the low seventies today, but I doubted most customers would arrive much before midday. In the height of summer, they'd often turn up by nine in the morning and leave long after the sun had set, but this close to the end of the season always saw a drop-off. At least, that was what Kadon had told me.

Kadon's gunmetal gray Aston Martin sat in his reserved space. It didn't surprise that me he was here already. He'd be champing at the bit, going through the figures from the last few days and making sure everything was in order. Kadon wasn't a descendant of the ridiculously rich Kingcaid family for nothing. Very little got past him. But outside of work, Kadon was as far removed from a billionaire as you could imagine. Shoulder-length, messy, blond-streaked hair, rarely dressed in anything other than casual clothing, fun-loving, and considerate of others. He was much more suited to hanging with the surfers who frequented Galiote Beach than in a shirt and tie and sitting around a boardroom table. Little wonder his father had put him in charge of this arm of the business.

I headed straight for Kadon's office. One rap on the door, and I pushed it open. I found him sitting behind his desk—but it wasn't the Kadon who'd left here a few days earlier.

My jaw dropped, and I burst out laughing. "What the hell happened to you?"

Chapter 2

Kadon

A wig? Why the hell didn't I think of that?

"DON'T SAY ANOTHER FUCKING WORD." I RAISED MY hand and glowered. Today wasn't the day to mess with me. Not that it changed Lee's reaction. She was the very last person to fear me, as evidenced by her laughter bouncing off the walls.

"Holy shit. My poor Samson." Flopping into the visitors chair opposite my desk, she flicked her lavender hair over her shoulder, propped her elbows on the polished oak, and fluttered her eyelashes. "Have you lost all your strength along with your luscious locks?"

I poked my tongue into my cheek and inhaled a slow breath. "I'm not kidding, Lee. It isn't fucking funny." I loved my long hair. It was me. I'd worn it long for years, never imagining a time when I'd cut it.

Until my mother, the indomitable Sandrine Kingcaid, had stepped in, and it was "Bye-bye, beautiful hair; hello, stupid short back and sides." And all for my brother's wedding. Nolen wouldn't have given two shits how long I wore my hair at his wedding, or anywhere else for that matter, but Mom... she'd insisted, and out came the scissors. My brothers and I had learned a long time ago not to argue with our mother. There was only ever one winner.

Spoiler alert: it wasn't any of us.

At least she'd let me keep it longer on top. Plus, it'd grow back. Eventually. Didn't stop me from being pissed, though. Add an unscheduled layover in New York, plus a nine-hour time difference, and *cranky* didn't describe how I felt this morning.

"What happened?" Lee couldn't stop her lips from twitching, not even when my scowl darkened.

"My mother. That's what happened. Something about not letting me ruin the wedding photos." I grunted.

"I kinda like it." She narrowed her platinum-gray eyes, scrutinizing me much as one would a prize bull at auction. "It suits you."

Her comments pulled a grin from me. If Lee liked it short, I might keep it this way for longer. Maybe forever. I spent most of my waking hours trying to figure out how I could make Lee look at me as anything more than a friend. I was still waiting. It was all that English prick's fault. His cheating ass had made her swear off men for the foreseeable future. She wouldn't think that way forever—I hoped —and when she decided she was ready to date again, yours truly would make damn sure I was right there, in the prime position to take advantage.

Not that I deserved her. I wasn't sure I deserved anyone after what I'd done, but especially Lee. She was *good*. Inside-out category of good. She'd spent years at the pinnacle of modeling, with sycophants flapping around her and telling her how perfect and marvelous she was. Yet despite that, she'd emerged with a humble approach to life that I admired the hell out of.

Wasn't she entitled to someone better than me? Someone who didn't carry around a ship-sized container filled with regrets and guilt and horror at what I was capable of. Only when breached did we discover our limits. If it weren't for my father and his power...

Fingers of depression descended, choking me, but before they could get too firm a hold, my therapist's suggestion to think of something nice popped into my mind. I chose my brother's wedding, remembering how happy he'd been as he'd made his vows, and after a few seconds, the dark thoughts retreated to the corners of my mind. They never truly went away. They never would. Nine fucking years, and even now I sometimes woke in the middle of the night covered in sweat and unable to breathe.

"Really?" I said. "You like it?"

"No." She laughed again. "I think we should get you a wig until yours grows back."

A *wig*. Why hadn't I thought of that? I should've told my mother I'd wear a fucking wig.

"Great. You almost had me there."

"Aw, poor baby." She rose from her chair and walked behind me, wrapping her arms around my shoulders. I bit back a groan and closed my eyes, pretending for a few precious seconds that this was real. Lee's arms around me was something I fantasized about far too often—along with many other fantasies, much dirtier than a simple hug.

And fantasyland was where they'd remain. Lee had friend-zoned me, and from the looks of things, I'd have to come to terms with that.

Even last month, when I'd mentioned to Lee that I had a date with an actress who'd pursued me for weeks, she'd patted me on the back and told me to have a great time.

I'd had a crap time, although I must have been a better actor than my date because she'd lost her shit when I'd declined her not-so-subtle hints for a hookup.

Nine months ago, I'd had more dates lined up than days in the week, my little black book bursting with the phone numbers of the hottest women to pass through Saint Tropez. Then I'd met Lee, and that was that.

The heart knew what it wanted—and mine had picked her.

Hers... had picked a douchewaffle named Benedict who'd crushed her heart in his meaty fist until there wasn't anything left.

I hated that bastard. I hoped his new wife cheated on him and then gave him crabs. Or syphilis. Or crabs and syphilis. I hoped his balls turned black and his dick fell off.

Vengeful? Me? Nah.

Lee released me and returned to her chair. She sat back down and reached across my desk, stealing my cup of French roast from our favorite coffee shop. "How was the wedding? Apart from the shorn locks, that is."

Her lips twitched. I scratched my temple with my middle finger. She laughed, holding up her palms.

"Okay, that's the last joke. I promise."

"It'd better be," I groused. "The wedding was great. Never seen two happier people. Shame it took them ten fucking years to get their act together."

She hitched a shoulder. "Sometimes it takes a little while for people to realize what's right in front of them."

Jesus. Tell me about it.

"Was great to spend time with the fam, too. It's been a minute."

Lee wrinkled her nose. "That American phrase confuses me. I mean, a minute isn't a very long time. Why don't you say 'while'? It's been a while. Or it's been a few months? Those make far more sense. Why 'a minute'?"

"I've no freaking idea. I've always said it. You say weird things sometimes, too."

"Oh yeah? Like what?"

I rubbed my chin, contemplating her question. *Dammit.* "Well... I can't come up with any right this second, but—"

"Aha! Gotcha."

"No. I'll think of something."

She pretended to file her nails. "I'll be right here, on the edge of my seat, waiting."

Lee's sarcasm was one of the first things I'd fallen in love with. She definitely had more English blood in her than French. Attending school in England had probably helped. Her French accent was so slight that I had to strain to pick it up.

I chuckled. "How have things been here?"

"Ah, the old 'let's change the subject' switcheroo. Everything's been fine. No drama. It's almost like you're not needed."

"You'd miss me if I weren't around."

"Yeah, like a boil on the bum."

"Lies."

She downed the remains of my coffee and aimed the cup at the trash. Of course, it went in. "Score! I did miss you." Her lips stretched into a grin, and her eyes twinkled —both signs that she hadn't finished.

I waited, one eyebrow arched in anticipation.

"I've had to fetch my own coffee."

"And there it is." I threw my hands in the air. "You're so predictable."

"It's your belief in my predictability that will ultimately be your downfall. I do have a funny story to tell you about the temp receptionist, though, if you're interested."

"Brigitte not back yet?"

Brigitte was my full-time receptionist. She'd called in sick the day before I was due to fly to Vegas for Nolen's wedding. I hadn't met the temp. Lee had taken care of the arrangements, even though it technically wasn't her job. She might have the title of VIP Operations Manager, but she took care of far more than our VIPs.

If only she'd take care of me.

"No. I spoke to her on Thursday. She sounded awful."

"I'll send some flowers and a gift card for a spa day or something."

"Already done."

"Lifesaver." I motioned with my hand. "So, the temp?"

"Her name's Claudine, and she's super sweet, but a little... green. Anyway, yesterday I was going through the upcoming bookings for next weekend, and I saw one that made me laugh out loud. She'd typed 'Vee Eye Pee' instead of 'VIP' against a booking for Sebastian Devereaux for Friday through Monday."

Sebastian was a senior board member of ROGUES, a company my family did a fair amount of business with, and an all-around great guy. If he was stopping by, I might drop him a line and suggest a round of golf.

"She didn't? God bless her."

Lee made a cross on her chest. "I swear it's the truth. She's magnificent with the guests, though. They adore her. She's delightful and caring and has this lovely way about her."

"That's the main thing. And who am I to judge? It sounds like something I'd do." I was dyslexic, something I'd worked hard to overcome. These days, I coped pretty damn well, but understanding the written word wouldn't ever come naturally to me.

"She's worth considering for a role for next season."

"I'll keep her in mind. Four weeks to go. How are you holding up?" I paid my full-time employees for twelve months, although the club only opened for eight because of the inclement weather in the South of France in the winter months. At this stage of the season, everyone was running on fumes. Given that this was Lee's first year, I expected her to feel more exhausted than my longer-serving employees.

"Not gonna lie, I'm tired. It's been a long year. But I'm used to being tired. Modeling looks glamorous from the outside but is damned hard work on the inside."

"Do you miss it? Modeling?" It was the first time she'd mentioned her former career since she'd taken the job with me, almost as if she'd completely washed her hands of it. If only I could leave my past behind so easily.

"No. I thought I would. It's all I've known since I was six years old, but I've seen a different side to life these past nine months since Benedict dumped me, and I like it. I guess it's proved to me I can do other things, that I'm not just..." She drew a circle around her face. "This."

"You know you're more than your looks, Lee." The press liked to downplay beautiful women, make them out to be nothing more than airheads. Funny how they didn't treat male models in the same way. Only the women. Misogynistic assholes.

She sighed. "Sometimes it's hard to remember that."

"I'll have my tattoo artist ink your arm with it if you like?" I was only half joking.

She shuddered. "Needles? No, thanks."

"Noted. So, what are you planning to do with your time off?" I kept the yearning out of my voice. No idea how. I couldn't bear to contemplate the four months stretching ahead of me when I wouldn't see her every day. While she got time off, I didn't. Although I based myself in Saint Tropez, I had fifteen other beach clubs around the world that came under my wing of the business, and we opened at least one new one a year, which always required additional attention. Some, like our property in Dubai, were four times as big as Saint Tropez, with four times the problems. While Saint Tropez was closed, I'd spend a large part of the winter visiting those other locations. I'd installed highly capable managers at each one, but that didn't mean I could abandon my responsibilities. The ultimate buck stopped with me.

Fuck knows, Dad has told me often enough.

"I'll tell you what I'm *not* doing with it." She reached into her purse and pitched a card onto my desk. I drew it toward me.

Sir Darren Grange and Lady. Rosalind Grange
request the pleasure of the company of
Miss Annaleesa Alarie & Guest
At the wedding of their beloved daughter, Fenella
To Benedict Oberon
At Grange Manor, Berkshire
From Thursday, November 5th to Saturday, November 7th
Accommodation provided
RSVP

I read it twice, mainly because I couldn't believe my fucking eyes. Benedict Oberon was a class A prick, but he'd outdone his douchery this time.

"Is he insane? And what's with the three-day extravaganza?"

Lee tapped pink-tipped fingernails against her thigh. "They're toffs. They'll want the maximum press exposure. And to answer your question about insanity, yeah, I like to think he is. In my darker moments, I picture him locked up in a padded cell with only his own ego for company, surrounded by a gallery of wronged women pelting him with rotten fruit and roadkill. Or paraded naked down the streets where a deafening crowd shouts, 'Shame! Shame!' Kinda like that scene with Cersei from *Game of Thrones*."

I chuckled. "It's good to have goals."

"All I have to do is figure out what mine are." She

sighed. "I'm working on it."

A chill surged through me. Lee had made it clear when she'd accepted the job at my beach club that it was only temporary, but the longer she'd stayed, the more I'd hoped she might decide this was her calling and make it permanent.

"You'll figure it out. And until you do, this job is yours."

"You're the best friend a girl could wish for, Kadon."

Oof. Just what I've always wanted.

"Stop. You're making me blush." I tapped my finger against the card, an idea developing in my mind, one that was more insane than Benedict inviting his ex to his wedding after the way he'd ended it, but it would give me a chance to get close to Lee. As close as I deserved.

Would it make me a bastard? Probably. But I'd lived through rock bottom. What else did I have to lose?

"Want to know what I think you should do about this?"

"Burn it?"

"I think you should go."

Her eyebrows flew up her head. "Then *you're* the insane one. Why the hell would I do that? So Benedict can humiliate me some more?"

"Hear me out. What's the best way to get back at an ex, and one who admitted he only dumped you for this new chick because her daddy could do more for his career than you could?"

Jesus, saying it out loud served as further evidence of how much of a fucking dick Benedict Oberon was.

She made a dismissive gesture with her hand. "Enlighten me, oh wise one."

"You turn up to his wedding with a new flame. One who's richer, more successful, and better looking than him. One who will treat you like a queen and show him what he gave up in the name of ambition."

She rubbed her furrowed forehead. "And, pray tell, where do I find this godlike creature?"

I'm going to hell.

I pointed at myself.

Lee laughed. "You're not serious."

I tried not to let her reaction slice my already damaged heart into a million pieces. "Deadly. We know each other well enough to pull this off, and imagine the fun we'd have."

"You're nuts."

"Think about it."

She got to her feet, shaking her head. "Mad, mad American."

"Promise me you'll think about it."

Suddenly, persuading Lee to be my fake girlfriend overtook every rational thought inside my brain. It was a ridiculous, stupid idea, but that wouldn't stop me. Pretending Lee was mine, even for a short time, might be the closest I ever got to living out my fantasies. And who knew? Faking it might lead to us making it.

I didn't deserve her, but that wouldn't stop me from giving it all I had to win her heart.

She gave me a quizzical look, followed by another shake of her head. "Nothing to think about. I'm not going. End of story."

Pivoting, she left my office with a cheery wave over her shoulder, leaving hope scattered like confetti behind her.

Chapter 3

Leesa

Ohh, buddy.
You messed with the wrong chick.

"Mr. and Mrs. Devereaux. Welcome to Kingcaid Saint Tropez." I handed our VIPs (or Vee Eye Pees, according to Claudine, which cracked me up every time I thought about it) glasses of crisp champagne. "I'm Leesa Alarie, the operations manager. We're so pleased to have you." I beckoned to our bellhop, who scurried over to take their bags. "Please follow me. Your bungalow is ready for you."

Kadon's beach club had various levels of membership. The lower levels entitled guests to use the main pool, the day beds, two of the restaurants, and direct access to the private beach. They could pay an extra six hundred euros for a cabana, which included a ceiling fan, a refrigerator stocked with a variety of soft drinks, a phone, and a fifty-inch TV. From there, levels of service and comfort increased. Those who paid an extortionate membership fee received access to a private bungalow, boasting a sitting area, a bedroom and a fully equipped bathroom, complimentary spa treatments, and a butler who attended to their every whim.

"Great to be back. And it's Sebastian and Trinity. We're not ones for standing on ceremony." He scanned the immediate vicinity. "Is Kadon around?"

This was the first time I'd met Sebastian Devereaux. According to Kadon, he'd normally spend two or three weeks of the season at the club, but this was his first visit since I'd started working here. Kadon had said he was a down-to-earth guy. Looked like he was right.

"He's on his way. I warn you, he's mentioned golf once or twice."

Sebastian chuckled. "Yeah, he's sent a couple of texts about it, too."

He put his arm around his wife and looked at her with adoration. I'd often wished Benedict would look at me like that. He never had. He'd put it down to his staid English upbringing. Said he struggled to show emotion, but that didn't mean he didn't feel it. Back then, I'd believed him. Stupid me.

"Too bad for Kadon that my wife trumps him every time."

"You can play if you want to," Trinity said. "I'm sure I can amuse myself."

"Nope. I've barely had time to breathe these last few months. You're my priority."

I almost swooned. *Where do I find one of these men?*

"Seb." Kadon strode over, hand outstretched. "Great to see you. It's been a minute."

I stifled a giggle. Kadon caught my eye and narrowed his. I beamed at him.

"Sorry I missed you at Nolen's wedding last weekend," he said to Sebastian.

"Yeah, I tried to shift things around, but it wasn't possible. Ryker said it was a terrific day."

"It was. I hope Leesa has been taking care of you."

Funny how he called me Lee when it was only the two of us, but Leesa in a professional capacity. Not that the why of it mattered. I loved the fact that Kadon was the only person to call me Lee. It solidified our special relationship. I'd never had girlfriends, not really. The modeling world was a competitive one, and it always raised suspicion if someone tried to be your friend. Usually, they had a hidden agenda. I'd gone into modeling at such a young age that I hadn't even made school friends. A tutor who'd traveled with me had provided most of my schooling.

"She has." Sebastian threw me a wink. "She's even tipped me off that you're still rambling on about golf."

Kadon faked a shocked expression, his hand clutching his chest as if in the throes of heart failure. "You traitor. And here I was thinking you had my back."

I tapped a finger against my bottom lip. "Hmm, aren't you the one who drums into us that our guests are our top priority?" I wouldn't normally jest in front of our VIPs, but Kadon had made it clear that Sebastian was a friend of his and an all-round great guy. It gave me the confidence to be myself. "I'm only doing your bidding, dearest boss, and making sure I arm Sebastian with a rebuttal. He's here to spend time with his lovely wife, not play the most pointless game in the world with you."

Both Sebastian and Kadon sucked in a sharp breath. Trinity beamed.

"Finally!" she expelled. "Someone who thinks the same as I do. It *is* a pointless game. A perfectly pleasant walk ruined; that's what they say about golf. And it's true."

"You're lucky I love you despite your hatred of my beloved hobby." Sebastian pressed a kiss to his wife's temple.

"You're lucky I love *you*, despite your *love* of your pointless hobby."

Ohhh. I liked Trinity. I liked her a lot.

"So that's a no to a game of golf, then?" Kadon asked.

"Another time, buddy. If I can find a space in my calendar, I'll swing over to Dubai this winter. Drop me a line when you're planning to be there."

"Sounds like a solid compromise."

"Shall I show you to your bungalow before Kadon tries another tactic to get his own way?"

Sebastian sniggered. Trinity's beam grew.

"As if I would."

"We both know that's a lie."

This time, Sebastian didn't contain his laughter. "You're magnificent, Leesa. You're what Kadon needs to hold him to account. Be careful someone doesn't poach her, buddy."

"You're right. She is magnificent, and I'd hate to lose her. But I'd never hold her back if she chooses to leave."

"Oh, stop with the praise. I'm almost blushing."

I settled Sebastian and Trinity at their bungalow, made sure their butler had noted down their food and drink preferences, and arranged for the masseuse to stop by after lunch. I left them my phone number in case they needed anything and promised to swing by during the day, then returned to the reception area to greet my next set of guests. The club had seven bungalows that housed the most important VIPs, and all of them came under my care. Despite the lateness in the season, they were full this weekend, which would keep me on my toes right through Sunday night.

By twelve o'clock, all my guests were in their bungalows, and so far, I hadn't had to deal with a single drama. Long may it continue, although I doubted much time would pass before my phone rang. I grabbed a coffee and was on my way to the staff lounge when a news item on the TV behind the main bar caught my eye. I stopped dead in my tracks.

"Dom, can you turn that up?" I jerked my chin at the bartender.

"Sure." He picked up the remote control and increased the volume.

Sliding onto a bar stool, I cupped my hands around my coffee mug and stared at the TV screen with growing horror. Benedict and his soon-to-be wife, Fenella, were standing outside *our* favorite Japanese restaurant in Kensington, talking to a journalist about their upcoming wedding. I couldn't turn away, transfixed to the screen.

And then I heard my name.

What the ever-loving fuck?

My jaw slackened until I was sure I'd never clamp it shut again. I couldn't believe my ears. The journalist posed a question about regrets. Did Benedict regret our breakup and how he handled it?

"Of course." Benedict's smarmy grin drew wide. "I'm not proud of breaking up with Annaleesa so soon before our wedding day. And she was so *broken,* you know. She cried and cried and begged me not to leave her." He painted this pretend-to-give-a-shit expression on his face. "It was rather pathetic actually."

Pathetic? I clasped my mug hard enough to shatter it. Oh, I'd kill him. If I ever got my hands on that bastard, I'd—

"We've invited her to our wedding." His chest puffed up as if he'd won the fucking peace prize. "You know, to say no hard feelings. I doubt she'll come, but we're generous people, and Annaleesa once meant a lot to me." He gazed down at Fenella. "But when you find the one, you know." His lips pulled back from his perfect toothy smile.

I swayed in the sudden grip of rage and grabbed the edge of the bar. I took several deep breaths. *I'll show him broken. A broken fucking nose.*

"Won't it be strange," the reporter continued, his question aimed at Fenella. "To have your fiancé's ex at your wedding?"

"Not at all. Leesa and I were once very close."

I snorted. Close, my arse.

"But, as my beloved said," she continued, blinking up

at Benedict, enthralled, "we don't expect her to accept the invitation. I mean, it'd look a little sad, don't you think? A woman alone at her ex's wedding."

My breakfast almost came back up.

The reporter posed another question, but the blood rushing through my ears drowned out the response.

I seethed. How dare he? That fucking prick. If justice existed in the world, there'd be a live-streamed video of rats gnawing off his balls. Hell, I'd even pay for the production costs. Then again, wrongdoers rarely got their come-uppance.

Broken. Begging. Pathetic. A woman alone.

Twat.

Both of them were twats.

Except... I drummed my fingers on the bar. This time, they'd messed with the wrong chick. Benedict might have ended our relationship, but I'd have the last laugh.

I grabbed my coffee and made my way to Kadon's office. He wasn't there. I slid my phone from my pocket and shot him a text to meet me in his office. He arrived shortly afterward.

"I'll do it," I blurted.

He gazed at me quizzically, one eyebrow lifted in an expression reminiscent of a baddie in a cheesy eighties movie.

"Do what?"

"I'll go to the wedding. I'll be your fake date. I mean"— I pointed at his head—"you already have an appropriate haircut. Why waste it?"

Both eyebrows crept up his forehead. "What's changed? Last week, you were determined not to go."

Tracie Delaney

"Benedict fucking Oberon is what's changed."

Kadon scratched his cheek. "Are you coming down with something? Weird-itis?"

I made a face at him. "Funny. No, I just saw him on TV giving an interview." I briefed Kadon on what I'd heard. "Screw him. He invited me, never expecting I'd turn up. So I'll turn up all right. And with a date, too."

Kadon's eyes brightened. "Not *just* a date. Your long-term boyfriend. We've been going out for, what, six months? I think six months sounds good. It's not right after he dumped you, but it's close enough for him to feel aggrieved. I mean, there he was, breaking your heart and all, then three months later, you're like, 'Cheers, jackass. I found someone better.' It's perfect."

Excitement curled in my gut. "It *is* better. And he deserves this. I've always hated the fact that I crumbled right in front of him when he broke things off. Looking back, I realize now that my response gave him the upper hand. He knows he broke my heart. But this way, he'll have to question that belief. Brokenhearted ex-fiancées do not hook up with someone new a few short months later."

"Exactly." Kadon replaced his evil eyebrow with an evil grin. "This will be epic."

My excitement ebbed. "God, but will it? What if he sees right through the charade, and that gives him even more power, more satisfaction? 'Poor Annaleesa,'" I mimicked. "'Had to hire a fake boyfriend to save face.'"

It'd be out-of-this-world fantastic to turn up to Benedict's wedding with someone far smarter, far richer, and yep, far better looking, but if Benedict guessed our relationship wasn't real, he'd wring the crap out of my discomfort.

26

"Relax. He won't see through the charade."

"How do you know?"

Kadon moved in, wrapping his arms around me. He pulled me tight to his muscular chest and stroked my hair. "Because we're gonna make it so damn convincing. That's how."

"But he knows me so well."

"Wrong." He drew back to look into my eyes. "He *knew* you. He knew the person you were nine months ago. You're not her any longer. You're confident and sassy, and you're rocking a demanding job, charming the pants off every VIP who comes through the front gates. You're so much *more* than when you were with him. And believe me, he's going to see that and question his choices."

I nibbled my lip. "Really?"

Kadon kissed my forehead. "I guarantee it. Let's rub the bastard's nose in a pile of shit so big he'll smell it for the rest of his miserable life."

"I like the sound of that."

"Me, too." A broad grin edged across his face. "This will be fun."

"We'll have to make sure we don't trip up. We should do a couple of question-and-answer sessions. Y'know, things like favorite movie, or the name of our first pet, schools we attended."

Kadon rubbed his chin. "That's a good idea. Why don't I swing by in the morning? I'll bring pastries from that patisserie you love so much."

I nudged him with my toe. "See. You already know the way to my heart."

Chapter 4

Kadon

**I'm an idiot. Or maybe a genius.
The jury is out.**

BALANCING A BAG FILLED WITH PASTRIES ON TOP OF two caramel lattes, I made my way to Lee's front door. She must've been watching out for me because the door opened before I reached it. She stole the pastry bag and took a deep sniff, then cradled it to her chest as if it was the equivalent of Gollum's "precious."

"You know the way to a girl's heart." Spinning on her heel, she disappeared into the kitchen, which overlooked a small but well-stocked backyard. By the time I'd followed her, she had plates set out on the counter and the pastries already apportioned.

"Anyone would think you hadn't eaten in a week."

"Listen, mister. I spent twenty years having to watch every single morsel I put in my mouth. I'm making up for lost time." She took a huge bite of the almond croissant. A third of it disappeared into her mouth. She chewed, her eyes rolling back in her head. "God, that's orgasmic."

If anyone asked me how I did it, I couldn't say, but somehow, I managed not to emit a groan.

"You're so easily pleased."

"You have no idea." Another third disappeared. She plucked one coffee from my hand and peeled off the plastic lid. Blowing across the top, she sipped. "Ow, that's hot."

"Is it? What a surprise, considering it's made with hot milk."

She grinned, pastry crumbs on her chin only endearing her to me further. "You're learning, Kingcaid. That was almost good for you."

Dash poked his head in the kitchen, checked out who the infiltrator was who'd interrupted his morning, then padded over, head high and proud. He purred as he weaved in and out of my legs.

I'm honored.

Dash tolerated me, until he didn't. Tentatively, I bent down and scratched behind his ear. He wasn't fond of being touched by anyone other than Lee. I didn't know a thing about cat psychology, but it must have had something to do with being a stray. She was his savior, his person. Everyone else was treated with the highest level of suspicion.

"It's odd how you're the only one he comes anywhere near. If anyone else stops by, he runs and hides."

I sent a grin her way. "He's a brilliant judge of character. That's why."

"Oh God. I fed you that one, didn't I?" She facepalmed. "Wake up, Leesa."

Laughing, I pulled out a chair at the breakfast bar and sat beside her. I removed the lid from my coffee, too, and drew my pastries toward me. Tearing off a hunk of the pain au chocolat, I slipped it into my mouth. Delicious. "You're right. I am learning."

Dash jumped up on the countertop and almost dipped his tail in my coffee. I picked him up and put him on the floor. He gave me this look as if to say, "Touch me again and you die," then, tail pointed straight up, he almost pranced into the next room.

Normal service has resumed.

"That cat is a law unto himself. He puts up with me, but only on his terms."

"It's true." Lee nodded sagely. "We're all stooges in his world domination plan." Plunking herself on the stool next to mine, she sighed. "Okay, so I've been thinking."

"Uh-oh. Never a good idea this early in the morning."

I received a dig to my ribs for my troubles. "Kadon! I'm being serious."

"Fine. Fine." I held my hands up on either side of my head. "What have you been thinking about?"

"This fake dating thing."

Ah... the fake dating.

Fake for her. The opposite of fake for me.

Spending three days as Lee's boyfriend was about as real as it got. Not that I could ever tell her that. I'd thought about it. Too many fucking times. But what good would it do? Was there anything more painful in the world than to tell someone that you loved them and have them not say it back? Or worse, for them to say something like "I'm sorry."

God. It gave me the shivers to even think about it. I might as well say, "Here's my balls. Squeeze 'em until they pop."

"What about it?" I brushed pastry crumbs off my hands and reached for a tissue to wipe grease from my fingertips.

"I couldn't sleep last night. I... I don't think it'll work, Kadon."

My heart skipped at least three beats. Sure, I'd never have Lee for real. I didn't fucking deserve to have her for real. But goddamn, Universe, let me have this one thing. This one tiny speck in time where I could pretend I had the funniest, kindest, most beautiful woman in the world on my arm and know that every man in the room was looking at me and burning up with jealousy. Even Benedict.

Especially Benedict.

That man would wake up one day and realize the price he'd paid for success wasn't worth a dime.

I cleared my throat. "Why not?"

"I don't know. It's... I'm not an actor, and neither are you. If it was only the wedding, then perhaps I could do it. But it's three days. How are we supposed to keep up the pretense for three days?"

All too fucking easily.

"Look. We're best friends, right? So we're already close. We laugh together, we tease each other, we're natural in our interactions. None of that has to change. All we have to do is something like hold hands in public and dance at the wedding."

If I wasn't careful, I risked appearing desperate, but to have my dream dangled so close only to have it snatched away was not happening.

Was. Not. Happening.

Goose bumps peppered the back of my neck as I waited for her to consider my rebuttal. The silence physically hurt me, but the right play here was to keep quiet. Let her think about it properly.

And if she still wasn't happy with the arrangement, I'd... I'd...

Ah, fuck. I got nothing.

She nibbled the corner of her mouth, then urned her seductive gray eyes on me. Twirling a lock of her lavender hair around her finger, she nodded. "Yeah, I guess you're right."

Relief loosened the coiled muscles in my back, and my shoulders relaxed.

"I am right." I dropped my half-eaten pastry on the plate and reached for her hands, encasing them in mine. "Look, Lee, you deserve your shot at revenge. You've earned it. Let me do this for you."

An inner voice muttered, "For *you*, you mean."

It wasn't wrong. But what Lee didn't know wouldn't hurt her. The only person at risk of getting hurt was me. And as I was the catalyst for the entire situation, then I got to decide whether or not I could handle it.

Spend a few days in England, bank a few memories,

have a fun time rubbing her ex's nose in it, then return to our normal lives.

What could possibly go wrong?

Lee rubbed her lips together. "Are you sure?"

"Positive. I wouldn't have suggested it last week if I wasn't. Come on. It'll be fun." I pushed the remains of my plate away. Lee stared in horror at me, then at it, and then back at me.

"You're not going to finish those?" She jerked her chin at the leftover pain au chocolat and the untouched kouign-amann, which, in my opinion, was far superior to the humble croissant. This morning, though, my appetite wasn't there, and after Lee almost backed out before we'd begun, what little I'd had, vanished.

I patted my stomach. "Gotta take care of the six-pack."

"Well, I don't." She snagged the pain au chocolat and polished it off in one mouthful.

As close to her lips touching yours as you're gonna get, dickhead.

"So, are you in?" I pressed.

She swallowed. "I guess."

"Great."

I reached into the inside pocket of my jacket and removed a sheet of paper. Laying it on the kitchen counter-top, I smoothed it out. "I noted down a few questions before I left the house this morning."

"Oh my God. Look at you, you little organizer. I planned to wing it."

"That works, too. We can use these as prompts if we run out."

She plucked the paper out of my hand and scanned it. "Wow. How did you think of all these?"

"I didn't. Google did."

"Ah. Full marks for ingenuity. Zero for effort."

"Not true. The effort was thinking to ask Google in the first place. And it's efficient, too. Why re-create the wheel when it's already been done?"

"Hmm," she grumbled. "Let's see." She ran her finger down the list. "Ah, here's a nice cheesy one to start with. Famous person you have a crush on."

You.

Sometimes it was easy to forget that Lee had spent most of her life in the glare of publicity. She had an Instagram following of over ten million, and even though she'd given up modeling more than nine months ago and hadn't posted any new content since then, her following continued to grow. Newspapers and magazines still ran old pictures of her, and strangers occasionally stopped her in the street whenever she went out in public. At least at my club, she enjoyed some privacy. A large number of my clients were as famous, or more so, as she was. Not to mention that most of them were so wrapped up in their own egos that they barely gave her a second look.

"That's easy. Margot Robbie."

"Good choice. She's gorgeous."

Not as gorgeous as you. Not even close.

"What about you?"

She gave it some thought. "I don't know. I met so many when I modeled, and honestly, the old saying to never meet your heroes holds more than a grain of truth. But if I had to pick one, I guess... Elvis."

"Elvis? He's dead."

"So?" She tapped a perfect, round fingernail against the sheet of paper. "Show me where in the rules it states they have to have a pulse."

A laugh spilled out of me. "I knew you were going to be trouble."

"Okay, we need to speed this up. Otherwise, we'll be here all day. Where did we first have sex?"

I almost choked on my own saliva. "Jesus, Lee. That's a bit of a leap from celebrity crushes. No one is going to ask that."

"Ya think? Let me tell you, these kinds of people are far more likely to ask that than which celebrity we'd like to bang. So... where did we do it? Who made the first move? Did you make me come, or were you selfish and blew your load before I'd warmed up?"

Fuck.

I fidgeted in my seat, my cock getting far too excited. Stupid thing didn't realize we were playing a game. Or rather, it had a game of its own it'd like to play.

Wouldn't we all?

When I was a kid back in Seattle, I'd taken drama classes as an outlet for an overactive imagination. I could do this. All I had to do was slip into a character that wasn't me, that didn't find her attractive, that was simply acting a part in order to help a friend.

I'd done it before.

I was used to pretending everything was peachy when the chaos inside my head ran riot. I knew how to put on a face, to make everyone around me think I was the carefree and untroubled surfer dude who ran a bunch of exclusive beach clubs.

These days, it was like wearing a second skin made of an impenetrable armor, and the only time I peeled off that second skin was when I found myself alone with nothing more than my personal thoughts.

"For our first time, I set up a picnic on the beach in this beautiful hidden cove, tucked away from prying eyes. I laid down a thick blanket so you'd be comfortable. We ate lobster rolls and caviar and drank Dom Pérignon. And as the sun dipped below the horizon, painting the sky in gold and yellow and orange, I kissed you and undressed you and made love to you. Afterward, I held you in my arms, and under the stars, we fell asleep. When we woke the next morning, bathed in warm sunlight, I made love to you all over again. And from that moment on, we both knew what we'd found. The other half of us."

I fell silent, but when Lee didn't respond, I arched a brow. "Good enough?"

Her throat bobbed as she swallowed, and she licked her lips. "I—um... Yeah. That's good enough."

If I didn't know better, I'd say she was flustered. Distracted was far more likely.

"Great. Oh, and just so you know, you came. Several times."

She blinked in quick succession. "Right. Okay, then. Good to know." She rubbed her forehead. "Would you excuse me for a minute?" Palming the back of her neck, she added, "Bathroom."

She jumped off the stool and disappeared toward the stairs that led to the second floor. Dash poked his head into the kitchen again, took one haughty look at me as if to say, "Are you still here?" and then slowly pivoted and went back the way he'd come.

Lee had done me a favor by leaving the room for a few minutes. It gave me time to collect myself. The character thing had failed miserably. Every word I'd spoken had come from my heart. I might not have rehearsed it, but what I'd described was how I'd imagined our first time together.

I was in big trouble.

This idea might have been mine, and at the time, I'd thought it a master stroke, but now I was having second thoughts. As much as I yearned for this to be real, it wasn't. There was no future for me and Lee. And if she found out this wasn't fake for me, would she think I was a manipulative asshole? I couldn't bear that. I should call it off.

I don't want to.

Yes, I do.

I should.

I'm an idiot.

Or a genius.

An idiot genius.

Ugh. I couldn't get out of my head. The idea of a three-day time frame where I got to put my arm around her and hold her hand and, *fuck,* maybe even kiss her when we needed to shore up our fake relationship for the benefit of Benedict and the other attendees... I wanted that. I craved that. I *needed* that.

I'd never have that.

And the worst thing of all to acknowledge was... I didn't deserve that.

Pulling the sheet of paper toward me, I jotted down a few answers to the stupid Google-sourced questions and left a space for Lee to write down hers. I didn't want to do this Mr. and Mrs. thing anymore.

If anyone asked us a question we hadn't prepped for, we'd have to improvise—and fuck the consequences.

Chapter 5

Leesa

**A shopping trip with my ride-or-die
is in order.**

KADON'S IDEA OF FIRST-TIME SEX WITH A NEW
partner had plagued me for the last several days. He'd
never struck me as a hopeless romantic, but that date.
God.

Talk about every girl's dream. He hadn't even used the
word *fuck.* He'd said 'make love.'

I'd almost swooned. I'd almost forgotten he was my
best friend and we were faking it. That was why I'd taken
myself off to the bathroom, dousing my face in cold water
when I probably should have dunked my nether regions in
an ice bath to put out the fire he'd lit with his sensual tale.

I'd never once looked at Kadon with any degree of

romantic ideal. He didn't do it for me like that. I loved him, dearly, but there'd been no sexual chemistry between us.

Well, color me screwed, because the sexual chemistry at my house twelve days ago had been off the charts.

I'd been relieved when he'd told me he'd written the answers and left space for mine. The remaining questions he'd pulled off Google were all pretty easy to answer, but after my stupid contribution to our "getting to know you" session, anything might have happened. Even a simple question such as favorite sexual position could have led us down the path of no return.

After giving myself a good talking-to, I'd concluded that my reaction to Kadon's dreamy date idea had been nothing more than sexual frustration. I hadn't had sex in over nine months. No wonder I'd reacted the way I had. I was a normal, red-blooded woman with needs.

A hookup would do it. One night. No strings.

That'd put out the flames.

Except I never went anywhere to meet someone for a hookup. And I'd never sleep with someone I met at the club.

Kadon—God bless him—had carried on as normal. And now that I'd posted the stupid RSVP, I'd committed us to seeing this thing through to the bitter end.

With only eleven days to the end of the season, things were slowing down at the club. Outside of the height of summer when every day was busy, Wednesdays were often the quietest, and today was no exception. I didn't have any VIPs due today, so I could take a few hours off. I needed a couple of new outfits for the wedding. After I'd given up modeling, I'd donated all my fancy red-carpet gowns and cocktail dresses to charity. I could hardly turn up to the wedding in yoga pants and a Kingcaid Beach Clubs T-shirt.

More's the pity.

I had the perfect man in mind to help me choose appropriate clothing. Or, more truthfully, I hated shopping alone.

All I had to do was convince him to come with me.

"Are you busy today?"

Kadon looked up from his computer, a pen clenched between his teeth and his eyebrows dipped in concentration. He always had that same look when deep in thought. I told him often enough that he'd need Botox if he carried on squishing his face like that.

He plucked the pen out of his mouth. "Depends. What've you got in mind?"

I narrowed my eyes. "So suspicious for one so young."

He chuckled. "What do you need, Lee?"

"A partner in crime."

"I gave up my bank-robbing days right before we met. Sorry. You're out of luck."

"Ohh. You're getting better, Kingcaid. We'll turn you into a sarcasm champ yet."

"Learned at the knee of a master." He tapped the pen on the desk. "Spill."

"I need clothes. For the wedding."

He gestured for me to get on with it. "Aaannnddd? You want time off? You got it."

"Well, yes. But more than that. I'd like a man's opinion."

It dawned on him what I was asking. He sat up

straight, a look I could only describe as horror leaching across his face.

"No. Nope. Not a chance. I hate clothes-shopping for myself. I'm not doing it voluntarily for someone else. Not even you. Besides, I know nothing about female... attire. Dresses and shoes and purses. Ask Liam. He's far more suited to this than I am. Tell him I said it was okay for him to take off for a few hours."

Liam was the executive chef for our VIP restaurant and a self-confessed fashionista. His abject excitement when Kadon had first introduced me as the new VIP Operations Manager still made me chuckle. Liam had clapped his hands like a performing seal and gushed about what a fan he was of mine and how he adored everything I'd done and how brilliantly I wore clothes. On and on, he'd extolled my so-called virtues while Kadon had stood off to one side, an amused grin lifting the corners of his mouth.

But I didn't want Liam's opinion, as valid as it would be. I wanted Kadon's. And I hadn't a clue why.

"I don't want Liam. I want you."

Kadon's entire demeanor changed in the time it took me to blink. His hazel eyes brightened, dread replaced by a spark of enthusiasm that had been absent a few seconds ago. Huh? Why was he happy I'd rather go with him than Liam? Kadon was the one who'd suggested Liam in the first place.

The more I got to know Kadon Kingcaid, the less I understood him.

I was probably reading too much into it, my nerves at this stupid upcoming wedding playing with my emotions. At least ten times a day, I swung between anguish at making such a stupid decision and pride in myself for calling Benedict's bluff and accepting the invitation to attend.

I wished I'd been there when Fenella's parents told him I'd RSVP'd. I'd bet his jaw had hit the floor.

Good.

The more I made him doubt he knew me, the more fun I'd have at his expense. Bastard deserved it for what he'd done to me.

Although... these last couple of weeks, or maybe longer, I'd started to get this feeling. Sort of like... relief. That might not be the right word, but I couldn't put my finger on it. Almost as if, had I gone through with the wedding, I'd have regretted it.

It made no sense. I'd been so *sure* Benedict was The One. Even after he had dumped me, leaving me crying on the beach where Kadon had found me and taken me under his wing, I'd spent days sobbing into my pillow, wondering what I'd done wrong.

I cringed to think about it now. I'd done *nothing* wrong. I hadn't cheated. I hadn't chosen a partner based solely on what her father did for a living and how that played into Benedict's political ambitions. All I'd done was love him and fund his extravagant lifestyle. And for what?

"You really want me to come with you?"

I rolled my eyes. "Duh. I wouldn't have asked otherwise."

"Okay." He moved several bits of paper around on his desk. They ended up in exactly the same position as before he'd started. I almost asked him if he was having an embolism. "Okay, then. Let me... I'll finish up here, and we can go."

Thirty minutes later, we were in Kadon's Aston Martin driving down the coastal road toward Cannes. My favorite boutique was located there, although I hadn't made a purchase with them for... gosh, it must have been two years or more. They'd kitted me out in the most beautiful Dior gown for the Cannes Film Festival that year.

I'd been dating Benedict for about twelve months by that point, and I recalled walking down the red carpet with my arm tucked inside his, flashbulbs blinding me, and feeling this incredible swell of joy. Most of the time, modeling had exhausted me, but that night I remembered as one of the happiest of my life.

Didn't last long.

I wound down the window and turned my face to the cool breeze. The weather had changed these last few days. I could almost smell winter in the air.

This would be my first winter in Saint Tropez. When I'd modeled, I'd usually spent winters in exotic locations. Bikini shots on the beach, aboard fancy yachts, draped across chaise lounges in dresses that cost more than most people's annual mortgage payments. All very glamorous on the surface, but beneath that, it was the loneliest existence. I'd found it easier to give up than I'd thought I would.

My decision had cost me a relationship with my parents, but it had given me a sense of peace and tranquility I'd never had.

I loved my new life but couldn't help worrying that what had started out as a temporary position working for Kadon was at risk of turning into a permanent career. I adored working at the beach club, and I met amazing and interesting people—even if a few of them were arseholes—but did I want to work there forever?

No. I didn't.

As for what I'd do instead, I hadn't the faintest idea. I tried not to worry about it too much. I was only twenty-six. It wasn't as if I had to figure out right this second what to do with the next fifty years. Twenty-six was nothing in the grand scheme of things.

I glanced at Kadon, his attention fixed on the winding coastal road. He and I were the same age, his future predetermined for him since he was young, in the same way as mine had been. Yet he seemed peaceful, content, and sure of where he was going.

Why couldn't I be like that?

Why had this sudden restlessness attacked me when I'd spent nine months content?

Perhaps it was because the end of the season was almost here, and I had a long winter ahead of me to sit with nothing but my thoughts. Kadon wouldn't be around. He'd be off visiting his other clubs, which left me here alone, with no family, no friends, no company apart from a cat who always looked as if he was plotting the downfall of humanity.

Or perhaps it was knowing that in a couple of weeks, I'd have to face Benedict and smile and congratulate him when all I wanted to do was set a pack of dogs on his genitalia and grab a bucket of popcorn to watch the show.

"You're making that face."

Kadon cut into my violent thoughts. I squinted at him. "What face?"

"The face that tells me you've got an asshole on your mind."

"That sounds... weird. And... ick. But also, am I really so transparent?"

"Yes."

"You're supposed to have your eyes on the road."

"They are."

"Then how did you see my face?"

He side-eyed me, a slight tilt to his lips. "What can I say? I'm a multitasker."

"With an answer for everything."

"That, too."

I drew a thoughtful breath through my nose, letting it out slowly. "I was thinking about Benedict; you're right. I'm half dreading, half itching for this wedding to get here already."

He reached across the center console and clasped my hand, giving it a squeeze. "It'll be fine, you know. Think of it as closure."

"Yeah. That's a good point."

"I have my uses."

I smiled at him and briefly rested my head on his shoulder. "I often thank my lucky stars you were out running that day. I honestly don't know what I'd have done without you these last nine months."

"You'd have been fine." He cleared his throat. "You're a survivor."

"I don't feel like a survivor. I feel like a victim."

"Well, you're not. You turned your back on the only career you'd ever known and picked up a new one as if you'd been doing it your whole life. You drew a line in the sand with your parents, even though it cost you more than you're willing to admit to yourself, let alone to them. You have enriched not only my life but also the lives of everyone at the beach club. You have to look at things through a different lens. That's all."

I gazed at him fondly. "You always seem to say the right thing to bolster my flagging self-esteem. You know that?"

"One of my many qualities." He chuckled.

"I've been thinking." I tugged on my lip.

"Uh-oh. This sounds ominous."

"About my future."

"Oh yeah?" His voice was soft, tentative, almost as if he guessed what was coming.

"I need to figure out what to do with the rest of my life, and right now, I haven't a clue."

He sighed, nodding. "I knew this was coming, but I've pushed it to the back of my mind. For selfish reasons, I don't want you to leave the beach club. Or me."

"I'd never leave you. You're my ride-or-die."

"Yeah, until you find The One and he steals you away from me."

I caught a wistful tone to his voice. Apart from me and his family, Kadon didn't have any close friends. At least, none that I was aware of, so I understood his worry.

In all honesty, I had the same concern. One day a wonderful woman would come along and steal Kadon from me, and I'd have to find someone else to listen to my woes day and night.

It hurt to even consider it. Which was the reason I rarely did.

"Never gonna happen. Whomever I end up with will have to accept that you're part of the package. Like Dash."

"You're comparing me to a cat?"

I clapped a hand to my forehead. "How silly of me. Of course Dash is more important." I laughed.

Kadon lobbed a glower at me. "Funny."

"I like to think so. Seriously, though, I mean it. If I met a guy, and he couldn't handle the fact that my best friend was also a guy, then he isn't the one for me."

"You say that now. But things change." There was that wistful tone again.

"Are you speaking from experience?" I'd often wondered if Kadon had suffered heartbreak in the past. He hardly dated, and I'd never heard him mention ex-girlfriends.

"Nah. But I know what guys are like. We're territorial bastards who don't like anyone with a dick coming too close to our woman. I'm resigned to losing you one day, though I hope it's not yet."

I could have sworn his voice cracked.

"Never." I put my hand over his on the steering wheel. "I mean it, Kadon. You saved me. You gave me a purpose, a job, even if I don't see it as a long-term career. You are my first-ever best friend, and you'll be my best friend until I take my final breath. And if the guys I meet can't hack that, well then... I'll stay a spinster and breed lots of Dashes."

He laughed, the forlorn droop to his shoulders vanishing, if it had been there at all. I could have misread his despondency.

"First, *spinster* is the worst word ever created. *Bachelorette* is far better."

"I'll give you that one. But worse than *moist*? Really? Or *squirt*? Or *flaccid*?"

He laughed harder. "Stop. Please. I'm trying to drive here."

"You started it."

"No, *you* started it with *spinster*."

"Oh, yeah." I rubbed my forehead. "There's a lot going on."

He gave me a playful smile. "You're crazy."

"True. Anyway, you said 'first.' What's second?"

His nose wrinkled. "Please don't breed lots of Dashes. If you do that, it's the end of the world as we know it."

I nodded. "True story."

Our banter-fest had yanked me from all the inward reflection I'd gotten lost in, and by the time he parked behind Boutique Noémie, I'd brushed off my self-pity and was ready to shop.

Look out, Benedict Oberon, because I'm about to show you what you threw away.

Twat.

Chapter 6

Kadon

Practicing or salivating?

Noémie the boutique owner, greeted Lee like the long-lost daughter she thought she'd never see again. Exclamations, hugs, twin-cheek kisses—real ones, not pursed lips kissing thin air. I stood off to the side while the two women spoke rapid French, too fast for me. I could hold my own when speaking to the locals—just—but this level of excitement was far beyond my language capabilities.

I waited for the melee to die down, then introduced myself as Lee's friend. It surprised me that the word *friend* didn't stick in my throat. I hadn't a clue how I'd kept my composure on the drive over here when Lee had said I'd be her best friend until her dying breath. I didn't want to be her fucking friend, goddammit. I didn't want her telling

53

another guy that she and I came as a package. I wanted to *be* the other guy. The only guy. *Her* guy. The Package.

Never gonna happen.

"So you are 'ere to give zee male point of view, oui?"

"It appears so." I caught Lee's impish grin and narrowed my eyes. "Let's just say Lee coerced me into it."

"What utter tosh," Lee exclaimed. "You couldn't get in the car fast enough."

I arched one eyebrow. "Recollections vary. Let's leave it at that."

Lee's grin widened. She loved teasing me. She lived for it.

I lived for her.

"Shall we begin?" Noémie asked. "I 'ave some beautiful gowns for a beautiful girl."

She took Lee by the arm, and the two women disappeared into the back. I wandered around the store, which took less than thirty seconds, helped myself to a bottle of water, then sat on a purple leather couch and waited.

Ten minutes later, Lee emerged from behind the screen door.

I swear I almost swallowed my tongue.

"Well, what do you think? I thought this would work for the night before the wedding."

Dear God, help me.

My ability to speak fled. Lee was wearing a bottle-green velvet dress with full sleeves and a neckline that made her boobs pop, and my mouth water. Cinched at the waist, it fell to the floor with a slit up one side showing off a perfectly toned leg. She twirled, giving me a rear view.

Fuck me.

Her ass looked... bitable. It was the sort of dress that made grown men sell everything they owned for a chance to run their hands over the shapely body encased inside.

I opened my mouth. Closed it again. Opened it. Nothing.

Speak, goddammit. Say something. Anything.

"That's... um... nice."

Anything but that. Jesus Christ.

"I mean... yeah, it's nice."

Someone cut out my tongue.

"Nice?" Lee quirked a brow.

"No. I don't mean nice. I mean... great. Terrific." I swallowed. "You look stunning, Lee."

She ran her hands over her hips. Lucky hands.

"I gotta say, Kingcaid, you're playing the fake boyfriend part to perfection, although it's just us. You don't need to ham it up yet."

"I'm practicing."

I wasn't practicing. I was salivating.

"So it'll do? For the stupid rehearsal dinner? I mean, who has a rehearsal dinner the night before the actual wedding? What are we rehearsing?"

"How not to kill the groom? But yes. It'll more than do. Benedict might swallow his tongue."

Lord knows I almost did.

"Good. Hope the bastard chokes on it."

She spun on her heel and disappeared again. I blew out a breath.

Get a grip.

Pretending to prepare for when we'd have to do this for real was one thing. But Lee had a pretty good radar. If I wasn't careful, she might figure out the truth, and then where would I be?

Up shit creek without a paddle.

Her next outfit spared my painful hard-on, although she still looked smoking hot. A fitted pale blue shirt that lay over the waistband of a pair of skinny jeans, and fuck-me boots in jet black.

"What's this outfit for?"

"Traveling. I want to show up looking good, but not as if I've made that much of an effort. Casual."

I gave her a thumbs-up. "Nailed it."

Her phone buzzed in her purse. She jerked her chin at the coat stand she'd hung it on after we'd arrived. "See who that is, would you? In case there's a problem at the club."

I grinned. "If there was a problem at the club, I think... I *think*... they may call me. You know. The boss."

She scratched her temple—with her middle finger. I laughed, flicking my wrist. "Next. I'll take care of any fires in your absence."

She whipped around, giving me a terrific view of her ass encased in those clingy jeans before she disappeared. I stared into space far longer than I should have, the image vibrant and, therefore, worth spending a few seconds daydreaming about.

Lumbering to my feet, I unzipped her purse. The weirdest thing for a guy was when a woman asked him to dig around in her purse. You might come across all sorts of things. My personal nightmare? Grabbing a pack of tampons, losing control of my hands, and spilling them everywhere, then having to get down on my hands and knees and scoop them up.

Lucky for me, I located her phone with minimal rummaging, and not a tampon in sight. I tapped the screen to wake it up. She had it locked, but her notifications were on—and blazing across the screen was a text from Fenella.

What the hell did she want?

If I had the code for Lee's phone, I'd delete the damned message. But then I'd have to tell her why I'd done that, so what was the point, really?

Goddammit.

Lee was already feeling all kinds of shit about this wedding without Bridezilla popping up in her messages wanting fuck knows what.

She emerged from the back for the third time wearing... a bathrobe. I tapped my finger against my lips, looking her up and down and taking my time about it. She still looked gorgeous, even in a shapeless robe. But I could hardly tell her that. So I reacted as she'd expect me to. With a sarcastic comment.

"Not sure that's the look you're going for."

She didn't need to know my thoughts had shot to... one little tug. A quick pull and I'd get to live out a dirty fantasy.

Her eyes rolled back in her head. "You're such an arse. The dress is a little long, so Noémie is quickly pinning it. Who was the text from?"

I grimaced. "Bridezilla."

Momentarily confused, she wrinkled her nose. "Bri—Fenella?"

"One and the same."

"What the hell does she want?"

She planted her hands on her hips. The robe parted slightly, giving me a glimpse of one creamy breast. I swallowed a groan and covered my groin with my hands. Jeans didn't tent like sweatpants, which, on one hand was a relief, but on the other, fuck, erections and denim were completely incompatible.

Someone in the fashion industry should get on that. If they solved that problem, they'd make a fucking fortune.

I held out her phone. "It's locked. Not that I would have looked if it hadn't been." How easily the lies tripped off my tongue. "Notifications showed her name. That's it."

She took it from me. I gave it a few seconds.

"What's it say?"

"The cheeky cow." Lee's eyes volleyed from me to the screen, then back to me. "She says she's 'so delighted, darling' that I've been able to put my embarrassment at getting dumped behind me to come to the wedding. Glad there are no hard feelings. Oh, and a parting salvo of 'the best woman won' with a stupid grinning emoji." Lee snorted. "Best woman, my arse."

I couldn't agree more. The best woman was standing right in front of me. No fucking contest.

Damn Fenella.

Lee's relaxed and joyous mood vanished in the face of that woman's cruelty. I hated that she allowed these stuck-up English "toffs" to get to her. They'd better fucking watch out, because I intended to make sure Lee emerged from that wedding not only with the upper hand but also with Benedict ruing the day he'd let the most incredible woman slip through his fingers.

Lee threw her phone onto the couch. I got to my feet and held out my arms.

"Come here."

She hesitated, only for a split second, before wrapping her arms around my waist. "I hate them."

"It'll be okay. We'll show them both you're the better person."

I stroked her hair, burying my nose in the silky strands. I doubted she'd notice the intimacy, but if she did, I'd tell her it was more practice.

I wished she were mine.

I wished I deserved a woman as good as this one.

I wished for a lot of things that wouldn't come true, but that didn't stop me from wallowing in the fantasy.

She sniffed, tightening her arms around me. "Perhaps I shouldn't go."

Coldness hit my chest. Not again. Every time I thought the issue was settled, something came up to snatch away the dream. This was my one and only chance to create memories to fulfill a lifetime of yearning. I couldn't let a single text from Fenella ruin my chance at pretending Lee was mine, nor hers at getting the closure so badly warranted.

I leaned back and clipped a finger under Lee's chin. "And let her know you're still hurt by what he did? No, babe. That's not what you do. What you do is walk in there with your head held high, like the fucking queen you are, and you show that bastard that you're the one who had the lucky escape. You're the one who's glad he's too blinded by his political ambitions to realize what he had. That's what you do."

Releasing her, I picked up her phone and handed it over. "Reply to her text."

"And say what?"

"Tell her you're delighted to come and share in her special day. That you're looking forward to it."

"What, no sarcasm?"

I grinned. "None. Trust me, this will infuriate her far more than if you rise to the bait. Because that's why she sent the text. To goad you into a response. Don't give her the satisfaction. Be the bigger person. That's how you win this game."

"You sound as if you have experience, Kingcaid."

I laughed. "It's like business. Never let the person sitting on the other side of the boardroom table know what your angle is. You smile sweetly, and when they least expect it, you play the winning hand." Bending down, I kissed her forehead. "Send the text."

She rubbed her lips together, then tapped out a message on her phone. "Done. I'll show her who the best damned woman is."

"That's my girl."

If only.

"Right. Get ready to have your socks blown off, Kingcaid, because I'm going to show that fucker what he threw away."

She'd already blown my socks off, and they weren't the only thing on the cusp of an explosion.

Five minutes of picturing balance sheets and Dad's five-year business plan, and I'd gotten myself somewhat under control. Until, that was, Lee reappeared in a sleeveless, one-shoulder, floor-length purple gown with ruffles on one side and at the waist.

But that wasn't the jaw-dropping part of the dress. No,

that part was how it cut away from midthigh almost up to her hip, showing off legs for days.

Days and days and days.

Tanned. Shapely. Gorgeous.

I mean, I'd looked at pictures of Lee from her modeling days. Course I had. What man in love with a woman wouldn't scavenge for any scraps he could get? But this... in the flesh... was orgasm-inducing. I was so fucking close to coming in my jeans.

The last time I'd had an uncontrolled orgasm was a few days away from my sixteenth birthday. Mrs. Bennington, a supply teacher. Newly qualified. Early twenties. A blonde bombshell who I reckoned modeled herself on Marilyn Monroe. She'd turned up to our class in a white blouse that clung to her ample boobs and a pencil skirt. The way her ass filled that skirt... Every student with a dick jizzed their pants. And those who said they hadn't were gay or liars.

"Wedding day. Thoughts?"

Thoughts?

My thoughts were *not* for public consumption. My thoughts were of ripping that dress right down the front, pressing her up against the wall, having her wrap those delicious legs around my waist, and powering home where I fucking belonged.

Except, I didn't belong there. I would *never* belong there. And I somehow had to come to terms with that fact.

"Don't look at me like that."

I rediscovered the ability to talk. "Like what?"

Jesus. My voice rasped like a forty-a-day man. If she

didn't know I was turned on before, she'd fucking know it now.

"Like you want to tear off my dress. Is this you practicing again? Because if you are, dang, Kingcaid, you might want to call Spielberg and have him put you in his next movie."

"Practicing?" I blinked. "Yeah, sure. I'm practicing. Glad it convinced you."

"Are you okay?" She peered at me. "Your cheeks are red."

"They are? I guess it's kinda hot in here." I wafted my hand in front of my face. *Hot* didn't begin to describe it. I had a furnace in my pants.

"Kadon."

I lifted my eyes to hers... and I could have sworn something passed between us. A spark of... desire.

No.

I'd imagined it.

Lee adored me, but as her best friend, not her lover. Not even as a one-night hookup.

"Kadon," she repeated.

"What?"

Whether God had decided to save me from myself, or Lucifer was fucking with me, Noémie appeared from the back room, pins gripped between her teeth and a roll of tape in her hand. Oblivious to the sexual tension zinging through the air—at least from my side of the room—she crouched at Lee's feet.

If Lee and I had shared a moment, then what did that mean? Was she starting to look at me differently? Or, far more likely, I was seeing what I wished were true rather than something that *was* true.

"Five more minutes, chérie, and we are done."

I already had been. Done to a crisp by the fire in my groin.

Chapter 7

Kadon

Thank you, French air traffic controllers.

"You're not going to believe this."

I sidled past Lee, giving Dash a wide berth. He might tolerate me most of the time, but it was almost as if he knew I was the one responsible for stealing his momma away for a few days. I'd seen this narrow-eyed look before. It said, "Watch out, 'cause I'm gonna slit your throat while you sleep."

If the little shit ever grew opposable thumbs, I was doomed.

"Believe what?" She followed me into the kitchen. "I've made tea."

Before I'd met Lee, I couldn't understand the English obsession with tea. Now, I preferred it to coffee. If Home-

Tracie Delaney

land Security ever got wind of that, they'd bar me from going back home to America.

"Thanks." I took the cup she offered me. Blowing across the top, I sipped. "The French, in their inimitable Frenchie wisdom, have decided on an impromptu three-day air traffic control strike. Which means we can't fly to Heathrow as planned."

"You're kidding." Lee blew out a heavy sigh. "So what do we do now?"

"I called my father and asked if the company jet was free. It isn't. Our only other option is the Eurostar. We'll have to drive up to Paris and catch it from there." I cursed. "We'd never put up with this shit in the US."

She pushed a plate of cookies at me. "Brace for some shocking news. The French aren't Americans. They like to strike. It's a way of life."

I grinned at her sarcastic sideswipe and bit a cookie in half.

"It's a nine-hour drive to Paris, so I suggest we make the drive tomorrow, stop overnight somewhere close by the train station, and then take the Eurostar over to London on Thursday. From there, we can pick up another car and head out to Berkshire."

"What a faff. I think the universe is telling me not to go to this bloody wedding."

"You don't believe in that shit any more than I do."

"True. Oh, I meant to show you the wedding gift I chose for them. I haven't wrapped it yet." She snickered. "Wait there."

She ran upstairs. A couple of minutes later, she returned holding a large box which she planted it on the

66

kitchen counter. I checked out the picture on the side and laughed. Lee had bought the gaudiest fruit bowl I'd ever seen. A scalloped pattern of reds and blues and greens, it was the class of gift an Auntie Maud would buy for a niece four generations younger.

Or, as was in Lee's case, a fuck-you gift.

"It's genius."

"Isn't it?" She gave me a wicked grin. "I picked it up at a charity shop the other day. The lady who served me said there'd been no interest since some clever bugger donated it a few months ago."

"Color me shocked. It's hideous."

"Like the intended recipients."

I laughed. "That's the spirit. Remember that for the next few days and you're golden."

Leaving Lee to pack and ignoring Dash's evil stare, I headed back to my place to make the travel arrangements. Flying would have been a hell of a lot easier, and quicker. A direct flight from Toulon Hyères Airport to Heathrow only took a couple of hours. Our new travel arrangements would take two days.

The strike had provided me with an unexpected bonus, though. It meant I got to spend extra time with Lee. If that didn't shake off my salty mood, nothing would.

Plus, I got to stay overnight in Paris, the city of love, with the woman I loved. She might not have a clue, but I did. I could hold her hand as we walked beside the Seine and sell it as further practice for the main event.

Thank you, French air traffic controllers.

I made the necessary arrangements and waited for the confirmation emails to drop. A few seconds later, they came through. I was about to close the email program and put on my out-of-office reply when another email arrived.

My stomach fell to my feet, a tingling spreading across my chest. I blew out a steady breath.

Oh God.

And then I read the subject line.

Update.

Jesus.

My knees almost gave way. I wasn't sure whether I should feel relief or despair. Probably a little of both. Joseph, the investigator I'd hired a little over a year ago when the nightmares had become too frequent, always wrote "Update" in the subject line when there wasn't an update. If it were anyone else, I'd think he was trying sarcasm on for size, but Joseph Saunders was the most serious man I'd ever met. He made my cousin Johannes look like a stand-up comic.

I opened the email and read it, taking in one word at a time to make sure I neither missed anything nor confused the context. Dyslexia sucked, but we all played the cards as dealt.

Sure enough, he reported no news on the whereabouts of Samuel Collins, a kid I'd attended finishing school with in Switzerland. Given my dyslexic challenges, my father had sent me there to help me catch up on schoolwork.

Not for the first time, I thought about asking my dad for help in locating Samuel, but dredging up what had happened at that fucking school wasn't fair on my parents. I refused to revisit that time with them, especially when Dad had put his reputation on the line to bail me out of a hole.

No, not a hole.

A fucking chasm. A canyon.

A well deep enough to reach the earth's core.

The Swiss were adept at keeping secrets, but a year ago, after living with this since I was seventeen, I'd faced up to the fact that I'd never find peace until I found Samuel. However long it took to locate that kid and ensure he was okay, that despite what I'd done, he'd moved on to live a full and productive life, I had to do it.

I replied to Joseph, telling him to keep looking and reiterating he had an open-ended budget. Whatever resources he needed were his. All he had to do was ask.

Wednesday dawned bright and clear, although the weather forecast said to expect rain from Lyon north. I'd rented a car rather than take my Aston. That way, I didn't have the drag of figuring out how to get it back to Saint Tropez. The strike would be over by Sunday, so it made sense to fly home instead of doing this same trip in reverse. Depending on how things went in Paris, though, I might change my mind.

I put my suitcase in the trunk, leaving room for Lee's things. We should be good for space, unless she packed for a month rather than five days. I doubted she would. For a former model, Lee was the least fussy woman I knew, other than my mother, who was the most frugal of packers. She always went by the belief that as long as she had her passport and a credit card, she could purchase whatever she might have forgotten.

Lee was already outside when I pulled up at her house. One suitcase sat at her feet. The hideous fruit bowl was beside it, wrapped in silver-and-gold paper, and the couture dresses she'd purchased at Boutique Noémie a couple of weeks ago were in clothing bags draped over her arm. I jumped out of the car as she made her way down the path toward me.

"Here, give me your case." I plucked it out of her hand before she could decline the offer. "You can hang the dresses up on a hook behind the driver's seat."

"No Aston?"

"Thought we'd fly back, providing the strike is over, so rental it is."

"Ah. Makes sense."

She hung up her clothes and climbed into the passenger seat. As I joined her, I narrowed my eyes. "Why the long face? You still worried about the wedding?"

"No. It's Dash. He gave me that look when I bundled him into his pet carrier ready for Audrey to pick him up this morning. You know the one. The *How could you do this to me?* look."

"He's a manipulative little shit. He'll end up getting spoiled rotten, and when he comes back to you, he'll expect the same treatment."

"Yeah." She gnawed her lip and fiddled with the hem of her T-shirt. "He will be okay, won't he?"

"He'll be fine. You know Audrey. She'll probably feed him caviar and peeled grapes."

Lee chuckled.

"And she'll send you photographs, like you asked."

"True." Her eyes brightened. "You're right. Okay, let's get this show on the road."

We made good time along the A7, only getting held up for fifteen minutes at roadworks a few miles south of Lyon. After stopping off at a bistro for lunch we continued north toward Paris. We played car games on the way to break up the journey, and Lee took a turn driving to give my legs and back a rest.

I'd booked a suite at Le Meurice, one of my favorite hotels in Paris. A valet surged forward as I pulled in front of the entrance. As I'd expect from such an exclusive establishment, the bellhop had our luggage out of the trunk before either Lee or I had set foot outside the car.

Check-in took less than two minutes, and by the time we arrived at the suite, our luggage was already there.

"Which bedroom do you want?" I asked Lee as she crossed the expansive living room and opened the French doors to the balcony. "There are three, so take your pick."

She glanced over her shoulder. "Three?"

I shrugged. "What can I say? I like the view from up here."

"Me, too. I'd forgotten how gorgeous Paris is. It's been a while." Her eyes sparkled. "Note how I said 'a while,' Kadon. Not 'a minute.' Because that would be stupid."

"I think you've worn out that joke."

She hadn't. I wouldn't care if she teased me about cultural sayings for the next fifty years.

"Fair enough. It's not like you don't provide me with plenty of fodder."

I swept my arm from me to her in a grand gesture. "Pot, meet Kettle."

She giggled, stepping outside, where she took a deep breath. "Ah, Paris. The city of love."

I joined her. "Did you come here with... him?" It pained me to ask, but if she had, depending on what they'd done while they'd been here, I might have to change my plans for this evening.

"No. He said it was too touristy."

Jerkweed.

Paris was only too touristy for those with zero imagination. The city was crammed full with plenty of off-the-beaten-track gems hidden among the usual suspects. We didn't have time to see them on this trip, but I made a mental note to suggest we came back on another occasion.

I'd love to show Lee *my* Paris.

And I would, even if it was only as friends.

"Do you want to freshen up before dinner?" I checked my watch. We had an hour before we had to be down by the Seine for my surprise.

"That'd be good. Are we eating here?"

"No."

She canted her head. "Let me guess. Burger van? Falafel? Mexican street food?"

I tapped my nose. "You'll see."

"But what do I wear?"

Buck naked works for me.

"What you're wearing is fine. Jeans. A top. A light jacket." Paris was enjoying one of the warmest Novembers on record, which worked perfectly for my evening plans.

"So I was right. Greasy Burgers R Us."

I grinned. "You have thirty minutes. Make it fast. Take that bedroom." I pointed to the door behind the couch. "It's the best one. It has a view of the Eiffel Tower."

I took a quick shower and threw on jeans and a black button-down shirt. Grabbing a bottle of beer from the minibar, I wandered out onto the balcony to drink in Paris at night.

My chest ached, my heart yearning for her. I thought fake dating would be easy, but it turned out to be far more difficult than I'd imagined. My worst nightmare was tripping up and Lee guessing my true feelings. Having her pat me on the shoulder and tell me she loved me and all, just not like *that*.

It was an almost impossible line to walk. Everyone outside the two of us had to buy the whole boyfriend-slash-girlfriend thing, yet if I fully immersed myself in the role, it would stop being pretend and become all too real.

What if I slipped up? What if, in a moment of weakness, I spilled my true feelings?

No champagne for me this weekend.

"Ready?"

At Lee's question, I pivoted, checking my watch. "You have three minutes to spare."

She curtsied. "Despite what you might think of a former model, Mr. Kingcaid, I don't take three hours to get ready."

"Good to know." I set my half-finished beer on the bistro table and held out my arm. "Shall we go, Miss Alarie?"

The car I'd ordered from the concierge was waiting for us as we emerged from the hotel. Driving in Paris was difficult enough at the best of times, so I'd had the rental picked up earlier today.

I held the door for Lee, then hopped around to the other side. The boat launch was within walking distance, about thirty minutes from here, but as the sun dipped, it'd gotten a little chilly. And while I wouldn't mind Lee asking me to warm her up, I feared where that might end.

Every time I touched her, I had to steel myself not to encircle her waist, tug her flush to my body, stare into those mesmerizing eyes, and kiss her. I was in a constant battle with my libido, but if I wanted to keep our friendship alive, I could not let it win.

It. Like my desires were a separate entity. Sometimes I wished they were so that I could leave them at the hotel and enjoy a fun-filled evening with my best friend without all the baggage of a permanent semi and the streak of lust that had set up home in my stomach ever since she'd agreed to my fake-dating suggestion.

"Are you planning to tell me where we're going?" she asked as the car smoothly set off, merging into the busy Paris traffic.

"No."

"Why?"

"Because you'll find out soon enough."

"I don't like surprises."

I gave her a wide-eyed, incredulous stare. "Annaleesa Alarie, did you just flat-out lie to me?" I clutched a hand to my chest, hamming up my reaction. "I can't believe you'd look me, your best friend, in the eye and tell such a great big lie. I hope you're ashamed of yourself."

A peal of laughter fell from her lips. I didn't think it

was possible to love her any more than I already did, but she seemed intent on proving me wrong, even if she wasn't aware of the effect she had on me.

"Fine. I *love* surprises, but I also have an above-average level of impatience, and right now, that's winning."

"Too bad."

She pretended to pout, but she couldn't keep it up for long. A running commentary ensued of places she'd modeled but hadn't had time to truly appreciate. Lee didn't talk about her modeling days very much, but whenever she did, it always struck me as the loneliest of professions. She'd traveled extensively yet seen nothing.

If she were mine, I'd show her the world.

But she isn't. And neither should she be. You deserve to spend your life alone after what you did.

I squeezed my eyes closed, my brain throwing up an image of the lifeless body, lying there, a pool of blood spreading beneath his head, matting his dark brown hair.

I snapped my eyes open, nausea a whirlwind in my stomach.

The visions weren't as strong as they used to be, but when they came, they were a sucker punch to the gut. Would I ever find peace, or would the guilt I couldn't shake remain with me for the rest of my life?

I didn't even know if the kid I'd saved that night had made it. His parents had removed him from the school the very next day, and that was the last I'd heard. I'd asked Dad about him, but he'd said he didn't know. After a while, I'd stopped asking. Joseph *had* to find him. He had to.

If he didn't, I wasn't sure where I went from here.

To hell, probably.

Then again, I was already in hell.

"You've gone awfully quiet." Lee touched her pinkie to mine. "Are you okay?"

"Yeah." I forced a brilliant smile. "You're doing enough talking for us both."

She made a face at me. "Ha ha."

The car slowed, and I jerked my chin. "Okay, Miss Impatient. We're here."

I unclipped my seat belt and climbed out. She joined me on the sidewalk, her gaze on the cruiser in its mooring. "We're going on a boat?"

"A boat? Wash out your mouth. This is a beautiful sixty-foot cruiser that will make you feel as if you're floating on air. Paris from the water is stunning. What better way to spend the evening than with good food, a city built for love"—I risked slipping my arm around her shoulder—"and the best company a man could wish for."

She blinked up at me. The moon, in all its luminous glory, reflected in her eyes. Her lips parted, and for a split second, I thought she was going to rise up on her tiptoes and kiss me.

I longed for her to kiss me, to know what those soft lips tasted like, to feel the length of her body fused to mine.

"You almost had me there, Kingcaid." A dig in the ribs followed. "You're playing the part of boyfriend to perfection. But you needn't bother here. Let's save it for when we have to put on a show."

She might as well have punched a hole in my chest, ripped out my heart, and devoured it along with a full-bodied Merlot.

"Spielberg, here I come." How I sounded normal, I'd never know. But she bought it, flashing me a broad grin.

"Come on, then, stud. Show me a good time."

The real tragedy was that her idea of a good time and mine couldn't be any further apart.

Chapter 8

Leesa

I'm losing my mind.

KADON KINGCAID WOULD MAKE SOMEONE A FINE husband one day. He was caring, kind, and great company, had a face and body that modeling agencies would fight to the death over, and was the best listener I'd ever met. In my experience, men in general were dreadful listeners with short attention spans and a desire to speak only about themselves.

He also knew how to show a girl a good time. A boat trip down the Seine was something I'd wanted to do every time I'd traveled to Paris, but I'd only ever been here for modeling gigs, and those didn't come with spare minutes to myself. And like I'd told him, Benedict hadn't ever shown an interest in visiting. At the time, his disinterest had disappointed me, but now, looking back, I was glad I was here with Kadon rather than him.

Before we'd boarded, I would have bet more than a few quid that he was going to kiss me. And the most confusing thing of all... I'd wanted him to. I'd *wanted* Kadon to kiss me. Kadon. My best friend. The man I'd never looked at that way before. What the hell was wrong with me?

I blamed Paris. Like he'd said, it was the city of love and romance. And my emotions were all over the place knowing that tomorrow, I'd have to face Benedict and play nice and pretend he hadn't hurt me when we both knew he had. I hated the power that gave him over me. Plus, I was certain my poor brain was getting confused between what was real and what was fake. By Sunday, when all this was over, everything would go back to normal. I was sure of it.

"How are you feeling about tomorrow?" Kadon topped off my glass of wine.

"Can you read minds? I was just thinking about that." I drew figures of eight on the crisp white tablecloth. "I'm dreading it, but I hope it will allow me to close that chapter of my life for good. And if I can annoy Benedict a little, all the better."

"Oh, we'll needle him all right. By Sunday, he'll think he's slept on a pin cushion."

I laughed. "Now there's a happy thought."

"Trust me. I know men like Benedict. As long as he thinks he's got the upper hand, he'll behave like the smug asshole he is. However, when he realizes that you've not only gotten over him but are also already in another relationship, that will bug the shit out of him."

"At least I waited nine months. He didn't wait nine

fucking minutes."

He laughed. "And *that's* what you should say to him if he tries to play the injured party. Which he will. I guarantee it."

"You don't know that. You've never even met him."

"I don't need to have met him to know what he's like." He reached into his jacket pocket and slammed a hundred-euro note on the table. "Let's have a wager. I bet you, by the end of the weekend, Benedict will tell you something like he wishes you hadn't broken up but that he had to do what he thought was best for his career. In fact, I'll go one better and speculate he suggests an affair."

"He wouldn't do that. No way."

Kadon tapped his fingernail against the bill. "Then put your money on the table, Alarie."

Surely he wouldn't... right? Not even Benedict was that much of an arsehole. I mean, yeah, he'd as much as admitted he was marrying Fenella for who her father was rather than any deep love for her. But he had to at least like her. And that might grow into love.

If Fenella hadn't slept with him when he was with me, I'd tell her what he was like. But as far as I was concerned, they deserved one another.

"I'll take the bet." I added my own one hundred euros to Kadon's. He folded the notes in half and slid them into his wallet. Holding up his glass of wine, he waited for me to pick mine up, too.

"Let the games begin."

I rose the next morning as the sun bathed the Eiffel Tower in yellow and gold. While this bed might be one of the comfiest I'd slept in, the view from the window was more than enough to drag me from between the sheets and head to the window to take it in.

I loved Paris. I loved it more after last night. The view from the Seine aboard a sleek cruiser while enjoying amazing food, fine wine, and the best company, was a night I'd remember for always. The number of times I'd mused how lucky I was that Kadon had chosen that particular beach and time to go for a run. But as much as I adored seeing him every day and working at the beach club, it wasn't my dream career.

The issue I had to solve was that I didn't know what that dream career entailed. I wanted to do *good* in the world, to use my brain after all those years of strutting down a catwalk and posing for endless photographs, but I hadn't a clue what that looked like. What if I moved to Paris and became an artist, living in a tiny loft with a view of the Seine? Hmm. The problem with that idea was I couldn't draw for shit. Even stick men were above my capabilities. Nor could I dance all that well, so applying for Moulin Rouge was also out of the question.

I jumped into the shower and dressed in the second-skin jeans and shirt I'd picked at Boutique Noémie. Slipping on the four-inch stilettos that elongated my legs, I looked in the mirror. *Not bad, girl. Not bad at all.* I applied more makeup than usual and curled my lavender hair until it fell in endless waves down my back. I hadn't gotten dressed up like this in a long time. I only wore a touch of mascara and lipstick at the club and usually tied my hair in a high ponytail to keep it out of the clients' drinks.

"Fuck you, Benedict. You'll rue the day you picked your political ambitions over me." A chuckle made its way up my throat. He probably wouldn't, but it felt good to have the thought.

I found Kadon sitting at the large dining room table tucking into a sizable breakfast. Men were so lucky. They could eat mostly what they wanted without putting on a pound in weight. Not at Kadon's age, anyway. Perhaps as they got older. Women only had to look at a pastry and put on five pounds. Not that I cared all that much these days. I ate whatever I wanted, just not every day. But today, it'd have to be the fruit bowl. These jeans wouldn't show off to their best if I had to undo the button to let my belly hang out.

Kadon's jaw almost unhinged when he saw me. "Fuck, Lee. You look... I mean..." He let out a low whistle. "Benedict's gonna shit his pants."

"Ew. I do hope not."

"Seriously. I know I saw that outfit when you bought it, but Christ, you've gone all out."

"Go big or go home, right?" I pulled out the chair next to his and sat down. "It's armor. That's all. Underneath this"—I gestured to my face and clothing—"I'm a hot mess."

He caught my hand in his, wrapped his fingers around mine, and lightly squeezed. "I've got you. We've got this. You're going to be fine. I promise."

"My legs are shaking. God knows what I'll be like when we actually get there."

"You put your arm around me. I'll support you. Physically, emotionally, whatever you need to get through this weekend, I'm there for you."

His speech hit me right in my feels. I canted my head

and smiled softly. "I hit the jackpot the day I met you." Something crossed his face, an emotion too fleeting for me to catch, then he turned away and reached for the teapot, pouring me a cup and topping off his own.

"What do you want to eat? I ordered pretty much everything on the menu just in case."

"Okay, Richard Gere." I laughed. "Although, I am nowhere near as pretty as Julia Roberts."

He nodded. "It's true. Julia's a fox. Then and now."

I picked up a croissant and chucked it at him. "Arsehole."

His hand snapped out, and he caught it. Pastry crumbs rained down on the table. "Gotta be quicker than that, Lee. I played baseball when I was a kid."

I saw an opportunity to tease him, and I took it. "In the UK, we call that rounders, and it's played by little girls with pigtails during break time."

He gaped at me, pressing a hand to his chest. "You did *not* just diss my beloved baseball."

I shrugged, my grin both innocent and devilish. "I'm only educating you on cultural differences."

"You're lucky you're not my girl. I'd put you over my knee for insulting my favorite sport."

My belly flipped, something unfurling down there, something I hadn't felt in a very long time: desire. I'd deny it if I thought I could lie to myself and get away with it, but what point was there in contesting the bleeding obvious? *It's the situation, and the nerves. And the fact that I haven't had sex in months.* Yeah, that was it. Nothing more than that.

"Lee? You okay?"

"Um..." I shook my head. "Yeah, sorry. My mind is all over the place today. It keeps wandering off. I should put it on a leash."

He laughed, and the moment passed. "Eat. We have to leave in thirty minutes."

I hovered around the entrance as Kadon visited the reception desk to check us out of the suite and settle the bill. I'd insisted that I pay half. He'd given me a look that reeked of offense, and I'd withdrawn my offer. He hadn't let me contribute to last night, either. And, come to think of it, he'd booked the Eurostar tickets and hired the car. I wasn't anywhere near Kadon rich, but I had more than enough money to spring for half of this trip. I'd revisit the conversation at a more appropriate time.

I'd never been on the Eurostar, and after we handed over our luggage and the hideous fruit bowl, we strolled down the platform toward the first-class carriages at the front of the train. Ridiculous bubbles of excitement rose within me, like a shaken bottle of Bollinger, and I couldn't take the inane grin off my face.

"Y'know, the tunnels between France and the UK are an engineering miracle."

Kadon chuckled. "There are no engineering miracles. Engineering is an exact science."

"You know what I mean. It's incredible. That's all. Did you know they started digging separately and met in the middle? How amazing is that?"

"I didn't know that. Fascinating."

I caught the drawl to his voice and wrinkled my nose. "Ah. The sarcasm is strong in this one." Okay, it wasn't my best Yoda impression, but it was passable. Sort of.

He gave my shoulder a little shove. "Get on the train, woman, before it leaves without us."

I climbed up the steps, stopping at the top. I turned back to Kadon. "I've been thinking that we should practice a bit."

My heart beat faster as the words left my lips. After this morning's moment of yearning, and the mistaken almost kiss from last night, my dormant libido had kicked into high gear. I'd never do anything with Kadon. God, no. He was my best friend. I'd never looked at him that way, and neither had he looked at me as anything more than a friend. But perhaps I could *trick* my horny sex drive into thinking this was real. I mean, it fit with the whole fake relationship thing, right?

"Practice? Practice what? Getting on the train without falling over? Letting *me* get on the train before a line forms behind me? Yoda impressions?" His grin stretched a mile wide.

"Y'know, Kingcaid, if you carry on like this, I'll have nothing left to teach you. No, I mean we should practice faking it while we're on the journey."

He blinked a few times, then tapped his lip. "What did you have in mind?"

"I dunno. Hold hands. Sit closer than we normally would. Just be... you know, like lovers would be."

His eyes softened. "I can do that." His voice was so quiet I barely heard him over the bustling train station.

"Good." I cocked my head, beckoning for him to follow me. "Well, come on then, before the train leaves without us. God, you men. And you say women can talk."

His laughter followed me all the way to our seats. I

took the one by the window. If he wanted it, he'd have to wrestle me for it. Wrestling. God. My clit pulsed. At this rate, I'd orgasm from the rumble of the train on the tracks alone. When we returned to Saint Tropez, I had to find someone to help me scratch this bloody itch. It wasn't as if sex with Benedict had shattered windows or broke beds or anything. It was good-ish. Passable. It hadn't been as good as a couple of my former boyfriends, but they'd been more hookups. Models made the worst boyfriends. You had to fight them for the bathroom, and who needed that?

Besides, passion faded. Everyone knew that. Longevity was what counted.

Although... come to think of it, Benedict and I had completely omitted the rip-your-clothes-off phase where making it to the bed was too much to handle. And you didn't care if the dining room table dug into your spine or you got a cramp in your calf because your legs were in the air or wrapped around the guy's neck.

Kadon slid into the seat next to me. His outer thigh touched mine, and I almost leapt through the roof of the train.

For God's sake, Leesa. Calm your tits!

I should have brought a vibrator with me, something to take the edge off. Dry-humping my best friend's leg would win first prize in the Worst Idea Ever competition. If such a competition existed. Not that it would. What a ridiculous idea.

Okay, I'm losing it.

Goddamn Paris. The city demanded sex and I'd disappointed it. My penalty was the urge to rub my lady bits on... anything, really. It didn't even have to be a man's cock.

I mean, a cock would be nice. Better than nice. A deliciously girthy cock with a hint of precum beading the crown. Man, I bet I'd come in less than twenty seconds.

"Why's your face red?"

I startled out of my dirty thoughts and stared at Kadon as if he'd spoken a foreign language to me. "Huh?"

"You're red, like sunburn red, and it's November in Paris. And you keep wriggling in your seat. Have you got ants in your pants?"

"No, I haven't got ants in my pants." Or a cock. "And it's warm on this train." I fanned myself with my hand. "Do you have any water in your bag?"

He stood and reached up to the luggage rail above our heads. His shirt rode up, treating me to a sliver of toned muscle. My clit's excitement reached at least DEFCON 4. Maybe the onboard shop sold vibrators alongside coffee and donuts.

It wasn't even Kadon who interested me. I'd take any man. Okay, not *any* man. Like, I wouldn't proposition the eighty-year-old helping his wife into the seat across the aisle from us. I had *some* limits.

"Here you go."

Kadon passed me a bottle of water. I unscrewed the top that he'd already loosened and took several sips. Better. I set it on the table in front of me.

"Thanks. I needed that."

He frowned, angling his head to one side. "Are you okay? You're acting pretty weird."

"Yeah, I'm good. Nervous, that's all."

He took my hand. "I've got you, babe." Cradling my face with his other hand, he tipped up my chin, his hazel eyes boring into mine. I lost the ability to speak, to think, to do anything other than stare right back at him. My gaze dropped to his lips. He ran his tongue over them, and they glistened.

Fuck me, he had kissable lips. Thick on the bottom, slightly thinner on top. I'd never noticed them in such detail before, but they were like... designed for kissing. And that dimple in his chin. I had the urge to put my pinkie in it.

"Oh, dears, you're the sweetest things."

I tore my eyes from Kadon's and glanced over his shoulder at the elderly lady whose husband I'd used to defend my out-of-control libido. Her hand was pressed to her throat, and her blue eyes shone out of her wrinkled face.

"Excuse me?"

Kadon released me and twisted around to check out the lady, too.

"I mean, young love. Do you remember that, Frederick?" She gave her husband a pretty sharp dig in the ribs. "Remember when we were like that? Young, beautiful, couldn't keep our hands off one another?"

Frederick grunted something unintelligible and turned his attention to the window. The lady rolled her eyes. "Men. They get grumpier as they age, dear, so take advantage of this beauty while you can."

Kadon snuffed out a laugh just in time, covering it with a cough. I managed a "Thank you, I will."

He shifted his body, shielding me from view, and arched one eyebrow. "Well, beautiful. I think our plan might just work."

Chapter 9

Kadon

When women say they're fine, they're not.

Something was off with Lee.

In all the time I'd known her, I'd never seen her act this weird. She kept staring at me as if I had carrots sprouting out of my head, or kale in my teeth. And talk about fidgeting. Dear God, she hadn't stopped shifting in her seat during the entire train journey to London. I'd asked her twice if she was okay, and on each occasion, she'd brushed my concern aside with a breezy "I'm fine." Now, I might be a man and use *fine* as a descriptor more than I should, but I had enough experience with women to know that when they responded with "Fine," they were anything but.

It had to be the wedding. She was happy enough when we'd driven from Saint Tropez to Paris, her usual self when we'd sailed down the Seine. Even this morning I hadn't noticed anything out of the ordinary.

The problems had begun when she'd boarded this train. That had to be it. This was the last leg of the journey. Once we disembarked at the other end, we'd be in London, only ninety minutes from her coming face-to-face with Benedict.

"It'll be all right, you know."

She stopped cannibalizing her lip long enough to answer me. "I know."

"I mean it, Lee. Please don't worry."

"I'm not worried."

"Then what *is* wrong? And don't say 'nothing' or tell me you're fine. I can smell bullshit a mile off."

"You should see a doctor about that. Can't be healthy having your nostrils full of the smell of excrement day and night." She grinned at me, but it didn't reach her eyes, and I couldn't help but notice she'd avoided answering my question.

"I'll take it under advisement, but I want you to know that you can talk to me. About anything."

"I know I can."

She briefly touched my shoulder with her head, something she regularly did, and it always made my protective side rear its head.

"It's nothing, really. Nerves, like I said. I'm dreading seeing Benedict, but worse than that, I'm terrified he'll see right through our charade and call me out in front of everyone, use it as a battering ram to hit me over the head with. 'Ahh, poor Annaleesa. She's so brokenhearted I junked her for someone else that she's brought a *pretend boyfriend* to the wedding. What a sad little excuse for a woman. I had a lucky escape.'" She sighed.

"He won't see through it."

"How do you know?"

"Because I'll make damn sure he doesn't."

"How?"

I palmed my neck. "I don't know yet. I'll figure it out."

The train pulled into St. Pancras at five minutes after eleven in the morning. As we collected our luggage, I jerked my chin at Lee's wedding gift. "Still in one piece."

"Shame," she said. "I'd enjoy watching Benedict slice open his hand on a jagged piece of glass."

I winked at her. "That's the spirit. Come on, let's go."

"How far is the car rental place?"

I shrugged. "No idea. But it'll piss me off if the car isn't waiting for us outside."

She grinned. "Ah, you billionaires. Such spoiled creatures."

"I can't deny it." I grabbed her suitcase and my own, leaving her with the garment bags and that awful fruit bowl. If anything sent a message of Lee's disdain for Benedict, it was that bowl.

We weaved through the throng of people crowding the platform, emerging into torrential rain. "Gotta love London." I took shelter underneath a canopy right outside the station. "You wait here. I'll put these in the car and then come back for your stuff."

"Where is the car?"

I pointed at the cherry-red Ferrari parked by the roadside. Lee shook her head.

"Safe to say my hope to make a quiet entrance is effectively ruined."

"Meh. We don't want you making a quiet entrance. This is a statement car, and we're making a statement with it. One that says, 'Fuck you, Benedict Prick-a-thon.'"

A smartly dressed woman battling with an umbrella handed me a set of keys. I thanked her, then heaved our suitcases into the trunk. I opened the passenger door for Lee. Once I'd seen her inside, I sped around the hood and jumped into the driver's side. My hair clung to my head, water dripping onto the leather seats. I flicked on the heated seats and turned up the fan.

"Here." Lee handed me a tissue.

I gave her a *What the fuck?* look. "What do you expect me to do with that?"

"It's all I've got. Take it or leave it."

"I'll drip-dry."

"Look on the bright side. At least you don't have so much hair to dry." She chuckled.

"You're quite the comedian, Alarie."

"You know it, Kingcaid."

I grinned at her, running my hands around the leather steering wheel. "What a beauty this car is. If I like her, I might have to buy one."

"I was thinking the same thing myself." She tapped her forefinger against her lips. "And to be clear, if you think you're having all the fun, you're mistaken. It's a ninety-minute drive, so you get the first forty-five minutes, and I'm having the next forty-five."

"That's not fair. I have to drive out of the city. Can't

exactly take advantage of the powerful engine while nego-
tiating London traffic."

"Then you should have let me drive first."

"Okay." I reached for the door handle.

"Forget it. You picked a side. You're stuck with it now."
Her grin widened.

"Goddammit." I hit the steering wheel. "You duped me."

"No. You duped yourself. And I suggest you get a
wriggle on. A traffic warden is making a beeline for us."

She pointed at the uniformed warden striding down
the sidewalk in a determined fashion, her expression sour,
her lips pinched. I started the engine, checked the mirrors,
and pulled away. I could have sworn she looked disappointed as we passed.

I hadn't been to London for some time. I'd hoped the
traffic situation might have improved, but if anything, it
was worse. It took thirty minutes to drive a mile. I glanced
at Lee. "We need to renegotiate our agreed terms." Before
she could answer, my phone rang. "Can you get that? I
haven't connected my phone to the car."

She reached for my phone in the center console. "It's
Blaize."

I frowned. "What does he want?"

Dropping my phone in her lap, she pressed two fingers
to her temples. "Hang on a sec. I need to tune in to my
psychic abilities." She laughed. "How the hell do I know?"

"It was rhetorical." I flicked her with the back of my
hand. "Answer it for me."

"What am I, your secretary?" She picked up the
phone. "Lord Kingcaid's mobile. May I help you?"

I burst out laughing, cocking my ears to pick up Blaize's deep baritone. He was laughing, too, although I couldn't make out what he was saying.

"One sec." She tapped something on the phone. "Okay, you're on speaker. Keep the locker room talk to a minimum, please, Kingcaid brothers. There's a lady present."

Blaize laughed harder. I'd told him all about Lee, including my obsession with her, though I hadn't had the chance to introduce Lee to any of my family. I trusted him to keep my confidence. He'd never throw me under the bus like that.

"What's up, bro?"

"I believe you're in London."

I leaned forward and glanced through the windshield and up at the gloomy gray sky. "Have you got a drone following me or something?"

"No. I injected a tracking device into you a long time ago."

"I wouldn't put it past you."

"If I could've gotten away with it when you were a teenager, I would have. In case he hasn't told you, Leesa, he was a complete delinquent from ages thirteen to sixteen."

"All right, all right. Don't share all my secrets."

Blaize chuckled. "Mom told me you're going to a wedding."

"Yeah. Lee's ex." I glanced sideways at her, one eyebrow raised in query. I didn't want her to think I was speaking out of turn.

"Your brother has kindly agreed to accompany me as

my fake boyfriend so I can stick two fingers up at that jerk I almost married."

The pause on the line was less than two seconds, but I caught it. Lee, though, appeared oblivious.

"Is that right? What a stellar guy my brother is."

Yep, caught that, too. The drawl loaded with sarcasm.

"Yeah, he's a good egg."

"Aha!" I pointed at her. "Right there. A weird British saying, even if it has caught on in America. And that one is odder than 'a minute,' or 'a hot minute.'"

"Don't be ridiculous," she retorted. "There's no comparison. It might have started in Britain, but it's used the world over. 'A good egg' is a brilliant saying. And it has an opposite—a bad egg. What's the opposite of 'a hot minute'? A cold minute? Of course not, because that makes no sense."

"Actually, the opposite of a hot minute *is* a cold minute. It means a very short amount of time."

Lee's eyebrows flew up her head. "You're kidding?"

"Nope."

"Good God."

I laughed. Blaize wouldn't have the faintest idea what we were talking about, but it didn't matter. This was how it was with Lee and me. We lived in our own world most of the time.

"You two do remember I'm here, right? I mean, much as I'd love to play third wheel to such quick-witted repartee for the next several hours, I did actually call for a reason."

Lee mouthed, "I like him."

I mouthed back, "I do, too."

"Sorry, bro. What did you want?"

"I wondered if you had time for a coffee before you head off, or lunch maybe?"

My mouth fell open. "Wait. You're in London, too?"

"Yes. That's what I've been trying to tell you, but honestly, it's kinda challenging to get a word in. I'm over here for a couple of days on a business trip."

"I'd love to meet up!" I didn't see nearly as much of my brothers as I'd like, what with Nolen in Las Vegas, Blaize based out of Miami, and me an ocean away in France. "So long as it's okay with Lee." I side-eyed her.

"All good here, provided I'm invited. I'm not sitting on a wall in the freezing cold eating a soggy sandwich while you two dine on lobster."

"Ah. I'd hoped it'd be just me and Kadon, Leesa. I'm sure you understand. We don't see all that much of each other."

I immediately grasped the situation. Blaize was having a little fun of his own. Lee, though, didn't know him, so she didn't pick up on the nuance in his voice. She deflated, her shoulders drooping like lilies starved of water. Her smile fell.

"Oh. I see. Well then, I guess I could—"

"Kidding." Blaize laughed. "Well, would you look at that? I can hold my own."

Lee's jaw dropped. "You... you..."

"*Asshole* is the word you're searching for," I said. "Don't worry. I'll hold him so you can punch him."

"I probably deserve it."

"No 'probably' about it. Where shall we meet you? We're about a mile west of St. Pancras, on Euston Road by Madame Tussauds, but the traffic is horrendous. It's taken us forever to get this far. There must be a crash or something, because we're hardly moving."

"Hang on a second. I'll find somewhere close by." He went quiet for about thirty seconds. "Okay, got it. There's a great little bistro called Crumb on George Street. I took a supplier there last time I visited London. I'm not that far away. I'll be there in twenty minutes."

"I hope I get more than a crumb," Lee said. "I'm starved."

Blaize chuckled. "Definitely more than a crumb. I'll see you there." He cut the call.

"He sounds nice."

"He's great." I opened the navigation pane on the in-car system and tapped in *Crumb, George Street.* "Both my brothers are. In fact, my entire family is pretty darn special."

"You're lucky."

Her voice was wistful. I squeezed her hand. "It's none of my business, but perhaps you should call your parents."

"You're right. It is none of your business." She snatched her hand from beneath mine, then sighed. "I'm sorry. That was uncalled for. I... I'm angry at them. And disappointed. I gave twenty years of my life to modeling, yet Maman thinks I should have given more. I probably would have if Benedict hadn't dumped me, but now that I'm out of that world, I know I made the right decision, even if it was 'in haste,' as Maman bluntly pointed out."

"They want what's best for you. That's all."

"Aren't I in the prime position to decide what's best for me?" She wriggled in her seat, growing agitated with the direction of the conversation.

"Yes. Of course you are. That's not what I'm saying." I scrubbed a hand over my stubble. "You've every right to be angry. I just don't want you to have regrets. Someone has to make the first move."

"Yes, and it should be them." She crossed her arms over her chest. *Defensive mode activated.*

I let her stew. Lee's temper lasted about as long as an ice cream in ninety-degree heat. Sure enough, thirty seconds later, she unfolded her arms and rested them in her lap.

"I'll think about it. Okay?"

"Whatever you decide to do is good with me. All I want is for you to be happy."

I caught her smile out of the corner of my eye, and it warmed me from the pit of my stomach to the tips of my fingers. Why did she have to be so goddamn beautiful? And why, oh why, couldn't I make her see me as more than just a friend?

"I've said it before, but it warrants repeating. I'm so lucky to have you as a friend." Her mouth turned down for the briefest moment. "I've never had friends. Not really. Did I ever tell you that?"

The monotonous voice of the navigation system interrupted my response. I turned off Euston Road onto Gloucester Place.

"I don't have friends, either, other than you. I lost touch with my school friends, and I never went to college, so..." I shrugged. Dad had thought it better for me to go straight into the family business after what had happened in Switzerland, and he'd been right. With my particular learning challenges, I'd have hated college. I'd learned more in six months of shadowing Dad and my uncles than I would have in four years of further education.

"But you have your brothers and your cousins. I've often wished Maman and Papa had more kids."

It occurred to me that Lee rarely talked about her family. Maybe she couldn't get a word in with the number of times I talked about mine. That made me a shitty friend. I should try some gentle coaxing to encourage her to reach out to her parents. As much as she put on a brave face, it was clear to me she missed them.

"Do you know why?"

"Yeah. Maman had complications after having me, and her doctor advised her not to have any more kids. I guess they could have adopted, but for whatever reason, they didn't."

"What about modeling? You must have made a ton of friends there."

She laughed. "Ah, my dearest Kadon. Models aren't friends. They're *rivals*. And it wasn't as if I attended school like other kids. I had a tutor traveling with me."

God. What a lonely life she'd led. It broke my heart.

"Well, for what it's worth, you're never getting rid of me."

She put her hand on my knee, and I almost shot through the roof. Somehow, I kept myself attached to the seat. Not a clue how. I wished she'd superglue her hand to my leg.

"Ditto."

Chapter 10

Kadon

The best idea I'd ever had, or the worst?

"Trust you to arrive in a Ferrari." Blaize stepped forward and bear-hugged me. "You're such a cliché. Glad to see the luscious locks are growing back." He let me go, ruffled my hair, and then held out a hand to Lee. "You must be Leesa. Nice to meet you."

"And you. I've heard a lot about you."

"Don't believe everything my baby brother says, unless it's complimentary, then it's a hundred percent accurate." He gestured to the entrance. "I've already got us a table. Shall we go inside and escape the cold?"

I waited for Lee to pick where she wanted to sit, then took the chair next to hers, resting my arm along the back, the instinct to drop in onto her shoulder like Travolta did to Newton-John in Grease. Minus the ridiculous sneeze, of course. Blaize sat opposite, crossed his legs, and opened his menu.

"If you're starved, Leesa, I recommend the Diablo Burger. It's not exactly a date meal, but none of us here have to worry about burger juices running down our chins." He stared pointedly at me. Lee wouldn't know the purpose of his stare, but I did.

I studiously ignored him. "Think I'll have the salmon."

"I'll go with Blaize's suggestion and have the burger. And a sparkling water."

Talk about nailing a guy between the eyes. Not that I gave a flying fuck about burger juices dripping down her chin. If anything, all I'd want to do was lick them off. But it was more what Lee's choice said about us. That there *was* no us. That there never *would be* an us. We were friends. That was all.

I knew this. Yet every time further evidence presented itself, my chest got a little tighter, my lungs struggled to breathe, and my shoulders bowed that touch more.

Blaize beckoned over a hovering server. "Two Diablo Burgers and the salmon. One sparkling water and two Cokes. Thanks." He gathered up our menus and handed them over. "So, Leesa, what's with this wedding? Are you planning to slip laxatives in his drink and spoil his wedding night?"

Lee laughed. "I hadn't thought of that, but it's a great idea. I'll keep it in mind." She paused to allow the server to set down her water. "I had no intention of going, until Kadon suggested we fake it out and pretend we're a couple."

Blaize picked up his glass of Coke, his jade-green eyes on me. "Is that right?"

I fidgeted in my chair. "Yeah. Her ex is a dick, and I'm more than happy to help Lee stick it to him."

"I'll bet you are," he drawled, one eyebrow perfectly arched.

I widened my eyes and flattened my lips in a simple message of "Shut the fuck up." I had nothing to worry about. Not really. I was only picking up on the hidden meaning behind Blaize's comment because I knew him so well. Leesa appeared oblivious to the secret conversation going on between me and my brother.

Our food arrived, and our conversation turned to our cruise ship business that Blaize headed up. Lee listened with fascination as Blaize told her about his latest venture; in a few months' time, Kingcaid Cruises would launch a new ship that, as of now, would be the largest vessel in the world. One of our rivals would build a bigger one eventually, but for a while at least, we'd be at the top of the tree. Blaize had been working on this for about five years, and his palpable excitement as the maiden voyage grew closer plastered a grin on his face that wouldn't quit.

"We're sailing out of Miami on July 1. You should come. Our brother, Nolen, and his wife, Marlowe, are planning to sail with us for a week for their delayed honeymoon. They have a baby, and they wanted to wait until she's a little older before they left her for that length of time," Blaize explained.

"It's peak season," I said. "I can't spare my staff at that time of the year."

"I might not be working for you by then," Lee said with an air of casualness that stabbed me right in the gut.

"Oh?" Blaize crossed one leg over the other. "Why's that?"

"I'm not sure what I want to do with my life, long-term. I love working at the beach club, but it was only ever supposed to be temporary. Right, Kadon?"

"Right," I rasped, the single word sticking in my throat.

"Yeah, so once I figure out where I'm going and what I want to do, I'll move on." She dug me with her elbow. "He's far too nice to say this, but he'll be glad to be rid of me. I'm a pain in his butt most of the time."

"Yeah. Pain in my butt." I smiled weakly.

"Phew." Lee wiped her mouth with her napkin and dropped it on top of her plate. "You weren't kidding about that burger, Blaize." She rubbed her stomach. "I should have had the salmon. These jeans aren't made to house bloated bellies." Getting to her feet, she slipped her purse off the back of her chair. "Won't be a sec."

My eyes tracked her to the restrooms. The heat from Blaize's stare burned into my skin, and when I turned back to face him, he shook his head.

"Bro, she's beautiful and smart and funny, and perfect for you. But..."

I held up my hand. "I know. She's oblivious. Don't fucking rub it in."

He leaned back in his chair, laced his fingers, and propped them behind his head, stretching. "You should tell her how you feel."

"What? No," I spluttered. "I know where she is, and it isn't where I am. Have you any idea how painful it is to tell

106

someone you love them and not have them say it back to you?"

"No. Have you?"

"Well, no. But I can freaking imagine it well enough." I glanced at the closed restroom door. No sign of Lee. "I don't want to lose her friendship. If being friend-zoned is the only way I can keep her in my life, then so be it."

His smile was wry. "Can't be easy."

"Fucking understatement of the century."

"I can see why you're so smitten, though. She's a stunner, and I'm not just talking about her looks."

"Tell me something I don't know."

He rested his elbows on the table and propped his chin on his hands. "I don't want you to get hurt. You deserve more."

I snorted. "You and I both know that isn't true."

He registered my meaning, shaking his head. "No, Kadon. *You* think it isn't true, but you're wrong. What happened, happened. None of us can alter the past, although God knows, if it was possible, I'd do whatever it took to make it happen. You've gotta let it go, brother. You've suffered long enough."

My heart froze mid-beat, my ribs threatening to crush my lungs "Have I? Have I really? Do you think that kid's parents would agree with you?"

Blaize pursed his lips, breathing out slowly. "It was an accident."

"That I'm responsible for."

His nostrils flared, and he opened his mouth to say the same thing he'd been saying for over nine years—that I did a *good* thing that went badly wrong. On this occasion, he didn't get the chance to say it.

"Okay, Kingcaid." Lee rested her hands on my shoulders and squeezed. I almost shot through the ceiling. "I'm fueled, refreshed, and ready to stick two fingers up to the happy couple."

"Sounds good." I downed the remains of my Coke and stood to hug my brother. By the time we returned from Berkshire, he'd have flown back to Miami. "Call me."

"Will do." He hugged Lee, too. "It was wonderful to meet you. And for what it's worth, I agree with Kadon. Your ex is a dick."

"I think we can all agree on that."

Lee kissed his cheek, and a shard of jealousy sharper than cut glass sliced through my stomach, real and painful enough that I wrapped my arm around my middle.

"It was great to see you." *Even if not-my-girl just kissed you, you lucky bastard.* "Safe flight back to Miami."

"And you two enjoy the wedding." He lifted one eyebrow. "Sounds like it'll be a blast." Chuckling, he pivoted and set off down the street in the opposite direction to us.

"He's great. My envy is back now that I've met him." Her smile dissolved and her chest rose and fell with a wistful sigh. "What is it about humans that we always wish for those things we can't have, not because we don't have the will to make them happen, but that they're impossible to attain no matter what we do?"

"Families can be made as well as inherited. You might not have grown up in a big family, but that doesn't mean you can't create one of your own one day."

With me.

Her luminous eyes widened, and she moved into my body, wrapping her arms around my waist. "You always know the right thing to say at the right time. I love you, Kingcaid."

It wasn't the first time Lee had told me she loved me, and it wouldn't be the last. But it wasn't anywhere close to the way I craved to hear her say those three words with a completely different sentiment behind them. In a way, it was worse than not hearing them.

"Love you, too." The passion in my voice echoed through my ears. As always, Lee was oblivious to the difference between the way she said she loved me and the way I said it back to her.

"I'm driving the next bit." She held out her hand for the keys. "And before you say anything, I know I'm changing our agreement. But if I drive the last part, we're likely to have a crash. I'm already shaking at the idea of coming face-to-face with him again. We can swap over ten miles out."

I dropped the keys into her hand. "Fair enough."

By the time we returned to the main road, the traffic had cleared and we made it out of London and onto the M4 motorway with no further holdups. Lee filled the car with chatter, and I sat back and listened to her talk, only interjecting when required, but as we approached the ten-mile mark where we'd agreed I'd drive the rest of the way, she fell silent. Her tension was palpable. She'd stiffened, her shoulders hunched up to her ears, and the grip on the steering wheel had turned her knuckles white.

"There's a parking area up ahead." I pointed to the

sign, which stated it was a half mile away. "Pull in there and we'll switch."

I waited for her to bring the car to a complete stop and cut the engine, then took her hand and placed it over my chest, pressing mine on top. For sure, she'd feel how fast my heart was beating, but I didn't care. All that mattered was offering her some reassurance and comfort.

"I've got you, Lee. I know you're panicking, but this is where you get your closure." I flashed a quick grin. "And, unless I'm way off the mark, your revenge. 'Bout time Benny drowned in a taste of his own sour medicine."

She nodded, bit her lip, and said nothing.

"Talk to me. Tell me what you're thinking."

Pursing her lips, she blew out a breath. "What if seeing him again dredges up all those old feelings? I've come so far. I don't want to go back to that place where I couldn't breathe properly, where the might of his betrayal sat on my chest night after night as I lay staring at the ceiling with tears streaming down my face."

I fucking hated that bastard. For what he'd done to her all those months ago, and for the power he continued to have over her. I stood by my conviction, though. Once she saw him again, she'd realize what a pathetic excuse for a man he was, and she'd realize, deep in her gut, that she'd had a lucky escape when he'd chosen ambition over the love of a woman he hadn't deserved.

"I can't say for certain what your reaction will be, but, I dunno, Lee, I have this feeling that this is where you finally close the door on that chapter of your life and move forward into a far brighter future. But if you find that this is all too much, say the word, and I'll have you out of there in seconds."

She smiled. "A safeword?"

I smiled back. "If you like."

"Okay." She rested her head against the back of the seat and looked up at the roof of the car. "How about... *wiener.*"

I chuckled. "Aimed at Benedict, I presume."

"Correct. It not only means a tiny sausage, but also an irritating person. Both fit him perfectly."

"*Wiener* it is. And as much as I hope you don't have to use it, I can't wait to see how you weave that into a sentence."

"Maybe I won't." She unclipped her seat belt. "I might shout, 'Wiener!' at the top of my voice instead."

Laughing, I unclipped my belt, too, and opened the door. "I wouldn't put it past you."

We switched places. Fifteen minutes later, I turned off the country lane and through a set of wrought-iron gates with "Grange Manor" fashioned into the artwork. Lee shifted in her seat, sitting up straighter, and her shoulders hunched again.

"I've got you," I repeated gently.

"I know." She drew in a deep breath through her nose and blew it out. "I'm ready."

A couple of other cars were ahead of us as we arrived at the circular, graveled entrance where valets waited for the next guest. In the center, set in a large water fountain, was a stone figurine of a man with the smallest dick I'd ever seen. It was almost as if the artist had run out of marble and thought, *Meh, that'll do.*

I jerked my chin at it. "Think that's modeled on Benedict?"

Lee burst out laughing. "It's eerily fitting."

The valet motioned to me. I pulled forward, stopping in front of him. I unclipped my seat belt, catching Lee's gaze locked on a group of five people chatting by the stone steps leading up into the manor house. Three strangers plus Benedict and his betrothed.

Lee twisted the hem of her shirt, creasing it. "Oh God," she murmured. "I can do this, right?"

"A hundred percent." I tugged her hand away from her shirt. "Wait there. Don't move."

I exited the car and walked around to her side. Opening her door, I reached in with my hand. "Take it."

Her warm fingers clasped mine. As she stepped out, Benedict glanced over. His eyes flared in surprise. I'd wager that, despite her RSVP, he hadn't expected her to actually turn up, and especially not with another man on her arm.

An idea slithered into my mind, as slippery as a snake and potentially as deadly to my friendship with Lee if she didn't approve of my "fuck you" methods. And yep, I admitted, a significant part of me saw an opportunity that might never come along again.

Making sure his eyes remained on us, I curved my hands around Lee's face, tipping her head backward.

"Do you trust me?"

Her eyes widened, and she nodded. I pressed my lips to hers, and the world vanished.

What started out as a gentle kiss meant to send a message to her ex morphed into a passionate encounter, engulfing me in a fiery blaze of lust. Kissing Lee wasn't anything like the dreams that kept me awake at night. It was the moon, the sun, the earth, the stars. It was *everything.*

She was *my everything.*

Lee opened her mouth. A gasp of shock perhaps, or a need for air, but the undeserving fucker in me took full advantage. I slipped my tongue between her lips, wrapping it around hers in a sensual dance to the music in my head, my thoughts consumed with "I could do this forever."

Lee thrust her hands into my hair and pulled me closer. A soft moan vibrated in her throat, and my groin burst into flames.

This single shattering kiss had incinerated any second thoughts Lee had about our fake relationship. We had no choice but to see it through now.

Chapter 11

Leesa

I'm not in Kansas anymore, Toto.

WHAT IN THE NAME OF GOD WAS THAT?

My knees shook, aliens had abducted the bones in my thighs and replaced them with jelly, and an unequivocal dampness that should *not* be there gathered between my legs. Add to that the slight problem of losing the ability to speak, and I was toast.

There were kisses, and then there were *kisses*, and Kadon's kiss was splat in the middle of the latter.

Sweet Jesus. Save me from the urge to climb him like that giant oak tree we'd passed on the way up to the house.

Kadon Kingcaid was my *best friend*. I was *not* attracted to him. Nope. No. Definitely not. Before we'd embarked on this stupid trip, I'd never once looked at him or thought of him in that way. I could sort of forgive my reaction to

115

him in Paris. I mean... we were in *Paris*. The city of love. He could have been anyone and I'd probably have had the same reaction.

But this... this was new.

New... and scary.

Because that kiss had my mind tearing off in directions it had no business traveling.

I touched my lips, swollen from the intensity of his kiss. The reason he'd kissed me was as clear as a cloudless sky. I'd caught Benedict eyeing us right before Kadon had asked me if I trusted him, and I'd second-guessed his plan. But I'd expected a quick peck, a tender look, or him tucking my hair behind my ear. I had not expected him to rock the ground beneath my feet and change the trajectory of my thoughts.

I'm not in Kansas anymore, Toto.

I peeked up at Kadon to gauge his reaction to what had transpired between us and whether he was as shaken up as I was. I expected to find him dumbfounded, or befuddled, or contrite, or worried.

Instead, his smirk was steeped in smugness, he'd jutted out his chin in that cocky manner some guys perfected after they'd nailed a girl, and he'd raised his eyebrows in a deliberate fashion.

"Fine, so you can kiss," I muttered. "Make sure you put that on your resumé."

A chuckle rumbled through his firm chest. The chest that, seconds ago, had my boobs pressed flat against it. The chest that, suddenly, I couldn't stop staring at. The firm outline of his pecs, the breadth of it. The power in those muscles, honed through hours of surfing.

I lowered my gaze—and caught a definite bulge in his groin.

Oh, fuck. Abort! Abort!

I looked up so fast I almost lost my eyes round the back of my head.

"Annaleesa!"

Benedict strode toward us, a smile as fake as Kadon's and my relationship plastered to his face and showing off teeth so bright they blinded me. I considered reaching into my handbag for my sunglasses until I remembered it was November in England and sunglasses were normally surplus to requirements.

"Hello, Benedict." Zero tremor to my voice. Top marks. "You look well."

"As do you." He looked me up and down as if he were assessing a prize thoroughbred. "Marvelous, in fact."

Kadon pressed his palm to my lower back, a move meant to support me. Instead, electricity sizzled up my spine. It surprised me that my hair didn't stand on end from the static. I could power an entire city with the volts traveling through my bloodstream.

"Thank you." I leaned my head on Kadon's shoulder. "This is Kadon Kingcaid. My boyfriend," I added pointedly. More like pointlessly, considering the display we'd put on for the assembled guests and the happy couple.

Kadon held out his hand. "Nice to meet you, Ben."

I suppressed a chuckle. Benedict's eyes widened, and his lips mashed together.

"It's Benedict. I didn't know you had a boyfriend, Annaleesa."

Kadon arched an eyebrow. "Really? You look far more

like a Ben. Or a Benny. And, to be clear, Lee doesn't have to tell you a damn thing about her personal life, or, indeed, any part of her life."

This time I couldn't help it. A squeak escaped through my lips. I tried—and failed—to disguise it with a cough. Kadon sounded so genial, yet the menace behind his tone came across loud and clear.

Benedict's neck reddened, a pulse thrumming in his cheek. He puffed out his chest and stood up straight, but despite his best efforts, he fell three or four inches short of Kadon. "I prefer 'Benedict.'"

"Then I'll do my utmost to remember that."

Ohhh, Kadon was playing a superb game. I could kiss him. Except I already had. Or rather, he'd kissed me. Either way, we'd kissed.

Stop thinking about the kissing.

The problem was, I couldn't. Even with Benedict's offended cockerel routine and Kadon's blatant "You're a dick" response, the way Kadon's lips had felt against mine consumed every thought.

"Kingcaid." Benedict tapped his finger against his chin. "Why does that name sound familiar?"

"Kadon's family has businesses all over the globe." I could have added, "And his bank balance makes your future father-in-law look like a pauper," but I refrained. Kadon hardly ever threw around his family's wealth; therefore, it was hardly my place to.

"Leesa!" Fenella hurried over before Benedict could respond, all plumped-up lips, waving arms, and back-combed hair that she really should check for nesting birds. "Oh, I'm so glad you could make it." She enveloped me in a hug and air-kissed the space next to both my cheeks. "I wasn't sure, you know. What with everything that's gone on. But I always knew you were the sort of person who didn't hold grudges."

Oh, I hold grudges. And they're aimed right between the eyes of your cheating fiancé.

Benedict was the one who'd been in a committed relationship and had thrown it all away for someone he thought better suited to enable his political ambitions. All too often, women blamed other women for their relationship breakups, and while it took two to tango, I laid ninety-five percent of the fault firmly at Benedict's door.

"Good to see you, Fenella. Are you excited for the wedding?"

"Very." She stuffed her hand through Benedict's arm and nestled into him. "We can't wait. Can we, darling?"

"Nope." He barely glanced at her, his eyes locked on me.

Fenella didn't notice, too busy checking out Kadon. "And who is this?"

"Kadon. My boyfriend." It sounded more natural the second time around. By the time we left, I might have perfected it. Right before we went back to being just good friends.

I rubbed my chest. Why did that thought cause an unsettling feeling to weigh on me?

"Oh, this is marvelous." Fenella clapped her hands. "Look at you, Leesa. You've bagged yourself quite the hottie."

Benedict bristled, but either Fenella was oblivious to the undercurrent, or she didn't care. He grabbed her hand

and almost yanked her off her feet. "Come now, Fenella. We do have other guests to welcome." He dipped his chin at me, ignoring Kadon completely. "Enjoy the festivities, Annaleesa. I'm sure we'll see plenty of each other over the coming days."

I nearly said, "More's the pity," but swallowed the retort at the last second and formed a sickly sweet smile instead. "Sounds wonderful."

"Wait." Fenella gestured impatiently to a middle-aged gentleman standing off to one side. "Andrews, please show Miss Alarie and Mister..." She arched a brow.

"Kingcaid," Kadon supplied.

"And Mr. Kingcaid to their quarters." She waggled her fingers at me. "We're thrilled you're staying here as our special guests. Toodles, Leesa."

Benedict hauled her off with such force that she almost tripped over her feet. Kadon watched them go, then looked at me, an amused tilt to his lips.

"Quarters? Toodles?"

I grinned. "You're in the world of the English aristocracy now, my boy."

"If I shout, 'Fuck!' at the top of my lungs, will the women faint and the men challenge me to a duel?"

"I'm not sure. Why don't you test the theory?"

I should have known better than to goad Kadon. He opened his mouth. I clamped my hand over it in the nick of time.

"Don't you dare."

The breath from his chuckle warmed my palm. I released him with a warning glare. Andrews motioned for us to follow him. He led us into the main house and up two flights of stairs, then along a dimly lit corridor decorated in a dark green, heavy brocade wallpaper to a mahogany door at the end. He opened it and motioned for us to enter.

"A member of staff will bring your luggage up shortly. Please let me know if you need anything." He bowed, then backed out of the room.

I stared, open-mouthed.

"There's only one bed." I scanned around. A single door led to what I presumed was the bathroom. "There isn't even a couch." I opened the wardrobe door. "Or spare blankets."

"Lee, quit panicking. I'll sleep on the floor. I can use this." He pointed to the woolen throw draped over the end of the bed.

"It didn't occur to me that they'd give us only one room. I thought we'd end up with a suite, or at least a room with a couch. Do you think we should go stay in a hotel?"

"No, I don't. That would look odd, considering we're supposed to be a couple. Unless you want to tell them you're saving yourself." He winked. "It's not a problem. Truly."

I shook my head. "You can't sleep on the floor. They're so uneven in these old houses. You'll ruin your back. It's a big enough bed. I'm... I wasn't expecting it. That's all." I narrowed my eyes at him. "But if you snore, I warn you, you're relegated to sleeping in the bath."

Kadon poked his head into the bathroom. "Hate to tell you this, but it's only got a shower."

"Oh, for Christ's sake." I sat on the edge of the bed. "Are we being punished for faking it?"

He sat beside me. His thigh was too close, too warm, too muscular. An urge to fan myself overcame me.

"I don't think Karma works like that."

"Don't bank on it," I muttered, shifting away a few inches and hoping he didn't notice.

Someone knocked at the door and I leapt to my feet, taking the opportunity to put a bit of space between me and Kadon. A porter wheeled our luggage inside, handing over an itinerary for the next three days. I waited for the staff member to leave, then handed it to Kadon.

"You read that while I hang these dresses up." I unzipped the first garment bag and hung the dress on the rail, glancing behind me as Kadon groaned.

"What?"

"This is... so regimented. Like tonight, we're expected to attend a dinner so we can mingle and meet the other guests." He rolled his eyes. "As if we'll ever see any of these people again. After dinner, there's a fireworks display. Then tomorrow, the men are going pheasant hunting." He arched a brow. "Fucking barbaric sport, if you ask me. I won't be shooting a single fucking bird. Maybe I'll take aim at Benny instead."

I laughed. "And what are the little women doing while the men are out beating chests and shooting innocent wildlife?"

"Ah. You get to enjoy a relaxing spa day and extol the virtues of the male species."

"Sounds... like a nightmare."

"Yep. Then tomorrow night, there's the rehearsal dinner. And on Saturday, it's the actual wedding, which, wait for it, runs from one o'clock to midnight." He flopped back on the bed. "Kill me now."

I picked up the second garment bag and unzipped it. "It's at this point I'd like to remind you that this was your idea. If it were up to me, I'd be sunning myself on a beach in Barbados right about now."

But if I'd done that, I wouldn't have had everything I've ever known about kissing destroyed by a man that, two days ago, I'd never looked at with anything approaching romantic thoughts.

Kadon had turned me on, and now I couldn't turn myself off.

My face heated. I moved away before he noticed my red cheeks and asked me why I looked as if I'd stuck my head in the oven.

"Well, we're here now. We'll have to find some way to amuse ourselves. Let me know if you think of any ideas."

My stomach flipped as if I'd crested the Big Dipper. Ideas? Yeah, I had ideas. Too many.

And all of them filthy.

Chapter 12

Kadon

**If heaven was a person instead of a place,
I'd found mine.**

I stood in front of the full-length mirror fiddling with my cuff links while I listened to the sound of running water on the other side of the wall. My imagination was spinning out of control. A two-inch slab of wood, a.k.a. a door, was the only thing that stood between me and a naked Lee. Ever since I'd kissed her, I kept having dizzy spells.

Probably because my cock hadn't deflated after my lips had left hers and my body couldn't spare the blood for my brain.

And tonight... tonight, I'd get to sleep beside her, in the *same fucking bed.* How I'd kept my cool when we'd discovered the sleeping arrangements would remain a mystery. I'd vacillated between punching the air as if I'd made the winning touchdown in the Super Bowl and drowning in dread at how on earth I'd keep my hands off her all goddamn night.

The water stopped. I smoothed a hand over my hair, my heart thumping against my rib cage. I pictured her stepping out of the shower stall, droplets of water caressing her breasts, her waist, her hips. My fingers tingled like they did in the depths of winter, but it wasn't from cold. Far from it. If I took my temperature right now, I'd diagnose myself with a fever.

I ran a hand around the collar of my shirt and sat on the edge of the bed with my back to the bathroom. The least I could do was afford her a little privacy. Not that I expected her to emerge completely naked, but the way I was feeling, and with my libido running amok, even if she came out wearing a towel, I'd probably orgasm and ruin my dress pants.

The door opened, and I held my breath.

"It's okay. I'm decent."

I twisted on the bed, shifting my leg up as I pivoted at the hip. Lee was wearing a knee-length cream cocktail dress with her hair wrapped in a fluffy white towel. She hadn't bought this dress when we'd visited Boutique Noémie, so I guessed she must have owned it already. It might lack the red-carpet style of the two she'd bought there, but she looked like a million dollars in it. She'd eclipse every woman there tonight, even if she kept the towel on.

Lee was a class act. From the top of her head to the tips of her toes.

"Nice dress."

"Thanks. I've had it for a while. It's a bit tight. I'm not as slender as I used to be."

"You're perfect."

I meant it, too. My attraction toward Lee was multilayered. Sure, she had a smoking body and the face of a goddess, but Lee was one of the smartest women I knew. She also had a pure heart and an Olympic-standard wit that kept me on my toes and made me laugh every day. I couldn't stand the thought of her leaving my employ and days, or even weeks, passing by where I didn't see her.

"Oh, shush. I'm far from perfect. And you don't need to fake it when we're alone."

"What if they have cameras on us?" I grinned to hide the pain her comment had caused.

"Then, considering my performance over the 'one-bed-gate,' I'd say the game is already up."

"Fair point well made."

I lay down on the bed, my arms braced behind my head as Lee dried her hair and applied makeup that, by the time she'd finished, looked as if she weren't wearing any yet gave her complexion a fresh-faced natural beauty. It was a skill, I realized, and one she'd clearly perfected. Not that it mattered to me. She looked gorgeous with or without makeup.

She perched on the edge of the bed and slipped on her shoes. Standing, she smoothed her hands over her hips and angled her head to one side.

"Will I do?"

I ran my tongue over my lips and swallowed. "There won't be a woman in that room who stands a chance of eclipsing you." I hadn't meant to voice my earlier thoughts, but I couldn't help it. She might be faking, but *I* wasn't. I wouldn't get another chance to be so open with my feelings. If she questioned me, I'd say I was method acting.

She didn't, though. She smiled, leaned over, giving me a bird's-eye view of her cleavage, and kissed my cheek.

"You're too good to me, Kadon."

I sat up with my back to her so she wouldn't see my cock tenting my dress trousers and prayed for the fucking thing to deflate. "We're a team," I said, pretending to retie my laces to buy a little time. "We're good to each other." I stood and fastened my suit jacket, hiding my semi.

"Look at you. So handsome." She brushed her hands over my lapels.

Sticking out my elbow, I smiled at her. "Ready?"

She sighed. "As I'll ever be."

According to the itinerary, tonight's dinner was in the ballroom. Signs guided us down a hallway filled with paintings of what I presumed were familial ancestors. My knowledge of architecture would fit on the head of a pin, but I'd guess this place was hundreds of years old. Probably passed down through the generations. I preferred modern builds, like my place in Saint Tropez or the apartment I kept in Seattle for when I returned home, but I appreciated the history as we followed in the footsteps of people long since dead.

A few guests nodded to us as we entered the ballroom. Circular tables seating eight, ten, and twelve filled the space, dressed in crisp white tablecloths, polished silverware, and centerpieces of white lilies and yellow roses. Some tables were already full, and at the far end was a stage with gear set up for a band. A banner hung along one wall with "Congratulations Fenella and Benedict" emblazoned across it.

"And this isn't even the wedding, or the rehearsal dinner," I murmured to Lee as I scanned the seating plan. "Table sixteen." I took her hand—God, that never got old— and weaved through the tables toward ours, which was right in the middle of the room. "All these people can't be staying here, surely? I mean, the place is enormous, but it's not Buckingham Palace."

"Oh, they're not." She glanced up at me and winked. "We're special guests, don't you know?"

"Lucky us." I pulled out her chair and waited for her to sit, then sat beside her. Four other people were already sitting at our table, leaving two chairs currently free.

We introduced ourselves, and when the inevitable question of "How do you know the bride and groom?" came along, Lee smoothly replied, "Oh, we're old friends," then immediately turned the subject onto the other guests. It was a masterful tactic. Most people loved the opportunity to talk about themselves, and these four—distant cousins of the bride, apparently—took up the mantle with gusto.

Another couple arrived. We went through the same recitation, with Lee using her earlier approach to divert attention away from us. Dinner was a five-course affair, and as efficient servers cleared our dessert plates, the couple to Lee's left made their excuses and rose from the table. In seconds, Benedict appeared and plunked himself in one of the spare seats, almost as if he'd been hovering and waiting for the opportunity.

"Did you enjoy the dinner?" he asked, plowing on before waiting for an answer. "Better watch that figure, Annaleesa. You don't want to get fat now that you're no longer modeling." He guffawed, turning to the other guests. "Did you know Annaleesa used to be a top model? She gave it up when I broke off our engagement."

He made that stupid laugh again while I scrunched the tablecloth in my fists and envisaged the material running red with his blood. What a fucking prick.

"First, Lee doesn't need to watch her figure. She's perfect whatever size she is. And second, she didn't give up modeling because of you. She gave up modeling because she wanted a different life for herself." I let go of the tablecloth and traced the back of my hand over her cheek, smiling at her with the love I felt in my heart. A woman sitting across from us sighed wistfully.

"It didn't take you very long to land another rich guy, huh, Annaleesa?"

This jerk was walking a rapidly thinning line.

Lee beat me to a retort. Picking up her champagne flute, she traced her fingertip around the rim. "Considering I'm wealthier than you are, Benedict, I'd say you were the gold digger." She gestured around the room with its crystal chandeliers and expensive art adorning the walls. "Nice to see that hasn't changed."

Despite vibrating with anger at the fucking gall of this dickhead, I laughed. Lee didn't need me to come to her rescue. She was more than capable of handling this jerk herself.

"And as you brought up the subject of how long it took me to find someone else, it's only right to point out that I took a lot longer than you." She put her hand on my leg, I guessed as a warning not to react to his attempts to rile me, but my dick didn't know that. No, all my dick thought was "We're off." I wasn't sure how to break the news to him that the only action he was likely to see this weekend was attached to my wrist.

I draped an arm around Lee's shoulder, conscious that we had an audience hanging on to every word of this exchange. Not that I gave a flying fuck.

"That you're a cheating asshole worked out damn fine for me, so thanks for that, Benny."

"It's Benedict," he said through clenched teeth.

I made a dismissive gesture. "I'm never going to remember that. You're such a perfect Benny."

The two women seated at the same table as us snickered. Benedict reddened, muttered something I couldn't catch under his breath—more than likely an insult I'd lose zero sleep over—and launched to his feet, stomping across the room to the other side.

I put my lips close to Lee's ear. "Are you okay?"

She nodded. "I can handle him."

"I know you can. Doesn't mean I don't want to break his fucking nose for speaking to you like that."

I wouldn't. With my track record, I avoided any kind of violent encounter. Didn't mean those urges weren't there, especially with a douche like Benedict Oberon, only that it was best I didn't let my anger get the better of me.

"So, you used to be a model?" Jeanette, if I recalled correctly, propped her elbows on the table and rested her chin on her hands. "What a fascinating occupation. So glamorous."

"It isn't nearly as glamorous as it seems," Lee said.

"Really? All that travel to exotic locations and being photographed in clothes that cost as much as my mortgage. People telling you all the time how beautiful you are. Which you are," she added gushingly. "You're stunning."

"Thanks." Lee shifted uncomfortably. "But looks can be deceiving. Trust me, it's hard work."

Jeanette's husband—whose name escaped me— snorted. "Poppycock. It's nothing more than prancing down a catwalk in ridiculous outfits that no one is ever going to buy and smiling for the cameras. What's so hard about that?"

I half rose out of my chair, my glare fiery enough to take the skin off his face. "Hang on a sec—"

"It's fine, Kadon." Lee gripped my arm and tugged me back to a seated position. "It's not an unusual response when you don't know what you're talking about." She smiled sweetly at him, her passive-aggressive sideswipe going right over the dude's head. "There's an enormous amount of pressure on models, of unhealthy practices to stay thin enough to fit into those ridiculous outfits, as you call them. They're designed for size zero models, which basically means there isn't a day that goes by when you're not racked with hunger pangs that make you double over. I often skipped meals so my belly wouldn't pop in the latest clingy outfit."

"Yeah, but what's the odd missed meal when you get paid a hefty wedge for something that takes no talent to perform? Doesn't sound that hard to me."

One more wisecrack from this dick, and I won't hold back. Fuck the consequences.

"Piers," Jeanette said, giving him a sharp dig in the ribs. "Don't be so rude."

"It's a brief career." Lee continued with her patient explanation when Piers deserved to leave here with his arm in a sling. "A little like sports. We have to make hay while the sun shines."

"Yeah, but sports are proper jobs undertaken by men with talent. You're merely a pretty girl who used to get paid to appear in pretty pictures and now want to complain about how difficult it was for you."

This time Lee couldn't stop me from launching to my feet. I planted both hands on the table to prevent me from wrapping them around this jerk's neck. "Okay, buddy, that's it. Keep talking and all you'll do is prove to everyone listening what a misogynistic bigot you are, not to mention an idiot. In case it's escaped your notice, women play sports, too. Now do us all a favor and stay out of my way for the rest of this weekend. Because if you don't, there's a high degree of probability you'll leave here on crutches. Or worse." I took hold of Lee's hand and helped her to her feet. "Come on, babe. Let's go watch the fireworks before I'm tempted to pick this jackass up and sling him onto the bonfire."

I curved an arm around her waist and held her close to me as we filed out of the ballroom along with several other guests to go watch the fireworks display. Lee said nothing, and I feared I'd overstepped the mark. She'd been handling the prick with the big mouth perfectly fine all by herself, then I'd rushed to her defense, which might have looked like I didn't think she was capable of defending herself. And that couldn't be farther from the truth. But what sort of boyfriend would I be if I stood by and let Piers the Prick diss my girl in that way?

Except I wasn't her boyfriend, and she wasn't my girl.

Piers was a prick, though.

I picked up a blanket from a stack left for the guests and wrapped it around Lee's shoulders to keep her warm, leading her to a spot close to the bonfire. A staff member was toasting marshmallows on sticks, and I grabbed a couple, handing one to Lee.

"Peace offering."

She craned her neck and looked up at me. "For what?"

I kicked back my head. "For what I did back there. I should have let you handle it on your own."

"Are you kidding me? You were amazing. No one has ever stood up for me like that. I felt like a fucking queen."

Relief chased away the tension pinching the muscles in my neck. I grinned at her. "That's because you are a fucking queen."

Her mouth turned down at the edges. "According to Piers, I'm 'merely a pretty girl who used to get paid to appear in pretty pictures.'"

"There's nothing 'merely' about you, Lee. Not that I'd expect an imbecile like Piers to understand that. The man couldn't find his own ass with a map, let alone comprehend what a smart, funny, kind, amazing, sharp-witted woman you are. He's the man who never looks beyond the surface of anything. I pity his wife."

She touched her throat. "Kadon. Stop. You're going to make me cry."

She jumped at a bang overhead, and the marshmallow flew out of her hand, landing in the fire. I handed mine to her.

"I promise I haven't licked it or anything."

She laughed. "I wouldn't care if you had." Slipping her lips around the gooey marshmallow, she pulled the entire thing into her mouth. Another firework being set off masked my groan. Was it healthy to walk around with a permanent erection? I really should Google that.

Tucking her hand in the crook of my elbow, Lee rested her head on my shoulder as we watched the explosion of lights above us. Sparks flew into the air from the bonfire, and the logs crackled and spit.

I kissed the top of her head. She glanced up at me. Flames flickered in her eyes. I couldn't stop staring into their luminous depths. My lips parted. Hers did, too.

"Lee—"

She placed a fingertip over my lips. "Don't say anything. Just kiss me."

"Kiss you?" God, she was asking me to kiss her. *Asking me to kiss her.* And here I was, not fucking kissing her. *What the hell is wrong with me?*

"Benedict is watching us. Kiss me."

I deflated faster than a weather balloon struck by lightning. *Fuck.* I'd fallen into the trap of thinking this was real. The entire setup was bursting with romance, and while I wasn't faking a damn thing, I had to keep reminding myself that Lee was.

"Quick."

I bent my head and lightly pressed my lips to hers. If heaven was a person rather than a place, then I'd found mine, right here with her. The fireworks weren't exploding overhead any longer. They were exploding inside me. I deepened the kiss, wrapping my arms around her and tugging her flush to my body. I burrowed inside the blanket. It fell to the solid ground beneath our feet.

Lee made a sound, a mixture of a groan and a sigh. Were we still pretending? I wasn't sure anymore. She played with the hair at my nape, her fingers feathering over my skin and drawing a carpet of goose bumps to the surface. Despite the chill in the air, I wasn't cold. I burned. My hand found its way to her ass. I squeezed. She returned the favor, planting both her palms on my butt. She pulled me closer. My painfully hard dick found the friction it craved. I ground my hips, only vaguely aware that we weren't alone. I didn't care who was watching or whether our passionate display made them in any way uncomfortable.

Don't stop.

Never stop.

She broke away first, eyes wide, pupils blown. She touched her fingertips to her lips, swollen from our kiss. My chest heaved, the air visible as I panted. My heart was beating so fast it rattled my rib cage.

"Well." She blinked. "That was..."

She didn't have to finish her sentence. Even an idiot could tell she thought I'd pushed it way too far. *For fuck's sake, jackass.* I'd basically dry-humped her in front of half of England's aristocracy. We were supposed to be faking a loving relationship, not putting on a porn show for the unwitting wedding guests.

"I'm sorry. I overstepped the mark. Kinda forgot it was

you there for a minute." I hadn't forgotten it was her for even a second. How could I when she was the only girl on my mind? "Men. We haven't evolved all that much, have we?" I laughed through a narrowed throat. It sounded strained to my ears.

She faced the fire. "It's fine. Please don't worry."

"So I haven't ruined our friendship?"

"Of course not." She turned back to me and patted my chest, but the look in her eyes was one that gave me the chills, and not in a good way. "It was just a kiss, Kadon." She bent down and picked up the blanket, wrapping it around herself. I couldn't help but wonder if she was using it as a shield—or a message of one, anyway. "I think I'm going to turn in for the night."

I caught her arm as she took a step. "I can check into a hotel." I couldn't lose Lee over this. I *wouldn't.*

"No." She lowered her voice. "Don't do that. If Benedict finds out we're pretending, then all this will have been for nothing. We carry on as normal. If you're all right with that."

I nodded. "Okay."

"Give me fifteen minutes to get ready for bed, then come up."

"Sure." As she walked away, I felt the weight of a stare on the back of my head. I pivoted. Benedict was standing on the opposite side of the bonfire, his eyes aflame with envy.

Too bad, dickhead. You lost.

Then again, so had I.

Chapter 13

Leesa

Right guy, wrong girl.

On spaghetti legs, I made it back to our room. I stumbled inside and closed the door, resting my forehead against the cool wood.

This thing between me and Kadon was getting way out of hand. The kiss earlier today when we'd first arrived had rocked the foundations beneath my feet, but that second kiss... That was a ten on the Richter scale. If I'd taken a lie detector test three days ago, and the question was "Are you attracted to Kadon Kingcaid?" my answer of "No" would have passed with flying colors.

Now...

Now, I wouldn't dare take the test.

What's happening?

How could I find myself attracted to a man I'd worked

with every day for the past eight months and never once had the slightest romantic interest in? Was it a hormonal episode brought about by attending my ex's wedding? That had to be it. People didn't suddenly have the hots for their friends. That wasn't normal behavior.

Fuck. I wanted to do more than kiss him.

I grabbed my nightwear from the drawer beside the bed and ran into the bathroom. Stripping in record time, I turned on the shower and dove under the spray. My clit pulsed, demanding relief. I removed the showerhead out of the bracket, turned the setting to "massage," and aimed it right between my legs.

Leaning against the wall, I pulled and twisted and played with my nipples and fired heavy jets of water at my clit. I'd always been responsive to sexual stimulation, but the speed of my climax took me by surprise. I stifled a cry of pleasure, squeezed my eyes closed, and pretended Kadon was here with me. I pictured him naked, dripping wet, his big hand tugging on his cock, his eyes boring into mine as he pleasured himself.

My lower abdomen grew heavy, a second orgasm coming at me too fast. This time, I let my cry break free. My knees buckled. I dropped the showerhead and slid down the wall, splaying my legs straight out in front of me.

Good God. I hadn't had a release like that in months. Maybe years. Maybe never.

If that's what your imagination does, what would the real thing do to you?

Kill me. Probably. But fuck, it'd be a hell of a way to go.

No. Stop it. This is ridiculous.

I got to my feet, washed away all signs—and scents—of

sex, and dried myself off. Bracing my hands on the bathroom countertop, I stared at my reflection in the mirror. Sometimes I hated the way I looked. Sure, I was pretty, in that horrible societal way we categorized people, but my physical appearance had been as much of a curse as a benefit. That dick at dinner, Piers, had voiced aloud my greatest fears that I'd amount to nothing more than a pretty face and a nice body—until age crept up on me and stole my identity. Yet, along with the crippling self-doubt and worries, another voice had snuck in. One that said people existed who saw past the surface beauty.

People like Kadon.

His comments at the bonfire before we'd kissed had caused a swell of emotion within me, a tidal wave of gratitude and love. Perhaps this newfound longing for my best friend was an accumulation of events and circumstances. Being here, seeing Benedict again, having to play nice with Fenella, putting up with misogynistic men like Piers... once we left here on Sunday, surely these feelings would vanish. Then Kadon and I would go back to the way things had been before he'd come up with the crazy idea of pretending to be my boyfriend.

Phew. *I feel better now that I've worked through that.*

I cleaned off my makeup and moisturized all over, then slipped my nightgown over my head. I usually slept naked. Thank goodness I'd packed nightwear. Especially as I'd so stupidly assumed we'd have a suite, something with a living room and a bedroom at the very least. The funny thing was I hadn't a clue *why* I'd assumed that. I'd known all along we were staying here, at Grange Manor, rather than a hotel suite, and having replied on my RSVP with a note saying

I'd attend with a plus-one, no wonder they'd only given us a room with one bed.

I blamed the wedding and my panic at letting Kadon talk me into coming. Except now my panic had headed off in a whole new direction, one I hadn't considered for a single second... Sleeping the entire night next to Kadon. Even if it was in an emperor-sized bed, that wouldn't be an easy feat to accomplish. I sighed. *Here's to a sleepless night ahead.*

I flicked off the bathroom light and padded into the bedroom.

"Shit." My heart almost burst through my chest at the sight of Kadon sitting on the bed. "I didn't hear you come in."

"Sorry. I should have made more noise."

He finished removing his trousers and threw them over a chair. My greedy eyes drank in the sight of him in those tight-but-not-too-tight black boxer shorts. I'd seen his chest before. Many times. And his abs. But not after he'd kissed me like he had—twice—and not while standing in front of a bed big enough to writhe around on.

Stop thinking about sex.

Strike that.

Stop thinking about sex with Kadon.

Somehow, I averted my gaze, though it wasn't easy. I sat on the edge of the bed with my back to him.

"Which side do you want?"

"Either. I'm not fussy."

I wrung my hands. "Okay. I'll stay on this side, then. If it's all right with you."

His heavy sigh reached my ears. I glanced behind me. "What's that for?"

He pulled back the covers and climbed into bed, draping the sheets over his abs. "I know this was my idea, but I'm having regrets."

"You are?" I twisted around fully, tucking my knees to my chest and hugging them.

"I don't want to lose your friendship. You mean far too much to me."

I frowned. "Why would you say that? You're not going to lose my friendship. Where's this coming from?"

"I..." Another heavy sigh filled the room. "What happened at the bonfire was... wrong. So wrong. I'm sorry, Lee." He ran a hand through his hair. "I don't want you to think I'm... oh, I don't know, a perv or something and I'm going to pounce on you in the middle of the night."

So he wasn't interested in me after all.

I suppressed a curse. God, I felt like such an idiot. Thank goodness I hadn't told him I was over here coping with *feelings*. That would have made the situation a hundred times worse. At least this way I could leave here with my pride intact.

And my heart a little more tattered around the edges.

"You're worrying over nothing," I said with a breeziness I was *not* feeling. *I must be a better actress than I first thought.* "It's chemistry. That's all. Physical. I'm not embarrassed or concerned, and neither should you be."

He gnawed at his bottom lip. I couldn't take my eyes off his mouth. Those lips. God, those lips. Warm, soft, full. Thankfully, he was too busy staring somewhere over my right shoulder to notice me eye-fucking him.

"Are you sure?" He flashed me a look, then turned his attention to the bobbles on the bedspread, mindlessly plucking at them.

"I'm positive." I turned back the covers and climbed in beside him. At least three feet of space stretched between us, what with him perched on the end of his side and me perched on the end of mine. "Let's get some sleep. You have to shoot at some innocent creatures tomorrow, and I have to try not to drown Fenella in the hot tub."

His gruff laugh should have lifted some of the weight from my shoulders. It didn't. If anything, I felt as if the entire universe had set up camp there, grinding me into the ground.

"Good point." He switched off the lamp on his side of the bed, casting his half of the room in shadows. "Night, Lee."

"Night." I turned my lamp off, too. The room pitched into darkness. Stiff as a surfboard, I lay there, staring at the ceiling, listening to the steady sounds of Kadon breathing. I could tell the moment he'd fallen asleep. His breaths shallowed.

Out here in the countryside, dark really meant dark. I couldn't even make out my hand in front of my face. The inky blackness had its upside though: finally, I could stop pretending I was okay when I wasn't sure things would ever be the same again.

Barely conscious, I squinted through half-mast lids. Sunlight arrowed through a gap in the curtains, casting a triangular shard of light across the crimson and green swirls in the carpet. I peered at the antique clock on the nightstand. Eight fifteen. Ugh. I closed my eyes again. God, I was warm. Too warm. And tired. So tired, as if I'd slept like the dead.

I threw back the covers. Better. But still too hot. I shifted my weight.

Oh God.

Was that... was that...?

Yep. Yes, it was.

An erection nudged my lower spine. I forced my eyes open. A man's leg was on top of mine, and a large palm pressed firmly to my abdomen.

Slowly, I peeked over my shoulder even though I knew the identity of the man snuggled against me.

Kadon.

In my semiconscious state, I'd almost forgotten we'd slept in the same bed. How long had we spooned like this? All night? I couldn't remember a thing. My last memory was staring at the ceiling and feeling like shit after Kadon's confession that he'd devoured me by the bonfire not because it was me, but because he was a man and I was a woman. And not just *a woman*. A pretty woman. An *attractive* woman. We weren't talking intellectually attractive here. Physically. The bullshit I'd heard my entire life from both the modeling world and the press that surrounded it.

Oh, she's so pretty.

What a beauty you are, Annaleesa.

145

This picture will sell for thousands.

No, dear. Don't talk. Smile for the camera.

Would you be interested in doing porn? We could make millions together.

The same even breathing pattern I'd listened to last night told me Kadon hadn't woken up yet. Good. With any luck, I could slip out of bed and tuck myself away in the bathroom, and he'd be none the wiser of how we'd woken up with our bodies intertwined. I gently clasped his wrist and moved his hand to rest on his hip. One problem solved. He murmured but didn't wake. The leg was trickier. I had visions of me whipping my leg out from underneath him and him ending up on the floor, like that scene from *Friends* with Chandler and Janice.

I moved my leg an inch. He made this adorable snuffling sound that tugged on my heartstrings, then he rolled over. As carefully as I could, I placed my feet on the floor and got up. Tiptoeing to the bathroom, I closed the door before switching on the light.

I stared at myself in the mirror, as I had last night after I'd made myself come by imagining Kadon in the shower with me. Except then, I'd felt this tinge of optimism that maybe, just maybe, there might be a spark of *something* between Kadon and me.

Now, a depressive weight sat across my shoulders. It showed in my eyes, too. They were dull, and sadder than yesterday. *Pull yourself together, Leesa.* Nothing had changed. *Nothing had changed.* Kadon was still my best friend, and I was his. In a couple of weeks, the memory of this weekend would fade, and we'd go back to the way things had always been between us. A relationship based on mutual respect and filled with a healthy dose of banter and sarcasm.

Except... the saying that you couldn't miss what you'd never had wasn't all that useful when you'd had it. Not that I'd had it. More's the pity.

Jesus Christ, Leesa. I wished my damned mind had an off switch.

I grabbed a quick shower, taking care not to let my hair get wet. I was in the middle of brushing my teeth when Kadon knocked on the door.

"Lee, you in there?"

I turned off my electric toothbrush. "Yeah. Give me five minutes."

"Hurry up. I need to pee."

I smiled at my reflection. *See? Everything is fine.* Kadon was being his usual self. All this weekend needed now was for me to act the same way I always had.

"Do it out the window."

His chuckle seeped through the door. "Tempting offer, but I'll pass."

"Then cross your legs. I won't be long."

I resumed brushing my teeth. Five minutes later, I opened the bathroom door and performed this over-the-top bow.

"Your throne awaits, sir."

Kadon's grin did funny things to my insides. New things. Yet his grin was the same one he'd always had. Part of me cursed those two kisses. They'd taken off the glasses I'd worn around him and put on a new set with lenses that saw a very different man from the one I'd met back in February. But another part of me, growing louder with

Tracie Delaney

each passing minute, yearned for him to take back everything he'd said last night. Fanciful longings that were destined to bring disappointment and heartbreak.

"About time." He sidled past me and shut the door. I leaned against it and sighed. If I didn't figure out a way to extinguish these feelings, I was in for an even rougher weekend than I'd feared. Once we returned to Saint Tropez, it'd be fine. Kadon would head off on his round-the-world tour of other Kingcaid Beach Club properties, and I'd take myself off to somewhere warm and sunny and figure out the future.

Yeah. I'd do that. Everything would be fine.

I quickly dressed in jeans and a purple T-shirt that set off my lavender hair. I'd dyed it after jacking in modeling as a two-fingered salute to the blonde my manager had forced me to keep, a color I'd grown to hate. My actual color was a boring mousy brown, and I hadn't wanted to go back to that either.

Kadon emerged from the bathroom with damp hair and wearing only a towel around his waist. I swallowed a groan, my insides flip-flopping around as if all the bits had somehow untethered. I wouldn't mind if he was purposely trying to torture me, but he wasn't. He was only being himself, comfortable in my company, the way he'd always been.

While for me, the world had turned on its axis, and I hadn't a clue how to right it again.

"Ah, what a fun day we have to look forward to." I pretended to hold a shotgun and take aim. "Boom."

"I'm not shooting a damn thing, other than maybe your ex." He winked, then opened the drawer beside the bed

148

and took out a fresh pair of boxers. My throat thickened. He was naked beneath that towel. One little tug at the side and—

I averted my eyes, crossing the bedroom to peek out the window. A bright blue sky greeted me, dew dampening the extensive lawned gardens that stretched farther than the horizon.

"If you do shoot him, aim for his balls."

"Done." He appeared beside me, dressed in attire similar to mine. "You okay?"

"Yeah."

He put his arm around my shoulders and kissed my hair, releasing me far too fast for my liking.

"For what it's worth, you're bossing this weekend. It's hard, I know, but I truly believe that by the time we leave here Sunday morning, you'll have closed the door on this shitty chapter of your life and be ready to open a new one. The right guy is out there waiting for you to let him in."

He wandered back to the bed to put on his shoes. I returned my gaze to the view. Sadness enveloped me. The right guy had been under my nose all this time.

Yet to him, I was the wrong girl.

Chapter 14

Kadon

**What the hell did Lee ever see
in this pompous prick?**

I DESERVED A FUCKING MEDAL.

No, not a medal. An Oscar. If my beach clubs ever went under, I had a new career as an award-winning actor. After mauling Lee like a feral animal at the bonfire last night, I'd had a strong word with myself. If Lee caught an inkling that I was in love with her, it would be the beginning of the end of our relationship. Oh, she'd say all the right things, but it would change the dynamic, hanging over us like a rotting corpse.

Part of what I'd said to her last night was the absolute truth. The idea of losing her friendship made me feel sick to my stomach. I couldn't bear it if she wasn't in my life.

But the other part of my apologetic speech was a fucking great lie. What had happened at the bonfire wasn't wrong. Not for me.

It was the rightest thing I'd ever done.

Shame she didn't feel the same. And she never would. I'd thought I could handle the idea of being her fake boyfriend for the weekend, but if I'd considered it with my head instead of my dick, I'd have seen how it had all the elements to end in disaster.

Sunday couldn't come quickly enough.

We entered the dining room. The smell of freshly grilled bacon and hot, buttered toast reached me, and my stomach growled. It struck me as odd that the Granges had bestowed "special" status on Lee, allowing us to stay at the manor. By God, I wished they hadn't. A two-bedroom suite at a hotel would have been a lot less painful than lying beside her all night. I'd woken up with a boner to rival all boners, and the only thing that had deflated it was trying to do complicated sums in my head. At least Lee hadn't been there beside me when I'd woken. If she had, I couldn't say with absolute certainty that I'd have been capable of holding back.

A uniformed member of staff approached us. "Miss Alarie, Mr. Kingcaid, I hope you slept well. Please allow me to show you to your table."

I arched a brow at Lee. I'd never met this dude before, and from the slight shake of her head, neither had she. It made me wonder whether the Granges had given the staff photographs of all the guests to study. How weird was that? My parents hosted get-togethers often, both business-related and for pleasure, and not once had they expected their staff to memorize the guests' faces.

We sat at a table overlooking a lake with four pairs of swans floating across the surface, sending ripples of water to the edges. The pretentiousness of this place was so alien to me. My parents were enormously wealthy, but they didn't shove it down people's throats like the Granges seemed intent to do. Growing up, I hadn't lived in a two-hundred-room mansion. Our family home in Seattle wasn't small by any means, but my mom had wanted us to grow up in a house where she didn't have to send out a search party to let us know it was time for dinner.

"Can I get you some tea? Or coffee, perhaps."

"Coffee for me. Lee?" I needed the caffeine kick to get through today.

"Water, please." She scanned the room. "Do you think I could feign illness and escape this godforsaken spa day?"

"Only if I can do the same." I caught sight of Benedict and Fenella over Lee's shoulder. He spotted us, nudged her, and pointed, then made a beeline for our table. "Brace for impact," I murmured a second before Fenella hugged Lee from behind.

"There you are, darling. Are you looking forward to today? I can't wait for us to spend quality time together. It's been so long since we've had a good old girlie gossip."

It always struck me as odd how people so easily lied to themselves. From what Lee had told me, she'd known Fenella before she and Benedict had hooked up, but they weren't besties or anything. Fenella's behavior was as if they'd been joined at the hip. She did a great job of ignoring the truth that she was marrying the man who had ditched Lee for her.

Lee responded like a rock star. "I can't wait. I've been talking about how much I'm looking forward to it all morning, haven't I, darling?" Lee placed her hand over mine. I should be used to her touching me by now, but each time she did, electricity fired through my veins, setting my blood alight.

I fixed a sickly sweet smile on my face. "She's spoken of little else."

Fenella clapped her hands like an overexcited child. I managed not to laugh out loud. People who did that always amused me. It was the oddest thing for an adult to do.

"Wonderful. Do help yourselves to the buffet." She motioned to the tables weighted down with food as if we were incapable of finding the scrambled eggs on our own, then linked arms with Benedict, who hadn't spoken a single word during the entire exchange. He gave us both a curt nod, his eyes lingering on Lee a moment too long, and in there, I saw yearning.

I knew it.

The jerk still had feelings for Lee. Well, he could fuck off. He'd had his chance, and he'd blown it. Spectacularly. Only a prick would choose politics over the love of a woman like Lee, and Benny was at the top of the pile of pricks.

"We're meeting for the shoot at ten," he finally said, looking at me. "Out front by the statue."

"Oh, the one with the tiny dick, you mean?" I schooled my expression to one of innocence, but Benny caught my drift, loud and clear. Lee tried to hold back her laughter, her shoulders shaking. Benny's ears pinked up, and his lips became a thin white slash.

"Yes," he snapped.

I yawned, leaning back in my chair. "I'll be there. Can't wait."

He gripped Fenella's elbow and steered her away from our table. He'd only traveled a few feet when Lee laughed loud enough that he must have heard.

"You are so bad, Kingcaid."

"He got off lightly. I almost added 'like yours,' but I refrained. I should get a prize for such admirable restraint."

She laughed again. "I wish you hadn't refrained."

"There's time. After all, I have to find some way to entertain myself today."

"If you do make the comparison, please film his reaction."

I winked at her. "You got it."

K

I arrived at the meeting point at five after ten—dick move but I was beyond caring at this point—to find the assembled group dressed in tweed jackets and checked pants tucked into knee-high boots. They were all wearing flat caps, too, which did not belong on anyone under seventy-five. Clearly, I hadn't gotten the memo about the dress code. Not that it would have mattered if I had. I wouldn't be caught dead wearing that outfit.

"Ah, there you are, Kingcaid." Benny made his way through the group, looking me up and down with a disparaging sneer on his face. What a child. If he thought his stupid games would bother me for a microsecond, he was more of an idiot than I'd originally thought. And I'd set the bar pretty low.

"Would you like me to loan you some appropriate clothing?"

"You mean like what you're wearing?" I smirked. "I'm good. Besides, those pants would be half-mast on me." I loved a bit of passive-aggressive messaging. "I don't think the birds care either way."

He pursed his lips. "Pheasants."

I faked confusion. "Aren't they birds?"

"Yes, but we call them pheasants."

"Why?"

Benny's face grew redder than a ripe tomato. This was too much fun.

"It's the way it's done. The British way. I wouldn't expect an American to understand."

If he thought that trashing my culture would irritate me, he'd better ready himself for disappointment. I beamed.

"If you don't know the answer to something, it's okay to say you don't know." I jerked my chin at the other men gathered around chatting. "You should ask one of your countryside buddies if they know why you're so offended that I called them birds when that's what they are."

I could do this all day. The entertainment value was priceless.

"It doesn't matter. Have you fired a shotgun before?"

"Once or twice." He didn't need to know that I'd been captain of the shooting team at the finishing school Dad had sent me to in Switzerland, and if my attendance there hadn't ended so abruptly, I'd have had a good chance at getting picked for the Olympics. The only difference was we didn't shoot innocent birds. All this hunting shit was such outdated claptrap, a cruel sport hidden beneath a veneer of tradition.

"So you know the basics, then." When I nodded, he responded with a gruff "Good," then spun on his heel, shouted, "Okay, gentlemen, follow me," and marched off with his band of sycophantic minions trailing behind.

I glanced back at the house. I should have asked to join the women at the spa. I'd have had far more fun, not to mention spending the day with Lee rather than with this bunch of jerks.

My chest tightened, and my mind chose that moment to play our kiss by the bonfire like a movie reel in my head. If I concentrated hard enough, I could almost feel her in my arms, taste her lips, breathe in the scent of her body-wash and shampoo. Kissing her for show wasn't enough. I hankered for the real thing, but wanting something and being able to have it were worlds apart. If Lee had even an inkling of attraction toward me, then she'd say. Wouldn't she?

You haven't.

Yeah, but that was different. I was in love with her, and I couldn't face telling her and seeing shock paint her face, followed by her desperately trying to reassure me it was okay, that me loving her and her not feeling the same wasn't a problem. That we could carry on as we always had.

We wouldn't. If I told Lee how I felt, it would start a

chain reaction I didn't have the power to stop. No, it was better this way. As soon as we left here on Sunday, I'd rebury the feelings that being able to kiss her and touch her had allowed to surface. I'd head off to Dubai, then the US, as I did every winter season when my Saint Tropez property closed, and Lee... I wasn't sure what Lee's plans were other than taking a well-earned break. Regardless, they wouldn't be with me, which was what I needed to reset our relationship and get it back onto an even keel.

Shotguns lay on top of a wooden trestle table at the wooded area where the shoot would take place. Gundogs milled about, sniffing the ground. As I understood it, they'd bring back the birds after these bloodthirsty English toffs had snuffed out their lives by shooting them full of lead.

"Here, Kingcaid. Choose your weapon." Benny swept his hand over the guns. "Let's see what you've got."

What the hell did Lee ever see in this pompous prick?

I shook my head. "You know, forget it. I've changed my mind. This isn't my thing. I'll take a walk or drive into the nearest town or something."

"Squeamish, are you, old boy?"

Old boy? Jesus Christ Almighty. I'd somehow gotten sucked into a wormhole and transported back seventy years.

"No. However, I don't see where the joy is in killing innocent life."

Benny tilted his head to this side, his eyes narrowing. "Really? You surprise me."

"I'm not sure why you'd say that when you don't know me."

"Oh, I know more than you think." He picked up a

shotgun and cocked it, inspecting the chamber. Lifting it to his eye, he aimed it at the sky, then returned it to the table.

"Is that so?"

He nodded, his smugness reminiscent of someone who'd been told a great secret and couldn't wait to blab. "I wouldn't have thought killing innocent beings was something that would bother you at all, Kingcaid."

A chill ran down my spine, and my shoulders stiffened. Had he put inflection into his comment about innocent beings, or had I imagined it? My heart set off at a gallop, sprinting out of the traps like a thoroughbred at the races. I somehow schooled my expression, gazing at him with feigned boredom while I read his body language.

He was fishing. He had to be. Only a tight circle of people were aware of what had happened that night, and this joker was not in the pack.

Breathe. He doesn't know a thing.

"Well, like I said, you don't know me. Therefore, it's probably advisable to keep your opinions to yourself, *Benny*. I'm not interested in hearing them."

I turned away and walked across the field toward the house, flinching at the sound of gunfire permeating the air.

Sunday could not come quickly enough.

Chapter 15

Leesa

Something's afoot.

BENEDICT WAS SUCH A TWAT.

No wonder I often had the urge to regularly kick myself in the backside for how long it took me to realize his character was seriously flawed. There he was with all his cronies dressed in their stupid shooting getups, and he purposely hadn't told Kadon, who'd turned up in jeans, boots, a warm jumper, and a waxed jacket.

Benedict and Kadon held a brief conversation—what I wouldn't give to have bionic hearing—then Benedict walked away, laughing and chatting with his mates. Kadon followed behind, a solitary figure with his blond-streaked hair blowing in the wind.

I shouldn't have let him bring me here. Not because of me, but because of *him*. Benedict wasn't only a twat; he

161

was a vengeful twat. He didn't want me, but his ego didn't want anyone else to have me, either. I'd seen that look of longing in his eyes at breakfast. I might lose the bet I'd made with Kadon on the Eurostar yet.

"There you are." Fenella's high-pitched voice echoed through the ballroom from where I'd snuck off hoping she wouldn't find me. "I've been looking for you all over." She joined me at the window, her eyes tracking the group of men heading toward the woods. "Ah, there they go. Such a *manly* sport, shooting, don't you think?"

"No." My droll reply was lost on her.

She laughed that tinkly laugh and nudged me with her elbow. "I hope they bring back lots of birds."

I arched a brow. "The winged type or the human type?"

She hesitated for a second, then caught up with my sarcasm-loaded reply. "Oh, you are funny, Leesa. Come on. The girls have already gone across to the spa. Our massages await."

"Ooh, goody." I rubbed my hands together.

"I know." She sighed wistfully. "Think of all that relaxation. Just what we need."

I sighed, too, though for different reasons. Sarcasm was wasted on Fenella.

Invitations to the spa were extremely exclusive, even more so than those invited to stay at Grange Manor for the wedding. Nine guests, including me and Fenella.

I blew out a breath. It was going to be a long-ass day, as Kadon would say.

Wisps of memories strayed into my mind. Sleeping beside Kadon, waking up with his erection nudging me, the speech he'd made about the right man waiting somewhere in the wilderness for me to find him. Goddammit. The inclination to scream, "I've found him, and he's you!" had risen inside me like a geyser about to spew. Thank God I'd found the strength to contain my outburst. Like Kadon had said to me, I couldn't lose his friendship either. Something was better than nothing.

How tragic that it had taken two beautiful kisses to open my eyes, and now I couldn't close them to the truth.

"Everyone, this is Leesa." Fenella's introduction dragged me back to the present. "She and Benedict used to be engaged. Can you *imagine* a more unmatched pair?" More silly laughter.

I managed a weak smile and a raised hand. "Hi."

A few murmured greetings, and one girl budged up on the sofa to allow me room to sit. I almost told her I preferred to stand, but that might come across as snooty, and I had hours ahead of me in the company of these women. No point in making the day harder than it needed to be.

Fenella stood on ceremony, listing out all the "fun and wonderful" things for us to do today. Her idea of fun was diametrically opposed to my own, but I was here now. Might as well get the most out of it. Besides, a massage sounded nice.

"So you were engaged to Benedict?" the woman who'd made space for me asked when Fenella paused for breath. "I'm Pippa, by the way."

"Oh, yes, she was," Fenella interjected.

I hadn't even opened my mouth.

"He dumped her for me."

The triumphant tone to her voice encouraged my bitchy side to come out to play. *Gloves off, darling.* I'd always laid the lion's share of the blame at Benedict's door, but did Fenella need to take quite so much glee in rubbing my face in it?

"It's true. He was cheating on me for weeks before he broke off our engagement."

Fenella's ears went pink. *You started it, sweetheart.*

"But you know, with hindsight, you did me a favor, Fenella."

"Oh." She tilted her head to one side. "How's that?"

"Well, if Benedict hadn't broken off our engagement, I wouldn't have met Kadon." I made my eyes go all misty and stared off into space. "Benedict was so *boring* in bed. He was what I'd call a traditionalist."

I looked at Pippa rather than Fenella, although I caught sight of the other girls paying close attention, their elbows propped on their knees, leaning forward in rapt enthrallment.

"He thought that me on top was going wild." I laughed. This was too much fun. "Whereas Kadon... he's so *adventurous,* you know? Thrilling. Sex with him is such a rush. I can't get enough." I faked a little shiver. "Sorry. I was remembering what we did last night." I closed my eyes and sighed. When I opened them, I could have sworn the women had shifted their chairs a little closer.

"Perhaps you were the problem, Leesa," Fenella snapped. "Because with me, Benedict is an animal in bed."

Animal? Benedict? A chipmunk at best.

I'd love to say that out loud, but it seemed a step too

far. As much as Fenella needled me—and meant to—she wasn't the one I was mad at.

"Then I'm glad for you both. Maybe he's found the right woman for him. I hope that's true, for your sake."

Fenella's hands went to her hips. "What's that supposed to mean?"

"Nothing, other than you should keep an eye on him. That's all. Put him on a tight leash."

A little furrow appeared between her eyebrows. "Why?"

"Because of what he did to me. My maman always says that once a man eats in another woman's kitchen, then he's likely to get the urge to sample lots of different food in different kitchens, no matter what you're cooking for him at home."

Fenella's eyebrows flew up her head the second she figured out the message behind Maman's saying.

She pursed her lips and kicked one hip out to the side. "Lucky I'm a brilliant cook, then, isn't it?"

Pippa muttered under her breath, "You'll need to be."

I wasn't sure whether Fenella heard her. She whipped around and flounced off, grabbing one of the women as she passed and lugging her into the next room.

"I'm sorry," Pippa said when Fenella was out of earshot. "I've been cheated on and it's the worst. Fenella isn't a bad person, though."

"She shouldn't have cheated with someone she knew was in a committed relationship, but I lay the blame firmly at Benedict's door. She was the free agent. He wasn't."

"That's magnanimous of you. I'm not sure I'd be so forgiving."

I shrugged. "It's behind me now."

"For what it's worth, I think you came out on top. I've never liked Benedict. Now, your man, Kadon." She winked. "He is fiiiine."

I grinned. Pippa was my kind of people. "Yes, he is. And miiiine."

Pippa threw back her head and laughed. "How did you two meet?"

"On the beach, right after Benedict dumped me." At least I could be honest about this part of our relationship. "I was crying, and Kadon came over to check on me. We became friends, he offered me a job at his beach club, and the rest, as they say, is history."

"I bet he swept you off your feet the first time you did it." She gave my arm a little shake. "Be a doll and give me the deets. It's been an age since I had anything approaching a romantic liaison. And given the men I met at last night's dinner, vicariously living someone else's sex life is as much action as I'm likely to get this weekend."

I chuckled. "Remind me to take your number before we leave here."

"You got it. And stop stalling."

I felt all warm inside as I thought back to what Kadon had said at my house about our "pretend" first time. "Okay, well, it was—"

"Ready, ladies?" Fenella clapped her hands. That was such a weird habit. "Our masseuses await." She spun on her heel and, like a teacher with a class of five-year-olds, raised her hand above her head and cried, "Follow me!"

"Fuck, that woman has the worst timing," Pippa muttered. "This isn't over, Leesa. My imagination needs a little kindling. Or, in far cruder terms, my wank bank is running low, and you're the one to fill it."

I spluttered a laugh. "I'll do my best."

I left the spa at four o'clock with fewer muscle aches and a new friend. I'd always longed for girlfriends to gossip with, and Pippa might fit the bill. I was grinning at some of her antics when I pushed open the door to our bedroom. She'd turned a tough day into the most fun I'd had in a long while.

Kadon was lying on the bed with his arms braced behind his head and his ankles crossed. A half-eaten plate of fruit was on the bedside table with the remains of a cup of coffee beside it.

"Hey." I snagged a piece of pineapple and popped it into my mouth. "How was your day? Did you shoot anything? And by 'anything,' I don't mean Benedict."

"No shots fired. Not by me, anyway." He didn't look at me as he spoke. "I left them to it. Came back here."

"Why?" I stole an apple slice. "Sorry, I'm finishing your fruit."

"I didn't want to do it. That's all."

Still no eye contact. What the fuck was going on?

I perched on the end of the bed. "I don't blame you. You should have come to find me. I've had the best day at the spa. I met this woman, Pippa. She's fantastic. I think I've found a new best friend." I flicked his arm. "Watch out, Kingcaid. You might find yourself replaced."

"Your choice." He got up and wandered over to the window, tucking his hands deep inside his pockets.

I frowned. Something must have happened. This

wasn't like Kadon. I followed him, standing close enough to offer solidarity, but far enough away to give him space.

"Are you okay?"

"I'm fine."

He wasn't fine. He was far from fine. "Are you sure? Because—"

"For fuck's sake, Lee." He rounded on me. He had this look in his eye that I didn't like. He'd closed himself off. What I couldn't figure out was why. "I'm tired. That's all. I didn't sleep well, then I had to put up with your ex and his cronies for thirty minutes longer than any sane man should have to endure. I'm glad you had a good day, but I didn't. So do me a favor and back off. Okay?"

I lifted my hands to either side of my head. In all the time I'd known him, Kadon had never raised his voice to me.

"No problem. I'll leave you to it. Call me when you're in the mood to act like a normal human being again."

I'd taken two steps when Kadon grabbed my arm. "I'm sorry. Fuck, Lee." He let me go, running the same hand he'd stopped me with through his hair. "Your ex is a class A dick."

Ah. Benedict must have said something terrible to rankle Kadon this much, but whatever it was, he didn't seem to want to talk about it. He'd share when he was ready. I wouldn't push him.

"Tell me something I don't know." I relayed the conversation I'd had with Fenella about cheating.

"Glad you stood up for yourself. And your mom sounds like a smart woman."

"She loves a good analogy."

"I hope to meet her one day."

I clenched my teeth. "Stop pushing me."

"I'm not." Cupping the back of my neck, he dropped a kiss on top of my head. "I'm gonna go for a walk before dinner, see if I can shake off this bad mood."

He didn't invite me to join him. I motioned to the door. "I'm about ready for a nap anyway."

Flopping onto the bed, I closed my eyes. First chance I got to question Benedict on what he'd said to Kadon to get him all riled up, I'd take it.

And if I didn't like what I heard, *I'd* be the one to shoot that twat in the balls.

Chapter 16

Kadon

If wishes were kisses...

THE FIRST TIME I'D SEEN LEE WEAR THE BOTTLE-green velvet dress, at Boutique Noémie, I'd almost swallowed my tongue.

The second time, I *did* swallow my tongue.

Coughing so hard that it wouldn't have surprised me if I puked up a pair of lungs, I rubbed my chest. Christ, the burn. Not fun. Lee thrust a glass of water at me.

"Here, drink this. What brought that on? Did you swallow a fly?"

She laughed while I soothed the fire in my throat. "I think I breathed in at the wrong time," I rasped. "And there's no need to laugh. It fucking hurts."

"Aw. Poor baby." She massaged my back in clockwise circles. "Better?"

Nope. Now my groin burned, too.

It took little contact from Lee for my dick to stand at attention, and the poor bastard had barely had a chance to deflate since we'd left Saint Tropez on Wednesday.

"Yeah, thanks." I stood up with my back to her to hide the giveaway bulge in my pants. "Won't be a sec."

I disappeared into the bathroom, closing the door behind me. Groaning at my reflection in the mirror, I braced both hands on the sink and willed my erection to deflate.

God, that dress. That body.

She'd done something different with her tits, too. They popped even more than they had when she'd modeled the dress for me in Cannes.

"Gonna be a long night, Kingcaid."

I straightened my bow tie, wishing a painful death on the person who'd invented the damn things. I hated suits at the best of times, but tuxedos belonged in a special place in hell. My brothers lived in suits. They'd always fit in so well with the billionaire lifestyle with their designer clothing and expensive watches and perfectly groomed hairstyles.

Whereas me? I was most comfortable in casual gear, or in swim shorts, riding the perfect wave to the shore.

Sometimes I questioned whether my parents had brought the wrong baby home from the hospital.

"Kadon." Lee knocked on the door. "We have to go."

"One sec." I had a final look at myself. "Do not rise to anything that asshole says, okay?"

Earlier, I'd walked six miles, and yet I still couldn't shake the prickles racing over my skin. The logical side of me recognized that I was overreacting. My father had many talents, and burying bad news was one of them. Although, *bad news* wasn't how I'd describe what had happened in Switzerland.

A *clusterfuck* was far closer to the truth.

I kneaded my chest. Why did guilt sit so heavy, like a slab of concrete, weighing me down and making it difficult to breathe? Time was supposed to be a healer, but it turned out that self-disgust and remorse didn't play by those rules.

Taking a deep breath, I plastered a smile on my face and opened the bathroom door.

"Ready?"

She laughed. "I've been ready for ten minutes. It's you who's running late." She dusted her hands over my shoulders, then patted my chest. "Looking good, Kingcaid."

Everything south of my midriff clenched. I stuck out my arm. "Let's go knock 'em dead."

We made our way down to the ballroom. I glanced at the table plan. Oh, good. They'd mixed up the seating, so I wouldn't have to sit on my hands to avoid punching Piers if he dared make another misogynistic comment to Lee. I was forever conscious of the dangers of striking out. How the consequences of something so seemingly innocuous could ruin your life.

But goddamn, when it came to pricks like Piers, or Benedict, it wasn't the easiest thing to do.

I took Lee's hand and headed over to the other side of the room.

She tugged me in the other direction. "Wait, there's Pippa. Come on, I'll introduce you."

A redhead in a floor-length, fitted black gown rose from her chair, meeting us halfway. She enveloped Lee in a tight hug. They both started talking simultaneously, then laughed.

"Kadon, this is Pippa. She saved my life at the spa today."

"Figuratively speaking." Pippa shook my hand. "It's good to meet you. Lee's told me all about you."

I glanced sideways at Lee, wondering what she'd said to Pippa. In my experience, women bonded easily. Lee could easily have told Pippa something closer to the truth. "Good things, I hope."

Pippa's eyes danced. "Oh, they were good." She looked me up and down. "Very, very good."

"Pippa!" Lee widened her eyes, a secret message passing between the two women. "Shush."

Okay, now I'm intrigued.

"Ignore her, Pippa. Tell me everything."

Pippa giggled. "I couldn't possibly. But suffice to say you came out rather well."

"Is that so?" I slipped my arm around Lee's waist and kissed the top of her head. "You can tell me later, Lee."

"It's a woman's responsibility to keep a man guessing, Kadon." She batted her eyelashes.

I tucked a lock of hair behind her ear, my eyes locked on hers. "And it's a man's responsibility to use all available tools in his arsenal to uncover every single secret."

"Oh yeah?" she whispered, her chest rising and falling with each breath.

I should win a fucking award for keeping my eyes on her face instead of dropping them to a cleavage I'd hack off an arm for a chance to burrow my face in just once. I lowered my head until our mouths were an inch apart. The noise of arriving guests muted, drowned out by the roaring of blood in my ears. Lee parted her lips, her eyes briefly dropping to my mouth.

"I'll let you torture it out of me later. In bed." I brushed my lips over hers with the faintest of touches. Electricity zapped through me, static lifting the hair at my nape.

"God, Leesa, you're a lucky bitch."

Pippa's untimely intervention broke the spell. Leesa blinked and took a step back. She opened her mouth, but nothing came out.

I stepped into the breach. "Sorry, Pippa. It's easy to forget we're not alone. That's what love does for you, I guess."

"You're not kidding. Look what you've done to her, Kadon. She's speechless."

I threaded my fingers through Lee's. "I guess we'd better sit down. Nice to meet you."

"We should meet up for a drink later. After dinner."

Lee's hand tightened in mine. I hazarded a guess what that meant. It must be exhausting for her to keep up this acting routine. Easier for me. I wasn't pretending.

"Another time. We'll be busy later." I stared intensely into Lee's gunmetal-gray eyes once more. She shifted her weight, a blush creeping up her neck.

Pippa giggled again. "I'll bet you will. You two enjoy yourselves."

I tore my eyes from Lee's and smiled a little at Pippa. "We plan to."

Lee landed in the chair I held out for her with a

thump. She dropped her purse on the floor and reached for the carafe of water. Pouring a glass, she downed it in one go.

"Thirsty?" I arched a brow.

"A little bit." She leaned toward me. "You're laying it on thick."

Was she scolding me? "Too much?"

"Not at all." She fleetingly touched my leg, more a brush as she moved than an intentional caress. Unfortunately for me, my body couldn't tell the difference.

"You could win a Tony Award with the performance you're giving this weekend."

"We aim to please." My voice came out husky. I poured myself a glass of water, too.

Another couple arrived, then a second and a third. I nodded through the introductions, using the time to gather myself. I wasn't an actor. I was a man in love and, for the first time, able to show it in public.

What worried me was whether I'd find it impossible to shove the toothpaste back into the tube come Sunday morning. I had a horrible feeling that I'd struggle to go back to pretending we were just friends. But what other choice did I have?

It crossed my mind to change my flight and travel to Dubai from London instead of Nice as I'd planned. I instantly dismissed the idea. I'd never let Lee make her way back to Saint Tropez alone. It was tempting, though. It sure would solve a lot of problems. Give me the breathing space I needed to get my head on straight.

"—Benedict. I mean, it takes balls to come here."

I dragged myself back to the present and tuned into the conversation. Lee was chatting with a guy in his early forties sitting on her left.

"I wouldn't say that," Lee said. "He and Fenella invited me, and I was happy to attend and celebrate their special day."

"But it's gotta hurt, right? I mean everyone here knows he dumped you for another woman."

"Sorry, who are you?" I glared at the jerk in the blue tux.

Who the fuck wears a blue tux?

"Barry Sanderson." He stuck out his hand. I left it hanging in midair. He withdrew, pretending he'd reached for the bottle of wine instead. "Freelance reporter. I'm not here in a professional capacity, though. Benedict and I are old friends. I can promise whatever you say won't end up splashed on the front of a tabloid."

"Good. I have deep pockets and a long memory."

Lee placed her palm on my leg.

Again.

Fuck. On the one hand, I wished she wouldn't. My dick needed a rest. On the other hand, I never wanted her to let go.

"To answer your question, Mr. Sanderson, I was the wronged party, so, no, it doesn't bother me that everyone here knows Benedict was the one who cheated on me."

She turned to me. Her eyes misted over, and, fuck, that look on her face. It was nothing short of adoration. Lee had this acting thing all sewn up. Either that or... or...

No.

Don't think it, even for a second.

She wasn't having feelings for me. She was playing the part we'd agreed to.

"Benedict did me a favor, Mr. Sanderson." She returned her attention to the journalist. "If he hadn't been unfaithful to me, then I wouldn't have fallen for someone ten times the man Benedict will ever be. I wish Fenella all the luck in the world. Believe me, she'll need it."

She shifted her weight, giving the journalist her back.

Masterful. Fucking masterful.

Our eyes met. Lust ignited in my stomach. She was giving me that look again, the one that, if she were mine, would compel me to lift her into my arms and carry her off to bed, and keep her there for several days.

But she wasn't mine.

Except...

Christ.

I couldn't stop these stupid thoughts that she might not be acting after all. I was enjoying this too much, but I shouldn't.

It's not real.

It is not real.

Even if it was, I didn't deserve a woman like Lee. She was worth ten of me. A hundred. She deserved to be with a man without skeletons rattling in his closet that, even now, I couldn't bring myself to deal with, to face up to. I'd run to my father that night for help, and I'd been running ever since.

Benedict's throwaway comment about *innocent beings* popped into my mind. The boy I'd killed had been far from innocent, but that did not detract from the facts, which haunted my dreams.

I was a murderer.

And no matter what I did, I'd never be good enough for a woman like Lee.

Chapter 17

Leesa

Damn. I'd lost the bet.

"Twelve hours and we're out of here."

My smile was as fake as our relationship. Kadon bought it, though, because his grin stretched wide across his face.

"Thank Christ for that. It's been *torturous*."

He wasn't wrong, but for me, the torture had been acknowledging my burgeoning feelings for a man I'd only ever considered a friend. Whereas for him, the torture had been surviving around a bunch of people polar opposite to him.

"Those speeches." He rolled his eyes and his head lolled back on his neck. "Dear God. I thought her father wasn't ever going to shut up."

I chuckled. "He's very proud of his little girl."

Unlike my parents. Okay, maybe that wasn't entirely fair. Maman had been very proud of me. When I'd modeled. Back then, she'd bored anyone who would listen with tales of how successful and beautiful and talented her daughter was. Bet she avoided those same people now, too *embarrassed* to tell them I'd voluntarily given up such a dazzling career.

Her words, not mine.

"Where'd you go, beautiful?" Kadon touched my arm. I stared at his tanned fingers against my pale skin.

An image popped into my mind. One of me and Kadon lying side by side, naked. Him, all bronzed, smooth skin and hard lines, with a dusting of hair across his chest. Me, pale and slim, with pink nipples and curves in all the right places. At least I had curves now, and thank goodness for that. The days of sticking-out hip bones, visible ribs, and thigh gaps were long gone.

Sometimes, I thought of myself as a rather odd creature. Women the world over craved for a body like I'd once had, whereas I preferred the shape I was now. An article I'd read once said that men prefer women with a little meat on their bones, something to grab hold of.

Wonder if that's true.

"Do you prefer skinny or curvy women?"

Kadon startled, his eyebrows shooting up his forehead and widening his eyes. "Um, why do you ask? And how is that a response to my question?"

"I'm curious. I was thinking about how skinny I used to be and how I'm not like that anymore. And whether men prefer the former or the latter."

"I can't speak for other men, but for me, I'm more

attracted to curvier women. My view on this, though, is that as long as the woman is happy in her body, it doesn't matter what a guy thinks. And any guy who tries to change a woman's body to suit his own preferences is with the wrong woman. Or, better put, she's with the wrong fucking guy."

Why did he have to say all the right things? It was as if he'd rummaged around inside my head, fished out all the answers that would make me go gaga for him, and regurgitated them in his own unique style.

"Where's this coming from?"

I shook my head. "Nowhere. Just musing on things." Yeah, musing on how Kadon preferred curvy women. I was a curvy woman. Bingo.

If only it was that simple.

Benedict caught my eye. He was spinning Fenella around the dance floor, but every time he faced in my direction, his gaze locked on me, like an Exocet missile. If things had turned out differently, it might be me up there, wearing a handmade wedding dress of satin and lace and drawing the attention of the crowd.

The relief that it wasn't me was almost indescribable. A lightness that made me feel as if I were floating on air.

"Want to dance?" Kadon held out his hand and jerked his head toward the dance floor.

I smiled, rose from my chair, and placed my hand in his. "I'd love to."

He led me onto the dance floor on the opposite side of Benedict. I'd wager he hadn't done that accidentally. He slipped one arm around my waist. I expected him to take my hand with the other. He didn't. Brushing my neck with the tips of his fingers, he curved his palm around the back of my neck where wisps of my hair had fallen out of my chignon.

I couldn't breathe.

Everything south of my belly button cramped, and goose bumps carpeted my skin. I slipped my arms around his waist and rested my head on his shoulder. A sigh escaped me, steeped in the deepest contentment I'd ever felt.

"Almost over."

He must have misread my sigh, and why wouldn't he?

"Yeah." I leaned back to look at him. "You made it more than bearable, Kadon."

"So you don't regret it?"

"Not for a second. You were right all along. I came here and got my closure." I glanced over my shoulder at the newlyweds. "That could have been me. The thought turns my stomach. In the end, he did me a favor."

"He's still a low-life, cheating asshole, though."

I smiled. "Yeah, he is. But that's Fenella's problem now."

He rested his chin on the top of my head, and his hand tightened on my waist. "You're wearing a different perfume tonight."

My pulse jumped. I *was* wearing a different perfume, but I wouldn't have expected Kadon to notice. Was he... could he... be having feelings for me? The same feelings I'd discovered for him?

No. That's crazy.

It was the occasion. That was all. I'd venture that lots of silly decisions took place at weddings, only for the couple to have second thoughts later. A bit like baby show-ers. They created this false realm where every woman there instantly wanted a baby. I was imagining things that weren't there.

"That's some nose you've got on you, Kingcaid." Look at me, reverting to sarcasm to hide behind. Who'd have thought it? "You're primed for a role at airport security. Sniffer human as opposed to sniffer hound." I laughed, ruffling his hair, which must have grown three inches in the last couple of months. "You've got the shaggy look to pull it off."

"No thanks to my mother."

We danced to another couple of tracks, returning to our seats when the lights dimmed and the live band came onstage. As the lead singer belted out the first line, I picked up my handbag and waved it at Kadon.

"Going to powder my nose," I shouted over the music.

I made my way outside the ballroom to the ladies' toilets across the expansive Victorian-tiled hallway. I fresh-ened up, applied a new coat of lipstick, and gave myself a final talking-to over this fantastical nonsense about me and Kadon. It was a good thing we were leaving in the morn-ing. By nine o'clock, we'd be on our way to Heathrow Airport, and by four in the afternoon, we'd be back in Saint Tropez.

A part of me wished the French air traffic controllers were still on strike and we'd get to enjoy another stop-off in Paris, but the far more sensible part of me called that a disaster waiting to happen. The last thing I needed was to fall at the final hurdle and spew out some twaddle under the influence of a crisp Sauvignon by propositioning Kadon.

Wherever I went to recharge my batteries, a holiday hookup with some fit, tanned guy should be at the top of my wish list when choosing a destination.

Hmm... Australia might fit the bill. Bondi Beach was crammed with gorgeous, bronzed, blond-haired Adonises. A few orgasms, and this imaginary attraction to Kadon would disappear in a hedonistic haze.

I felt better already.

Clutching my bag, I left the bathroom.

Oh, great.

Benedict.

What did he want?

"Have you got a minute, Annaleesa?" He palmed the back of his head, his lips pressed together in a slight grimace.

"I suppose so. Congratulations, by the way."

His brow furrowed almost as if he couldn't figure out what I was congratulating him for.

Good luck, Fenella.

"Oh, yeah. Thanks." He gripped my elbow. "Let's go somewhere quieter."

I wrenched my arm upward. "I'm fine here. What is it, Benedict?"

Pulling on his earlobe, he shuffled his feet as if the floor were suddenly hot. "I don't love Fenella. I never did. It's you I love."

I widened my eyes. "What?"

He cleared his throat. "I've missed you so much, Annaleesa." His eyes beseeched me. "Please forgive me."

I sighed. "Benedict..."

"Please, Annaleesa. I have to stay married to Fenella for the sake of my career. But that doesn't mean we can't be together."

Okay, the man was officially insane. "What on earth are you talking about?"

"An affair." He ran his fingertip down my bare arm. I almost threw up all over his expensive tux. "You could be my mistress."

Ah, hell... I'd lost the bloody bet with Kadon. This dickhead had cost me a hundred euros and having to suffer through Kadon's smugness for several hours when I told him he was right about Benedict suggesting an affair.

"You're *married*, Benedict. You took vows."

"So." He shrugged as if the words he'd spoken in front of the minister a few short hours ago had meant nothing.

Clearly, they hadn't.

"Have you lost your mind?"

"My heart, Annaleesa. I've lost my heart. To you." He frowned, almost as if he couldn't comprehend that I hadn't fallen at his feet at such an amazing offer. "We'd have to be careful, but I'm willing to do that for you. I thought you'd be flattered."

I burst out laughing. I couldn't help it. What a self-absorbed, egotistical jerk who, if I was reading the look on his face accurately, believed in his heart of hearts that I'd jump at the chance of rekindling our relationship.

The tips of his ears reddened, and a vein popped in his forehead. That thing always protruded when he was about to lose his temper or couldn't get his own way. How had I never noticed what a child he could be when we'd been together?

"No, Benedict. I'm not flattered. And, in case it's escaped your attention, I have a boyfriend."

"The Yank?" He spat out a bitter laugh. "He's not worthy of you."

My eyebrows flew up my forehead. "And you are?"

"At least I don't look as if I've rolled straight in off a beach."

"No. Just out of another woman's bed." I high-fived myself for that one.

"I didn't mean to cheat. I meant to break up with you before I slept with Fenella, but what happened, happened."

What a piece of work.

"That's okay, then. I mean, those penises do have a habit of burrowing into vaginas without the man they're attached to having any say in it whatsoever."

"You never used to be like this. You've always been so good and kind. Is that *his* influence?"

"No." I jabbed a finger at his chest. "It's yours. After you dumped me, I woke up from the nightmare I'd been living and realized I'd buried my true self." I threw my arms out to the side. "So this is me, Benedict, in all my sarcastic glory. Still want to hook up with me?"

"I love you."

I laughed again. This was like a comedy sketch. I expected it to be up for a BAFTA any day now.

"Go back to your wife, Benedict."

I turned.

He grabbed my elbow and spun me toward him. His

arms banded around my waist. "Don't go. Please. Give me another chance." He tried to kiss me.

"Get off me." I whipped my head to the side. "You had your chance, and you blew it." I rammed both hands against his chest, and he released me. "You made your bed, Benedict. Go lie in it."

"Annaleesa—"

"You heard her." Kadon tugged me behind him, putting himself between me and Benedict. He grabbed Benedict around the throat and shoved him against the wall. "Touch my woman again and I'll fucking kill you."

"Kadon, let him go." I tugged on his arm. "He's not worth it."

"I'm warning you, Oberon. You lay one finger on her and I'll put you in the ground."

Benedict grinned. "Well, you do have form."

Form? What was he talking about? Kadon stilled. His hand fell from Benedict's neck, and he took a step back.

"Let's go, Lee."

He captured my hand and led me away. A nerve thrummed in his cheek, and his nostrils flared. I'd never seen him so angry.

"I might not be perfect, Annaleesa," Benedict hollered. "But at least I've never killed anyone."

Chapter 18

Kadon

It's time to tell the truth.

As if I'd been doused in liquid nitrogen, I froze to the spot. The world around me imploded, falling in rubble at my feet.

How did he know? How *could* he know?

It was impossible.

And yet, the facts were indisputable. I sensed Lee's eyes on me, confused, questioning. Afraid? God, no, not that. Anything but that.

The past never stayed buried. I should have known it'd rise up, like a phoenix, and tear down the crumbling walls I'd built. After all, I'd never put that night behind me. It might as well have happened yesterday. The sights and sounds, the smell of blood, the lifeless body lying on the stone floor. The terror that had coursed through me when I realized what I'd done. It was all so fresh, so *real*.

"What do you mean?" Lee's muffled voice broke through the fog clouding my brain.

"Ask him," Benedict said. "He knows what I'm talking about."

I blinked, but the rest of me remained paralyzed.

"Kadon?" The confusion in her voice killed me. "Kadon, talk to me."

I shook my head. It wasn't a no. It was "I can't," but I couldn't form the words to tell Lee that. I gasped to control my breath. Benedict said something else, but the words were all jumbled in my brain, reminiscent of how I saw the written word. I couldn't make sense of it.

Pull yourself together.

Fire rampaged through my chest, my arms, my fingers and toes, and white spots filled my vision. I blinked again.

Breathe. He can't prove a damn thing. Besides, the case was closed.

Lee. Oh God. What would I tell her? She was bound to have questions, and I wouldn't lie to her. Not to her. She deserved the full and frank truth, but, Christ, what if she looked at me differently when she knew I'd murdered someone? What if she hated me? Or, worse, was scared of me? I couldn't bear it.

Benedict. That fucking bastard. I fisted my hands. The urge to break his face for touching Lee, for spewing his venom, for knowing the *truth* of the man I was, almost overwhelmed me.

No. Calm down. Breathe.

Of all people, I could not afford to lose my temper. I'd

spent nine years keeping myself calm, practicing mindfulness. I refused to let that fucking asshole ruin the work I'd put in. I refused to allow him to drag me back to the darkest of times when I'd wake in the middle of the night, sweating, sobbing, ruinous thoughts tempting me into a pit of despair.

"Let's go." I pulled on Lee's hand and made for the winding staircase that led us up to our room. She didn't say a word the entire time. I opened the door, motioned to her first, then followed her inside. The thud of the door closing echoed through my heart.

I'd never thought myself worthy of a woman like Lee, but that hadn't stopped me from hoping. Stopped me from *dreaming*. Those same hopes and dreams lay scattered around my feet like ashes in the wind created from the embers of my life.

I sat on the bed and stared at the floor. My back ached, my lungs lacked room to breathe, and my mind was nothing but mush. The silence swallowed me up like a wormhole sucking the life out of all the good in the world and propelling me to a life of loneliness.

"Here." Lee held out a glass of what looked like brandy. I took it from her, nursing the glass in both hands.

"Drink it, Kadon."

I knocked it back in one go. Fuck, that burned. Setting the glass on the nightstand, I forced myself to look at her. Emotions rippled across her face, the earlier confusion replaced by concern. She sat beside me. The mattress dipped under her weight. Her palm landed on my thigh.

"Don't." My voice sounded strangled. Nothing like me.

She kept her hand in place. "Please tell me what's going on. I'm worried about you. You're white as chalk."

I plucked at my bottom lip. "I don't know where to begin."

"Take your time. We've got all night." She caressed my cheek. I closed my eyes, immersing myself in her tender touch. I'd never come so close to crying in years. Not conscious crying, anyway. I'd woken up plenty of times with tears streaming down my face, but this was different. Raw. Visceral. Dangerous.

"I struggled academically my whole life. Did I ever tell you that?"

"No, you didn't."

"After my dyslexia diagnosis, my parents did everything they could to help me pull up my grades, but it wasn't only the struggle with reading that affected my ability to learn. It was the lack of interest in the whole academic scene. The pull to engage in outdoor pursuits or doodling on a drawing pad or working with my hands was far more powerful. But I was also acutely aware of my place in the family, and the expectation that I'd take over one of the businesses someday, just like my cousins and brothers."

Running my hands through my hair, I took a breath. It had been so long since I'd spoken about that night that I'd forgotten how fucking hard it was.

"Nolen, my eldest brother, was the diligent, hard-working son. Blaize, whom you met the other day, is basically a fucking genius. Then there was me. The odd one out."

"You mean the kind, generous, funny, bighearted, talented-in-so-many-ways-I-can't-count-that-high son?"

I smiled for about a second. "If you say so."

"I do say so."

I heaved a sigh. "You're right. I know children aren't all the same, but when you're born into a family like mine, it's hard not to beat yourself up when you fall short."

"I can't even imagine."

"When I was sixteen, my father sent me to this finishing school in Switzerland. They boarded sixteen- to eighteen-year-olds. The school was well known for helping kids who struggled academically, and boy, they delivered. I blossomed under their tutelage. It was unbelievable. They helped me see things differently. I have a lot to thank those teachers for."

"Sounds wonderful."

"Yeah, it was." I nibbled on my thumbnail. "The first year at least."

"What happened?"

"The son of the principal happened." A chill ran over me, like when people say someone walked over their grave. I shivered. I didn't believe in that stuff, but even I had to admit the timing freaked me out. I hadn't talked about him out loud in years. Not since... not since the police interviews.

Her brow furrowed. "Go on."

"He was a year younger than me, so he only joined when I was in my second year. You'd never have guessed it, though. He was a right brute of a kid. Over six feet tall, built like a tank. He could easily have passed for early twenties. And he used his size advantage to bully the less-developed kids."

"He sounds like a treat."

Her sarcasm brought a much-needed smile to my face, even though I couldn't hold it.

"There was this one kid, Samuel, who took the brunt of it. He was probably the smallest of us all with the added challenges of a cleft lip and a squint in his right eye. Henry, the principal's son, treated him like his personal whipping boy. He'd steal his money, punch him when he thought no one was looking, and basically terrorize the poor bastard."

"Didn't anyone speak up?"

"Oh, yeah. A few of us did, me included."

"What happened?"

"She refused to believe us. We ended up with a month of detention and our weekend privileges revoked for six weeks."

"Can't be easy to accept that your son is a bullying twat."

Whenever Lee said *twat*, I couldn't help smiling. Today was no exception.

"No. I guess not. But it left us powerless. I thought of telling my dad, but I was worried he'd take me out of the school, and I was making so much progress that I hated the idea of leaving and losing the gains I'd made. So I kept my mouth shut, put my head down, and worked."

My stomach clenched. I needed another drink to get through this next part. I picked up the brandy glass and crossed over to the drinks cabinet. Waving the bottle at Lee, I said, "Want one?"

"Yeah."

I poured two glasses and returned to the bed, retaking my seat next to her. On many occasions, the urge to hold Lee consumed me, but none more so than right now. Too risky, though. My emotions were bubbling close to the surface, and the last thing either of us needed was for me to blurt out that I loved her, then tell her I killed a kid.

Relationship disaster right there.

"This one night, I woke up starving. I'd missed dinner because I'd wanted to finish a paper, and even though I was making great strides with reading and writing, it took me longer than kids who didn't suffer with my particular issues. The kitchen was always open, although we weren't allowed to cook anything."

My bones chilled. I rubbed up and down my arms. Fuck, this was hard.

"Take your time."

I blew out a stream of breath through pursed lips. "I made a turkey sandwich and poured a glass of milk. I was on my way back to my room when I heard someone crying as I passed the library. I went inside. The place was almost pitch black, the only light coming from a lamp left on the desk where the school librarian worked."

I drank half the brandy. My heart thumped against my ribs. I could see it, as if I were standing there watching the unfolding horror from outside my body. A bystander but not really.

"You don't have to tell me if you're not ready."

I shook my head. "It's about time. This thing... it's a poison, eating me from the inside. Telling you might be the cure I've searched for since it happened." I set down the glass. "Give me a minute."

I stood, paced, rubbed my lower back, paced some more. The jumble of words forming the basis of an explanation gathered together in my mind, as if a magnet was in the center of a circle and each word was powerless to resist the pull. Slowly, as if by magic, they made a sentence, then a paragraph. I remained standing but found the courage to look Lee right in the eye.

"I crept toward the crying. I didn't want to intrude on someone's privacy if they were having a moment. Lots of kids got homesick as the term progressed." I took several deep breaths. In through the nose, out through the mouth. My heart flopped about inside my chest so much that I considered the possibility that the arteries had detached. Although if that were the case, I'd be dead.

Like Henry.

Fuck.

"Breathe, Kadon. You're freaking me out. Here, squeeze my hand."

I held on to her, my one sliver of stability. If I didn't know any better, I'd say we were on a boat in rough seas. The floor beneath my feet undulated. I slumped onto the bed.

"He... the bully... Henry... he had Samuel. He had S-s..." Ah, fuck. *I can't do this.* I pinched the bridge of my nose.

"I think we should stop."

"No!" I swallowed. "No. If I don't do this now, that's it. I'll never be able to tell you, and I don't want to keep secrets from you. Not from you. Not anymore."

"Okay, okay." She ran her free hand up and down my arm.

I took several more deep breaths. No idea where it came from, but a calm settled over me. Maybe Lee was passing her strength to me through our joined hands. I locked eyes with her again.

"Henry had Samuel bent over a table in between the bookcases. Samuel's pajama bottoms were around his ankles, and Henry was..." Nausea ripped through my stomach.

Lee's hand flew to her mouth. "Oh God, Kadon. No."

"I lost it, Lee. This surge of anger, of blind white rage, overtook me. I must have blocked out what happened because the next thing I remember was Henry lying on the floor with blood gushing from the back of his head. Samuel pulled up his pants and ran screaming from the library. I slumped to the floor. That's where the school nurse found me. The rest of the night is a blur. Blue flashing lights, the principal's agonizing cries, police asking me questions. My dad arrived the following afternoon, and somehow, he made it all go away."

"What happened to Henry?"

"He... died. Samuel told the authorities that I hit Henry, and he fell and cracked his head on the corner of the table. Blunt force trauma, according to the coroner."

She steepled both hands over her nose and mouth and just... stared. At me, at the floor, out the window. I understood her state of shock. I was in the same place. It had taken me nine years to tell anyone outside of the authorities and my family.

Even if it cost me my friendship with Lee, I'd never regret her being the one I finally confessed to.

"The boy, Samuel. What happened to him?"

"I don't know. His parents came to pick him up the next day, and I never saw him again." I worried my lip, stopping only when I tasted blood. "I never paid for it, Lee. My father whitewashed it away, as if it never happened. But it did happen. Henry was a living, breathing human being, and I killed him."

"Henry was a rapist."

A shudder racked my body, the images from that night as clear today as they were nine years ago. "Yes, he was, but that didn't give me the right to act as judge, jury, and executioner."

"Kadon, it was an *accident*."

I shook my head. "No. An accident is where no one is culpable. I heard that same excuse so many times from my parents and my brothers after I returned home to Seattle, but they were wrong, and you're wrong. If I hadn't lost my temper and hit him, Henry would be alive today."

"And Samuel? What would have happened to him if you hadn't stepped in? Have you thought about that?"

I had, many times, yet I always focused on the life I'd taken rather than the life I'd saved. If I knew what happened to Samuel, I might get some closure. All I'd ever wished for was that, unlike me, he'd been able to put those horrific experiences behind him and move on with his life. He deserved to be happy.

I hadn't yet figured out whether I deserved the same.

"You should try to find him. Samuel, I mean."

I gave her a watery smile. "Funny you should say that. I've had a private investigator on the case for about a year, but so far, nothing. The authorities sealed the records because we were minors, and the Swiss are world class at keeping information secure. It's their superpower."

She encased both my hands in hers. "You'll find him. And when you do, that's where you'll find your peace."

I prayed she was right.

Chapter 19

Leesa

**Ever felt as if you're the ball
in a pinball machine?**

"WOULD YOU RATHER I CHECKED INTO A HOTEL tonight?"

I whipped my head around so fast I pulled a muscle in my neck. Massaging it, I glared at Kadon. If he asked such a stupid question again, I'd clip him around the ear. Or pull out his pubic hairs with tweezers. "Of course not. Why would you think that?"

He hitched a shoulder. "I killed someone, Lee. I wouldn't blame you if you called it quits and I never saw you again."

"Oh my God. Really, Kadon? Is that the kind of person you think I am?" I narrowed my eyes and crossed my arms.

He kept his gaze averted, and what I saw broke my heart. My happy-go-lucky, kind and generous, surfer-loving best friend was a shell of his former self. He looked... devastated. Destroyed. At the end of a tether pulled taut for too long. What had happened to him was so huge I couldn't even empathize. I could try, but I couldn't feel what he was feeling. What I could do, though, was stop him from falling any further into a pit of despair and give him a good old-fashioned shake.

"Get ready for some tough love." I counted each point on my fingers. "One, stop with the self-pity. It doesn't suit you."

He drew his head back quickly, but I continued.

"Two, I'd like to think I'm not that shallow. Friends stick by friends when times are tough, and if they don't, then they weren't friends at all. And three," I tapped the third finger. "Accidents happen. I know I've already said that, but it's worth repeating." I turned sideways, crossing my legs yoga-style, and drew his hands into my lap. "I can't even imagine the kind of scars an experience like that causes, but I believe internal scars heal like external ones do. The thing is, Kadon, healing starts with forgiving ourselves, and you..." I looked him squarely in the eye. "You're not there, are you?"

"No." He rubbed his lips together. "I'm not sure I ever will be."

"Not with that attitude you won't." I hadn't a clue whether I was making things any better by being so blunt. I wasn't a therapist. I could make things ten times worse. But Kadon and I had always been into straight talking. He'd given me more than my fair share of tough-love speeches in

the first few months after Benedict had dumped me. Now
it was my turn to do the same for him.

"Tell it like you see it, Lee."

I risked a grin. "You know me."

"Yeah. I do." His eyes glazed over, his attention somewhere behind me, although I doubted he was looking at
anything in this room. I'd wager that he was back there, in
Switzerland, on the night it had happened.

"Kadon." I stroked his face, his stubble rough beneath
my fingertips. "Why don't you get some rest? You look
exhausted."

"How does Benedict know?" His brow furrowed. "The
only people who know what happened that night are my
closest family members, the Swiss authorities, and
Samuel's and Henry's parents. Plus the school nurse,
whom Samuel ran to that night. Benedict wouldn't have
come across any of those people in his day-to-day life."

"I don't know. Maybe he doesn't. What if he was
fishing?"

"It's a hell of a line to cast." He shook his head. "Not
that it matters. The police carried out a thorough investigation, and they didn't put me in prison, so I guess they were
satisfied that it wasn't intentional."

"Because it *wasn't* intentional."

"Or my dad paid them off. He had the contacts and the
money to do it."

God, Kadon. "They wouldn't have covered up something so huge if they thought there was a case to answer."

"Wouldn't they?" He laughed, but the sound was
nothing like my Kadon. It was all bitter and twisted and
filled with self-loathing. "The world of enormous wealth is

powerful, Lee. A boy died. Because of me. Parents grieved. Lives were ruined. Yet somehow, it's never come out. Tell me that's got nothing to do with wealth."

If he didn't quit castigating himself, I might have "It was an accident" tattooed on him somewhere visible. "I understand you want to take responsibility, and it's admirable. But Henry had some culpability in his own demise." I held up my hands as he opened his mouth. "I know. I know. He didn't deserve to die. I agree. Of course he didn't. But you didn't mean for him to die, did you?"

"No." His voice was so small and sad that my heart shattered for him.

"Then I repeat: it was an accident."

"Yeah." He rubbed his eyes.

"Say it with conviction." I grinned.

"Thank God for you, Lee." He ran his thumb over my knuckles. Back and forth, back and forth, his eyes cast down and his shoulders hunched.

The air around me shifted, and my breath caught in my throat. *Kiss him.* The thought echoed around my head like a ball hitting the sides of a pinball machine. I edged forward. Kadon chose that moment to cease the tender swipes of his thumb across the back of my hand. His chin came up and our eyes locked. Something shifted in his expression. I couldn't place it. A mixture of determination, confusion, and uncertainty. I lost count of how long we stared into each other's eyes. A second, two, a minute. An hour. Butterfly wings flapped against the walls of my chest and my stomach, and I had this sense of lightness, as if I were floating on air.

"Lee," he rasped, his pupils dilating. In this light, they

made his eyes look almost black. I held my breath, antici-pating his next move. And it'd better be to kiss me.

If he kissed me, I'd dare to believe that there might be the beginnings of something special happening between us.

If he kissed me, I'd—

His lips collided with mine. I gasped at the suddenness of it, even though I'd wished and prayed for his kiss. His tongue surged between my lips, wrapping around mine, his hands delving into my hair, angling my head to his liking. This kiss wasn't like the others we'd done for show. It was rough and tinged with a desperation I felt, too. He leaned into me. I landed on a stack of soft pillows. Kadon lay on top of me, nestling between my spread thighs. I wrapped my legs around his waist, and *God*, he was hard.

I groaned into his mouth. It spurred him on. A warm hand burrowed underneath my dress. The sound of fabric tearing froze his hand in place. His lips broke away from mine.

"I think I ripped your dress."

"Rip it again," I whispered. "Tear it to shreds. I don't care. Just... don't stop."

"Fuck, Lee."

He took me at my word. The dress split up the side, the stitching working loose. Lust ignited inside me. I clawed at his jacket, somehow wrestling him out of it. His shirt disap-peared. Trousers, too. My heart took off at a sprint, rattling my rib cage hard enough to snap the bones in two. My skin was on fire yet clammy to the touch. I felt *crazed*, rabid. Animalistic.

Kadon groaned. "Christ, no panties."

Oh, yeah. I'd forgotten I hadn't worn underwear. They ruined the line of the dress.

"You're killing me."

"Don't die yet." I peppered his neck with kisses. "I need you."

He stilled. Rearing back, his hazel eyes bored into me. "Do you?"

I wasn't the shy and retiring type, but lying here with Kadon looming over me and only a thin layer of underwear between me and his cock, I came over all coy. I was fine in the moment, when our libidos were in charge and our instincts drove us forward, but pausing to ask a question had pulled me out of fantasyland and into a stark reality.

My best friend and I were about to fuck.

Heat crept up my chest and over my cheek, and even my ears felt hot. My tongue grew to twice its size. Not literally, but enough that speech was impossible, and every drop of saliva had evaporated. Gone. Vanished. I couldn't even swallow.

"Lee?" He nuzzled my neck. "Talk to me. Tell me you want this as much as I do."

How was this happening? Was he doing this as a way of quashing the dark cloud that had descended over us unexpectedly, or had his feelings for me changed on this trip, too, like mine had for him?

Jesus Christ. Say something.

Nope. Zero words came. I waited for him to look at me, and I nodded. That'd have to do as confirmation of consent. His gaze dropped to my mouth. I parted my lips, an invitation he accepted. Our teeth clashed, tongues fought for supremacy, hands roved and explored and touched places I'd never imagined we would. Not us. Not me and Kadon. But as the last shreds of my tattered gown landed on the floor beside the bed, exposing me to him for the very first time, the *rightness* of what we were doing hit me. A wrecking ball that demolished everything I'd thought up to this point and opened my eyes to something so wonderful and pure and perfect.

His lips left mine. I sucked in a deep breath, my lungs burning for oxygen I'd deprived them of. Tonguing my nipple, he brought the nub to a stiff peak. The graze of his teeth made me gasp.

"God," I croaked. *Is that the best you can do?* "Don't stop." *Better, but clichéd.*

He gave each nipple equal attention, driving me to the edge of insanity. His stubble sanded my skin, but I didn't care if I came out in a rash. I only cared that his lips and his tongue and his teeth kept doing what they were doing. I found myself on top without the memory of Kadon moving me. I settled over his cock, rocking my hips back and forth. He groaned softly, his hands clasping my hips.

"Sit on my face, Lee."

My mouth popped open. I'd had oral sex before, but not like that. What if I suffocated him?

"Don't deny me a fantasy I've had for far too long."

Say what now? How long was 'far too long'? Longer than this weekend, that was for certain. Had I been blind to Kadon's feelings for me? Was I that dumb? "How—"

He placed his forefinger over my lips. "Can we talk afterward?"

Without waiting for an answer, he shifted me up his

body, shuffling down the bed to meet me halfway. My thighs tensed.

"Lee, I don't have a twelve-inch tongue. Get lower."

His fingers dug into my hips, and he forced me to sit right over his face. My only saving grace was that he couldn't see the blush creeping over every inch of my skin. One sweep of his tongue, though, and my embarrassment fled. I gripped the headboard and rode him, rocking back and forth, seeking more friction. My clit throbbed and pulsed. God, please let this go on forever. I'd happily live my life riding Kadon's face, but my stupid body didn't get the memo entitled "Let's make this last." I peaked, hovered, and fell, crying out, tremors and vibrations consuming every part of me. Even my toes clenched so hard that they cramped.

I knelt up. Kadon's lips were shining, covered with my cum. Another bout of self-consciousness caused a flush of heat to blanket my body, enough to imitate lying out in the sun all day without sunscreen.

"You taste better than I dreamed of." He licked his lips.

I ducked my head. I'd always been fairly secure during sex, but I couldn't shake the conscious thought that the man lying beneath me with my cum dripping down his chin was Kadon. My best friend. The man who, until a few days ago, I'd never thought of romantically. Now, I couldn't turn it off, and discovering that there was a high chance he felt the same way about me, only for a lot longer, it... it shocked me to my foundations.

"Lee." Kadon's fingertips, roughened from spending so much time in the ocean, brushed my cheek. "I don't have a condom."

This was it. This was my chance to put a stop to the insanity and attempt to recover what remained of our friendship. We could put down one sesh of oral sex to a moment of madness, but if we went the whole way and fucked, we couldn't turn back.

Oh, who was I kidding? We'd already overstepped. But more than that, I didn't want to go back to the way things were. This weekend had opened not only my eyes but also a plethora of opportunities for happiness I'd almost given up on. All these months, my dream guy had been right there in front of me, and I'd been too determined to protect my battered heart from any further damage that I'd refused to see. Well, my eyes were open now.

"I don't care. I'm on birth control." An unplanned pregnancy wasn't the only consideration, but Kadon would *never* put me in danger. If there was a one-millionth of a percentage point chance he might have an STI, he wouldn't do it.

"Are you sure?" Veins corded his neck from the strain of holding himself together.

Actions spoke louder than words. I inched down his body, hooked my fingers into his boxers, and tugged them down his legs. His cock sprang free, the tip glistening with precum. He was circumcised, something that wasn't widely practiced in Europe. Kadon's was the first circumcised cock I'd ever seen in the flesh—and I couldn't stop staring at it. So smooth, yet hard. A thick, steel rod wrapped in a tightly fitted satin coat.

A laugh simmered in my throat at the flowery language echoing in my head. I swallowed it down. I was pretty certain that laughing while staring at a man's cock might be

211

misconstrued, and I imagined men were *very* easily spooked if they thought a woman found their precious manhood amusing.

I ran my gaze over his defined abs, the firm chest with a smattering of dark hair, his broad shoulders, and ended at his stunning face. He really was a work of art, a man who'd have conquered the modeling world if he'd chosen that as a career. As I looked into his eyes, my amusement vanished and lust took over. I gripped his erection and lowered myself down an inch at a time. A hiss spilled from his lips as I bottomed out.

"Jesus Christ. Fuck, that feels so damn good, Lee." He bucked his hips, reaching up to cup my breasts. "Grind on me."

I circled, bearing down, gripping him with all my strength. His lips parted, his eyes squeezing shut.

"Fuck, yeah, that's it."

He bucked again. I met him beat for beat, sweat dripping between my breasts and beading my brow. Dear God, the man had stamina. He sat upright, cupping my cheeks, his mouth crashing on mine, and still he kept up this relentless rhythm. My clit swelled and pulsed and throbbed, teetering on the edge of heaven. I dove my fingers into his hair, digging into his scalp, and I met his ferocious kiss and frenzied thrusting hips with a savagery of my own. Who even was I?

I liked sex as much as the next person, but this... this was on a different scale. I lost myself, biting and clawing and bouncing on him, my heart beating wildly.

"Need more," he grunted.

He pulled out and flipped me over. Tugging me to the

edge of the bed, he stood up and gripped my ankles. Spreading my legs wide, he drove his hips forward.

"Look, Lee. Look how fucking hot we are."

I glanced down. The sight of him powering into me, all hard and thick and lustrous, and I came undone. My cry of ecstasy echoed around the room. Vaguely aware of Kadon grunting through his release, I forced my eyes open. This, I did not want to miss.

For the love of all that's holy. Waves of pleasure washed over his face, erasing the earlier pain that had scored my heart. Pride tightened my chest. I'd done that. I'd given him a few precious moments of peace after sharing a trauma that had shaped his life for so many years.

He collapsed on top of me, his face buried in my neck. He didn't stay there long, rolling onto his back and taking me with him. Tucking my hair behind my ears, he gazed at me with a look I hadn't seen before. Adoration, longing. Love? Not friendship love. Genuine love. The kind that lovers shared. The burning questions I'd had before stuck in my throat. What if I was reading more into this than there was? Men said all kinds of crap when they thought they might be about to get their dicks wet. What if all Kadon had needed was oblivion? To forget, if only for a few minutes, and sex had been a good way to achieve that. What if I was a convenience and nothing more? There and available, and oh-so willing.

"Lee."

"Yeah?"

"I need you to know something."

"What?"

"I'm in love with you."

213

Chapter 20

Kadon

The genie is out of the bottle.

I'D DONE IT NOW.

Stepped off the cliff's edge.

Let the genie out of the bottle.

Dropped the atomic bomb, and numerous other ridiculous clichés that described the current situation.

In simple terms, I couldn't unsay what had been said.

The number of dirty dreams and fantasies I'd had about Lee was in the hundreds. Thousands, even. But not a single one had come close to the reality. The taste of her cum, the smell of her skin, the feel of her pussy clamping around my dick and her small but perfect tits in my hands —all those experiences were unimaginable before I'd had them.

Once wasn't enough. Not nearly enough. But now that I'd blabbed that I was in love with her, what happened next might not be up to me. What if all she'd wanted was to make me feel better after finding out I'd killed someone nine years ago? A pity fuck. God, was there anything shittier than that? Lee loved me. I had no doubts about that. But it wasn't the same kind of love I felt for her.

Why hadn't I kept my big mouth shut?

"Kadon, I... I—"

"Don't say anything." I raised my shoulders off the bed and brushed my lips over hers, then gently rolled her to the side. "I don't expect you to say it back. But I owed you the truth."

"How... how long?"

I grimaced. Earlier, I'd said we'd talk afterward, but now that it had come to it, I couldn't find the right words. I feared that whatever I said, I'd come across as weird at best, creepy at worst. And what if she resented the fact that I'd lied to her for pretty much our entire relationship? Or she saw through my suggestion that we fake our relationship this weekend as a way of me getting closer. And now that we'd fucked, she'd have every right to feel duped.

"A while." I caressed her face. "Look at you, Lee. It isn't possible not to love you. You're beautiful and kind, and you have a sharp wit that I adore. I can't imagine my life without you. Please don't think badly of me."

"Kadon." She brought my hand to her lips and kissed the tips of my fingers. "I could never think badly of you. Why would you say that?"

"Because I lied to you. For months."

"You didn't lie. You kept your feelings to yourself, which you've every right to do."

"Lying by omission is still lying."

She shook her head, a soft laugh spilling from her lips. "Kadon Kingcaid, you're a daft bugger at times."

I grinned. "Wow, what a compliment."

"Honestly, I could shake you. I admit that before this weekend, I hadn't looked at you in that way. But after you kissed me when we arrived, something changed. You opened my eyes when I didn't even realize they were closed. I wasn't sure how to tell you I was over here wallowing in feelings and freaking out about them."

"And you call me daft."

She grinned. "Fine. We're *both* daft." Tucking into my side, she kissed my shoulder. "I don't know about you, but I'm exhausted. I know we have a lot of talking to do, but can we save it for the journey home."

I reached down and pulled the covers over us both. "Get some sleep. We have the rest of our lives to talk."

Having Lee fall asleep in my arms might be the single most wonderful moment in my entire life. As long as I took out the sex. Because that was on another plane, another planet, another universe. But being able to hold and touch and kiss this woman and not have her reject me stirred something inside me, a dormant sense of worth.

For so long, I'd wallowed in burdensome guilt, and I'd deserved to. But perhaps the time had come for me to acknowledge the truth. I'd never intended to kill Henry. Not even close. All I'd wanted was to save Samuel, to get that brute off of him and put an end to the horror.

Where was he?

Why couldn't Joseph find him?

He had to be out there somewhere. People didn't just vanish without leaving a trail. Even if he'd died, there'd be records. Evidence that he'd existed, that he'd lived, that he'd been loved. That he'd mattered.

I hadn't even known him all that well, yet the events of that night had bonded us in a way I could neither explain nor shake. I didn't want to, either. I only wanted to find him, to know that he was okay, that he was happy. Married, possibly, with children. I *needed* to know that Henry's abuse hadn't ruined his life. God only knew Henry's death had ruined mine.

Until Lee.

I gazed down at her. She had to be dreaming. Her eyelids were darting from side to side. I kissed the top of her head.

"Dream of me, baby."

Closing my eyes, I let sleep take me.

K

I woke to the sound of the shower running. Groaning, I rolled over in bed and rubbed my eyes. I squinted at the clock on the nightstand. Seven thirty-five. We hadn't planned to leave until ten o'clock. Lee must be eager to be on her way, and I couldn't blame her. We'd done what we came to do, and my dreams of our fake relationship turning into a real one might come true. If it wasn't for Benedict's suggestion that he had an idea of what had happened in Switzerland, I'd call this weekend a major success.

How the fuck did he know? If he did and wasn't fishing like Lee had said. I didn't buy that, though. If he was fishing, he might have accused me of being a playboy, or into polyamorous relationships, or some weird kink that'd turn Lee off. But to blurt out what he had... no way had that been a shot in the dark.

For years I'd lived with the fear of what I'd done making it to the press, but so far, my father had kept a lid on it. He had the power and the contacts to close down any attempts at a story. I'd have to tell him about Benedict, though.

I rubbed my brow. Wasn't looking forward to that. Dad and I hadn't spoken about that night in a long while. We had in the beginning, but over time, it'd stopped being a conversation piece between us. He thought I'd moved on because I let him think that. To know how much I'd suffered would hurt my father terribly. He'd blame himself, and that was the last thing I wanted. My dad was one of the best humans on the planet.

I couldn't hide from the conversation, though. Dad would need to get his lawyers ready to quash any signs of an ambitious journalist breaking the story. NDAs remained in place, but times changed, as did laws of different countries. Dad needed to know so he could line up a defensive strategy. Just in case.

I threw back the covers and got out of bed. I raised my hand to knock on the bathroom door, then changed my mind. I'd surprise her, slip into the shower with her, and give her three orgasms before breakfast.

The shower stall was steamed up. I slipped inside and captured Lee around the waist. She startled in my arms.

"Jeez, Kadon. You scared the shit out of me."

"Didn't you hear me?"

"Duh!" She pointed at her face. "Does this look like a person who heard you?"

"I don't know. What is that supposed to look like?"

She palmed my shoulder. "Funny."

"I thought so." I moved my hands to her ass and tugged her against me, bending to kiss her. Would I ever get used to being able to kiss her and put my hands on her ass? "You taste of mint."

"And you taste of morning breath."

I grinned. "Is the honeymoon over already?"

I expected her to laugh. She didn't. Fear curdled in my stomach. She'd changed her mind. She was about to tell me that what had happened between us was a mistake and it was over before it'd begun. I readied myself for a broken heart, one that I'd never recover from.

"I dreamed about you last night."

Not what I'd expected her to say.

"You did? What was I doing?"

She glanced down at my cock. "Stroking yourself while I watched." Her eyes lifted to mine. "You know the other day, when I left you by the bonfire?"

My head spun at the change of direction, but I went with it. "I remember."

A small smile lifted the corners of her lips. "I was so turned on after that kiss. I came back here, dove into the shower, and made myself come with that." She jerked her chin at the showerhead. "It has a rather good massage setting. Worked almost as well as a vibrator."

Lust chased away fear. I shivered, despite the heat from the water. My dick throbbed and tingled. Lee had made herself come while thinking about me.

Fuck.

A day ago, I wouldn't ever have imagined a time when Lee and I would be standing naked in a shower talking about masturbation, yet here we were. She wasn't running from me. She was taking things to the next level.

"Show me." I unhooked the showerhead and handed it to her. "Make yourself come. I want to see."

She took it from me, turning the dial until a single stream of water pulsed from the middle of the showerhead.

"Make *yourself* come." Her eyes traveled to my groin. "I want to see."

Bracing a hand on the tiled wall, she turned the showerhead upside down and aimed it at her clit. She hissed. Her eyes closed for a moment, bliss etching across her face. I couldn't look away. Was I dreaming? If I was, then I hoped I never woke up.

I wrapped my hand around my dick and gave it a single pull. Lee hissed again. Her eyes were open now and locked on my cock. I couldn't stop looking at her. Every emotion, every feeling, every lick of lust played out for my viewing pleasure. A tightening around her eyes, a clenched jaw, a soft sigh, a twitch to her shoulder, a shudder of pleasure ricocheting up her spine.

This was the most intimate sexual experience of my whole life, and I never wanted it to end.

"You're beautiful."

Eyes half-mast and heavy with lust, she smiled. "You're beautiful."

She adjusted the angle of the showerhead, and her hand crept over her flat abdomen, brushing along her ribs and cupping her right breast. She circled the nipple with her thumb, groaning as it peaked.

Jesus Christ Almighty.

I pumped harder, fucking my hand, my hips pistoning. She wasn't watching me now, lost in her own hedonistic moment. She rested her head against the tile and angled the showerhead closer to her clit. Her moans grew louder, her finger plucking at her nipple. Every single cell in my body was invested in this moment with her. I was drowning in ecstasy. She was the most magnificent sight. I imprinted the images in my mind. A bit too early in our relationship for me to suggest I film her, but fuck, one day. One day.

My balls tightened, a heat spreading throughout my lower abdomen. My calves twitched, and the first jet of cum shot out of me.

"Kadon, God, I'm coming."

I snapped my eyes open, unaware I'd closed them. Euphoria was written all over her face, her eyes fixated on the cum spurting from the head of my cock. It slowed, then stopped. She aimed a jet of water at my hands, washing off the cum. Replacing the showerhead, she pulled me under the hot spray. Standing on tiptoes, she eased my head down to hers and kissed me.

"I thought I tasted of morning breath."

"I don't care." She cupped my face. The intensity in her gaze stopped me in my tracks.

"What's wrong?"

"I need to tell you something."

Oh God. I tensed up. "Go on." My voice trembled.

"I think I'm in love with you, too." She shook her head. "No, I *know* I'm in love with you."

Relief weakened my knees. I held on to her for support, encircling her waist. "I thought you were breaking up with me," I croaked.

"After that performance? And last night, too? Not a chance." She stole another kiss, although it wasn't stealing when I gave it freely. From now on, all my kisses belonged to her.

"Kadon, this is all so new. We're both bound to have wobbly moments. But as long as we talk to each other, we're solid. I should have said it last night, but I was so... overwhelmed. I wanted to be sure."

"And are you?"

Her eyes softened. "A hundred percent."

I shaved while Lee dried her hair in the bedroom. It gave me a few moments to absorb my change in fortune. I'd never thought I'd hear Lee utter those words. She often told me she loved me, and I did the same to her, but while mine always carried a hidden message of being *in love*, hers never had.

Until this morning.

Despite her assurances, I couldn't shake the fear that she was telling me what she thought I wanted to hear. No. Lee wouldn't do that to me. Honesty and integrity were woven into her, like the rings on a tree. If she said she was in love with me, then she was. I guessed sometimes things happened that woke us up to the truth of what had stared us in the face all along.

If I'd known all it'd take was a passionate kiss by a roaring fire, I'd have dragged her to a bonfire on the beach long ago. The surfer set was always having bonfires and drinking and toasting smores.

"Kadon, phone." Lee passed my cell through the bathroom door.

I took it from her, frowning. Julian, my Dubai manager, was calling me. What did he want? As one of my most proficient managers, he rarely called, even in emergencies. There wasn't much Julian couldn't handle. And I was due a visit there next week, too.

"Julian. Everything all right?"

"Actually, no. Sorry to call you this early." His breath hitched. Was he crying?

"It's not a problem. What's wrong?"

"My mother died."

Ah, hell.

"I'm so sorry, Julian. What can I do?"

"That's why I'm ringing. Lucas is on vacation for two weeks. I can ask him to come back early, but—"

"Don't do that. He's entitled to his vacation. I'll fly over today."

"Are you sure?"

"Positive. Go be with your family. The club will survive for a day without you. I'll organize my flight and take care of things until you're able to return. No rush."

"Thanks, Kadon. I appreciate it."

"I really am sorry, Julian. Please let me know if there's anything I can do."

"I will."

He hung up. I exited the bathroom, half my face covered in shaving foam.

"What's wrong?" Lee asked.

My expression must've given me away. I twisted my lips to the side. "How do you feel about spending a few weeks in Dubai?"

Chapter 21

Leesa

Pretty does NOT mean stupid.

BRILLIANT SUNSHINE REFLECTED OFF THE CRYSTAL-clear blue waters surrounding Dubai, twinkling like a million diamonds cast adrift. The FASTEN SEAT BELT sign illuminated above my head. I clipped the belt into its housing, the smile I'd had in place since we'd boarded making my cheeks ache.

Audrey texting to tell me Dash was having a whale of a time and had commandeered her favorite chair, too, had kicked off my good mood. And returning to one of my most treasured vacation spots had kept it high.

"I love Dubai. It's been a while since I came here, though. I bet it's changed a lot."

Kadon brushed his hair off his forehead. I swore it'd grown at least an inch this weekend alone. Good thing, too.

He could stop bitching about it now. Besides, I much preferred the longer, surfer-dude style to the cropped cut his mother had coerced him into having for his brother's wedding.

"It's one of those places that seems to change every month. At one time, Dubai had something like seventy-five percent of the world's cranes to satisfy the amount of construction work going on."

I arched a brow. "Look at you, Mister Know-It-All."

"Mister Know-All-The-Useless-Facts is more like it."

"I found it interesting."

"Did you?"

"No."

He laughed, reaching for my hand. "Our relationship might've shifted, but you're still the same old Lee."

"Less of the old." I sniffed. "I'm in my prime."

His eyes roved over me, lingering on my boobs. They might not be huge, but that didn't seem to stop Kadon's obsession. *Guess he's a tit man.* Although, come to think of it, he'd felt my arse every time I'd gone to the bathroom on this flight, so who knew?

"You're definitely in your prime."

"Men. Such obvious creatures."

"We are." He nodded sagely. "It's an affliction we're born with. There's little point in fighting it."

"How women put up with men is a mystery."

"It's the D." He flashed a grin.

I tried to keep a straight face, but it was impossible. I was too busy enjoying Kadon's lighter side. After what he'd gone through, he deserved to have some fun, and I'd make sure he did. He might have to work on this trip, but we had the evenings and early mornings to enjoy.

Also... he wasn't wrong. I mean, I loved him for more than his dick. I wasn't that shallow. But the things he could do with it... my, oh, my.

The speed of our relationship morphing from best friends to lovers made my head spin. Who'd have thought two kisses would have the power to change everything? Not me.

During the flight, I'd studied him when he wasn't looking, trying to figure out how I'd been so blinded to how he felt about me. There must have been some signs, surely? Even Oscar-winning actors weren't that adept at hiding their feelings. Yet I'd blundered through my new, unexpected life, oblivious to my best friend's yearning for more.

When I'd modeled, I'd often read articles in the press about "airheaded pretty girls," and I'd strived hard to debunk that idiotic myth. "Pretty doesn't mean stupid" was a line I'd trotted out to more than a few journalists over the years, but deep down, I'd always feared that my looks were the only thing I had to offer. Yet even they hadn't been enough to stop Benedict from straying. Not that I was the least bit bothered about *that*. Not any longer. I'd had the luckiest of escapes.

The plane touched down with a bump, and I shifted a few inches forward in my seat as the captain applied the brakes. Our taxi was short, and as we emerged into the heat of Dubai, I dropped my sunglasses in place and took Kadon's hand to walk down the steps.

A limousine idled at the bottom of the steps to whisk us to the VIP terminal. I wasn't unused to such luxurious treatment. When I'd modeled for the big magazines, they often used to fly the models to their shooting locations by private jet. It still impressed me, though. The sumptuous furnishings, the bright and spacious atrium, the speed of passport checks. No waiting in line with tired parents trying to pacify overwrought kids, or groups of young men and women celebrating upcoming nuptials and making a racket as they staggered off the plane already half-drunk.

We exited the VIP terminal and climbed into a second limousine.

"Do you mind if we go straight to the beach club?" Kadon asked. "I'll have the driver take our luggage to the hotel, but I want to make sure everything is okay and that the staff aren't having any issues without Julian there."

"Of course not. This is a work trip. You do what you need to do."

He side-eyed me, a small smile tugging at his lips. "It's not all work." He ran his hand up the inside of my thigh. "I'll make sure of it."

"I'll bet you will."

"Complaining?"

"Nope."

His grin lit up his eyes. "Good."

"Will you see Julian on this trip?"

"If he wants to see me, yes. I've left the ball in his court. Losing a parent..." He shook his head. "I can't even let myself think about losing mine."

A deep, dark well of sorrow opened up in my chest. It was Christmas in a few weeks, and this was the first holiday season that I wouldn't be spending with my parents. Some days, I felt it was up to me to make the first move, but then at other times, I'd dig my heels in, determined that they were the ones in the wrong and therefore should be the ones to apologize.

But life was short. How would I feel if something happened to Maman and Papa and I hadn't tried to make amends? To at least attempt to build the bridges my mother had taken a sledgehammer to.

Kadon ran the back of his finger down my arm. "You're thinking about your folks, aren't you?"

"Yeah. I miss them. A lot. But I'm so mad at them. Maman said some terrible things when I told her I was quitting modeling."

"What sort of things? You never said."

"No. They hurt too much."

"I'm here if you want to talk."

I smiled at him, but it didn't stick. Sadness enveloped me. It came in waves, usually when I least expected it. My parents weren't dead, not like Julian's mother, but the loss and grief felt real.

"Maman pressed on one of my greatest fears." I stared at my hands. I really should get a manicure while I was here. My nail polish was chipping in places.

"Which was?"

"Ever since I was little and picked up by a modeling agency, I've been told I'm pretty and beautiful and gorgeous and all those *physical* descriptions. But I wasn't ever told I was good or kind, or a nice person, or thoughtful. Or clever. I grew up terrified no one would take me seriously, that I had nothing to offer the world."

"That's not true."

"I wish I could believe that. Deep down, you know? I

mean, I can logically say yes, you're right. I know I have brains. I know I'm more than a pretty face. But I only know those things when I'm on steady ground. The minute I'm knocked off-balance by a cutting article or a hurtful word, I find it all too easy to slip back into the belief that I'll never amount to anything more than the sum of my looks."

"Lee." His face twisted, my pain as hurtful to him as it was to me. I couldn't love him more.

"Anyway, when I told Maman I wanted to quit modeling at the height of my career, she... she..." I breathed in deeply. "She said I wasn't bright enough to do anything else and that I should wring the most out of my looks before they faded rather than throw away the only career I'd ever have."

"What the fuck?" Kadon's eyes smoldered with resentment, and he fisted his hands.

I pinched the bridge of my nose. "It's like... you know the very worst things you think about yourself, the thoughts you have in your darkest moments but you daren't say out loud in case others agree with you? Well, imagine the one person in the world who should support you agreeing that those terrible things you think about yourself are, in fact, true." I gestured out to the sides. "My mother, ladies and gentlemen." Pointing my chin at the privacy screen, I forced a smile. "Good thing that's up. This poor guy doesn't need to hear my woes."

"But this guy does."

Kadon unclipped his seat belt and shuffled over to my side of the limo, wrapping me in his muscular arms. I blinked away approaching tears. Kindness was one of those things that always made it difficult for me to hold back emotions.

"What about your dad? Didn't he have something to say about that?"

"Ah, Papa. He's always capitulated to Maman. It doesn't make him weak." No idea why I was defending my father, but I couldn't help it. "He's so in love with Maman that he always puts her first. Even above me, his only child. But I know he'll never stop trying to coax her into making amends. He'll just do it in a subtle way, one that doesn't yield instant results."

"When your mother said those horrible things to you, what was your response?"

"Ah." I grimaced. "Here's where you realize I'm as much at fault as she is."

"You bawled her out, didn't you?"

I bit my lip. "Li'l bit."

"Ouch. Then again, she shouldn't be able to say whatever she likes and get away with it just because she's your mother."

"No." I rested my head on his shoulder. "I don't want you to think badly of her. She's always wanted the very best for me. But on this occasion, she went about it entirely the wrong way."

"Parents. They're tricky people to handle."

"You don't seem to have any problems."

"Normally, no, but the conversation I had with my father while the captain was showing you around the flight deck wasn't a comfortable one."

"Why?"

"I told him what Benedict said. He's looking into it."

He bit the side of his cheek. "We haven't spoken about that night in years. I think he thought I'd buried it for good, and now, it's being dragged up again." He pursed his lips, breathing out slowly. "I've kept it hidden how much I've struggled, but it all came out, and he was so hurt that I didn't feel I could talk to him about it."

"You were trying to protect him." A shot in the dark, but Kadon's nod meant I'd guessed correctly.

"Yeah. When it happened, he was awesome while I fell to pieces. He's been... incredible. I wanted to, oh, I don't know, reward him in some way for supporting me by pretending I'd gotten over it and was moving on with my life."

"And you can."

"Not until I find Samuel."

"Did you mention him to your dad?"

"Yeah. He's got a few ideas, a couple of contacts, but even he admitted that if people don't want to be found, and they have the financial resources necessary to carve out a brand-new life, then they may stay hidden forever. And that's something I'll have to deal with, to find a way to cope with the guilt but not let it rule my life."

"I'm here for you, just like you're here for me."

He brought my hand to his lips and kissed my knuckles. "I know."

The car slowed, then stopped. I peered through the window as a security guard made his way to the driver's side. From what little vantage point I had, the setup looked similar to the Saint Tropez beach club, but a heck of a lot bigger with four manned gates guarding the entrance rather than only one like in France.

"This is our largest beach club," Kadon said. "We have the capacity for a thousand guests at any one time. And we're usually at or near capacity all year round."

Goodness. A far bigger enterprise than Saint Tropez. *Imagine being the VIP Operations Manager here? They must never sit down.*

Kadon led me through the club, stopping to talk to a few people. He introduced me to everyone as his girl-friend. That would take some getting used to, but I couldn't deny the little thrill of excitement that raced through me each time he did. I spotted major Hollywood stars, rock gods, and huge TV personalities lounging around on day beds, sitting at the bar drinking cocktails, and watching sports on the giant TV screens. I wasn't a stranger to celebrity—some people might have considered me one once—but I'd never felt like a genuine part of that world. I'd hovered around the periphery, waiting for a chance to dart back to my hotel room, change into comfy sweats, and veg out. I'd never gone in for the whole party scene. It'd earned me a reputation as a standoffish bitch when the truth was far from that. Truth didn't count for much in this world, though. Yet another reason I'd never regretted leaving it behind.

If only I could figure out what I *did* want to do.

I envied those people who had a clear vision from an early age. Like kids who, at five, announced they wanted to be a surgeon, or a teacher, or a lawyer. Okay, maybe not a lawyer. That would be one weird kid who had that as their dream vocation.

One thing I felt fairly certain about was that I wanted to help people. It was *how* that had me flummoxed. I kept hoping the answer would appear, like a genie from a bottle. *Ta-da!* An apparition with the answer to world hunger, global peace, *and* what Annaleesa Sabine Alarie should spend the next seventy years doing.

"Did you always know this was what you wanted to do?" I asked Kadon when he settled us in his office with a cold drink.

"Growing up, it was made clear that my family expected me to play some part in running the Kingcaid empire. I don't ever remember resenting the path I was born into. Gotta say, though, my dad picked the right business for me. Can you see me sitting behind a desk all day, pushing paper?"

"Um, Kadon, hate to tell you this, but you *are* behind a desk, and if I'm not mistaken, that pile of paperwork needs your signature."

He laughed. "Always a smart-ass. You know as well as I do that this business is about networking, building relationships, customer service, making the VIPs feel like they're the most important people in the world, even when there's a far bigger star two bungalows down." He tapped a fingernail on the desk. "Which, by the way, you're a natural at."

The game he was playing stood out like diamonds nestled among coal. He wanted me to stay on as his VIP Ops Manager, yet now that we'd moved from friends to lovers, it was even more important to create a professional distance. We risked disaster by spending twenty-four hours a day with one another. Which made me figuring out what the hell to do with my life even more crucial.

"You don't have to compliment me. I'm yours."

"Even more reason to compliment you."

He always knew the right thing to say. My frustration with myself ebbed away, and I grinned.

"Keep dishing out the good stuff and you're gonna get laid tonight."

He stood up, walked around the desk, and locked the office door.

"I never agreed to wait until tonight."

Chapter 22

Leesa

**There's a blast from the past...
an unwelcome one.**

I spent most of the following week chatting with the staff and guests at the beach club and lounging around by the pool while Kadon took care of things in Julian's absence. The funeral was happening in a few days' time, and Julian had asked Kadon to attend, after which, he planned to return to work.

While I'd expected us to return to Saint Tropez, Kadon had proposed that I travel with him on his annual tour of the other Kingcaid Beach Club resorts, most of which were in America and the Caribbean.

Sounded idyllic to me, although I'd persuaded him to

stop off at home for a couple of days so I could make sure Dash hadn't forgotten me. Not that Dash was the least bit concerned by my unplanned extended vacation. I'd called Audrey every couple of days since we'd arrived, and each time, she'd assured me he was fine and ruling the house.

Color me surprised.

"Where are we going?" I asked Kadon as we sat in the back of the limo belonging to the beach club. Well, it belonged to Kadon and his family, really. Everything did. He made my bank balance look like small change, yet he was one of the most grounded men I'd ever met. He never flaunted his wealth or treated his employees with anything other than the greatest respect.

"*Maekawa.*"

I wrinkled my nose. I'd heard of most of the restaurants in Dubai, and been to many of them, but *Maekawa* was a new one for me.

"Japanese?"

He nodded. "It opened a couple of months ago. A guy at the club recommended it. It's underwater. Gives a superb view of the marine life, apparently."

"Sounds gorgeous. I love underwater restaurants."

The maître d' seated us at a table beside the glass wall. Fish of all colors and types swam by, oblivious to the humans gawking at them. It struck me as a great place to come if you worried you might not have much to say to your companion. Not that Kadon and I had that issue. Our banter had remained relentless, despite having intimate knowledge of each other's body parts.

I'd feared that the change in circumstances would alter

the friendship side of our relationship in some way, but I needn't have been concerned. We remained best friends, with a heck of a lot of added benefits on the side.

I masked a tiny shiver of pleasure. Every so often, I woke up thinking I'd had a dirty dream, only to find myself embroiled in an even dirtier reality. In a lot of ways, I could kick myself for taking so long to realize what had been staring me in the face.

The man of my dreams.

When I thought back to my relationship with Benedict, there was no comparison to what Kadon and I shared. It wasn't only the amazing sex, but we had intimacy, friendship, and a genuine respect for one another. We'd always had the latter two, but I wasn't complaining about the recent additions.

"What are you thinking about?"

I blinked. "Sorry. I was miles away."

"Clearly, I'm failing at keeping your attention." His lips quirked up. Mine did, too.

"You're holding your own."

"That's it? Holding my own? One thing's certain with you, Lee. I'm never going to end up with a big head."

"If you must know, I was thinking about how lucky I am that you didn't give up on me when I showed no romantic interest in you."

"It was touch and go for a while. That's why I suggested the fake relationship. I hoped it might change things, and it did." His eyes widened. "Oh, shit. I meant to keep that to myself."

I laughed. "I knew you weren't to be trusted."

"It's true. I'm a terrible person, a rogue. You'd do well to stay far away from me."

"Wish you'd warned me about that before I fell in love with you."

His eyes softened. He half reached across the table for my hand, then withdrew. Dubai wasn't big on PDA, especially in unmarried couples, and while rare, the authorities had arrested tourists for simply holding hands or kissing in public. Better not to risk it.

"I should have ordered room service."

"It was your idea to come here. You—"

"Annaleesa? Oh my God. What are you doing here?"

I looked up, barely swallowing a groan. *Great. Just what I didn't need.* "Ayesha. Goodness, how nice to see you."

Lies. All lies. Ayesha Davenport, a fellow model, had made my life hell. She'd hated my guts, always craving the gigs I'd gotten, then bitching about me to anyone who'd stopped long enough to listen when I was hired instead of her.

I'd tried, God how I'd tried, to be the bigger person, to be nice to her. On each occasion, she'd thrown my kindness back in my face. In the end, I'd stopped trying.

She slipped off her fur coat, an odd thing to wear in Dubai. I sucked in a gasp before it escaped.

Fuck.

What had happened to her?

She looked... emaciated. Last time our paths had crossed, she'd been on the too-thin side, which wasn't at all uncommon for catwalk models. It was one of many sides of

242

the industry I despised. The dreadful pressure put on women to be almost skeletal. But this... this was on another level.

"You remember Daniel, don't you?" She beckoned her companion forward.

My jaw flexed. Daniel Romero was a top modeling agent, a man with many of the world's most successful models on his books. And an absolute bastard. He worked his models too hard, double and triple booking them, and raking in his fat fees. He lived a life of incredible luxury, amassed off the backs of the women he exploited. He'd tried to sign me on multiple occasions. I'd met each approach with a firm no.

Unfortunately, Daniel didn't take well to rejection. Frequently, he'd told lies about me to his immoral journalist friends, promising he could make the stories go away with a click of his fingers. As long as I signed a contract with him, of course.

Like I said, bastard.

"Oh, I remember."

Kadon lifted an eyebrow, evidently picking up on my flat tone. He glanced from me to Ayesha, then to Daniel, and back to me.

Daniel's lips thinned as he dipped his chin. "Annaleesa. You're looking well."

"Well?" Ayesha inspected me from head to toe, her eyes lingering on my rounder waist, more generous hips, and moderately larger breasts. "I wouldn't say that. I mean, you always were Little Miss Perfect, Annaleesa. You're not so perfect anymore." She giggled, covering her mouth with her fingertips, almost like a naughty child messing about at the back of the classroom. "You've gotten fat."

Kadon quivered, his eyes molten rage. I shook my head. *Don't react.* That one barbed comment showed everything wrong with the world I'd once inhabited. No one in their right mind could call a size eight woman fat, yet to Ayesha, who must be less than a size zero, my weight was something to vilify. When I'd modeled, I'd refused to drop below a size four, and even then, I'd known I was borderline malnourished and unhealthy. But at my worst, I'd never looked as ill as Ayesha did.

"Are you all right?" I ignored her comment about my weight. In my experience dealing with this particular individual, it was best to smile sweetly and refuse to rise to her insults.

"Of course. Why wouldn't I be? Now that you're off the scene and out of my way, I'm living my best life."

She linked arms with Daniel, gazing up at him as if he were a god. The fucking devil was a far better description. I glared at him. He stared back at me, his gaze belligerent.

Nothing had changed.

"I heard about your fiancé dumping you." Ayesha laughed. I expected her at any moment to rub her hands together in glee. "I'm not surprised you quit modeling after that. I mean, imagine the gossip you'd have been subjected to every day."

Yeah, and you'd have been the ringleader to every bitchy comment.

I kept the smile fixed on my face. Across the table, Kadon simmered. I touched him with my foot, a further warning not to rise to the bait.

"We've both moved on. I have a new man in my life." I sent Kadon a reassuring smile. "And Benedict is newly married to someone far better suited to him. Kadon and I recently attended his wedding."

"Really?" Ayesha gave a good impression of biting down on a bitter slice of lemon. "What an odd thing to do. Don't you agree, Daniel?"

Daniel, instead of listening to Ayesha's spiteful outpouring of bitterness, had zeroed in on Kadon. He blinked several times in succession.

"Kadon?" Daniel leaned closer, his eyes narrowed. "As in Kingcaid?"

Kadon dipped his chin, once.

"Wow. It's great to meet you, man."

He stuck out his hand. Kadon left it hanging in midair. Daniel, one of the most egotistical, self-absorbed jerks to walk the earth, took far too long to realize Kadon had no intention of shaking his hand. Eventually, he let it fall back to his side. "I'd love to talk to you about a business opportunity sometime. How long are you staying in Dubai?"

Kadon's icy stare would have shriveled the balls of most men. Daniel Romero wasn't most men. Thank Christ. One was enough.

"I'm choosy about whom I partner with."

"Yeah, me, too." Daniel guffawed. I resisted clamping my hands over my ears. "Seriously, I can meet you anytime, anyplace."

"That won't be necessary." Kadon shook out his napkin and relaid it in his lap. "If you'll excuse us."

Daniel, finally realizing Kadon had dismissed his offer,

snorted. "The rumors about your family are true. You are a bunch of stuck-up narcissists."

Kadon slammed his napkin on the table and rose to his feet. He towered over Daniel by a good half a foot. I almost let out a cheer when Daniel stepped back. One–zero to Kadon.

"This is a nice place, and because of that, I won't embarrass my girl by doing what I should, which is to put you on your ass. But let me be clear; if our paths cross again, you won't get off as lightly. So do yourself a favor and fuck off."

My chest burst with pride. If we weren't in an Arab country, and at risk of getting thrown in jail, I'd kiss the hell out of him.

"Come on, Daniel." Ayesha tugged on his elbow. "You don't need him, and she's a has-been. Let's not waste any more of our precious time on them." She swept away, the hem of her coat dragging along the floor.

"Who the fuck are those two charmers?" Kadon asked, returning to his seat.

I laughed. "No one important." I updated him briefly on them both. "I'm sure I've mentioned it before, but the modeling world is the epitome of dog-eat-dog. It's why I don't have female friends. Not those deep, tell-one-another-everything relationships. I've never had that. It's not surprising, given that I've modeled since I was six." I shrugged to hide the bite of hurt. "Ayesha, though, was one of the worst. I landed a lot of the jobs she went for, and she blamed me for it. And as for Daniel, he's a creep."

"If that's what modeling does to a person, I'm glad you got out when you did."

"Yeah." My gaze drifted over to their table on the other side of the restaurant. Ayesha's shoulder blades protruded through paper-thin skin. "She's made a big mistake getting in bed with him. A big mistake."

Only time would tell just how big.

Chapter 23

Kadon

A bolt from the blue.

"I DON'T WANT TO SOUND UNGRATEFUL, BUT I'M looking forward to getting home tomorrow." Leesa rubbed the right-hand side of her neck. "God, I'm so stiff. I used to get like this when I traveled for work. I need my own bed."

"I'm moving into your place, then?" I arched a brow, a smile pulling at my lips. "Here." I sat behind her on the bed and massaged the tight muscles. She groaned.

"God, you're good at that. Keep going."

"Are you sure you want to come to dinner tonight? Blaize will understand if you're too tired."

Blaize was driving up from Miami to Palm Beach, our final stop on the North American and Caribbean part of our trip. It was the last opportunity I'd get to see him for a while. I was only sorry I hadn't had time to fly over to Vegas to see Nolen, nor up to Seattle to visit Mom and Dad. Not on this trip, anyway. I intended to take Lee away for Christmas—although I hadn't sprung that on her yet—and then visit my family early in the new year.

There'd been many occasions where I'd thought of relocating to one of the clubs on this side of the world, if only to be closer to my nearest and dearest, but I loved Saint Tropez. And now that Lee and I were a couple, I had even more of a reason to remain in France. It was her home. Well, that and England, but I doubted she'd want to move there in a hurry and risk bumping into Benedict at the local grocery store.

"Jesus, you make me sound ninety." She rolled her neck to the side. "I'll be good to go after a shower."

A grin stole across my face. "Hmm, a shower. Sounds good."

"Alone."

"Ah, I see the honeymoon period is over already." I heaved a sigh. "I guess there's only one thing for it."

"What's that?"

I stood and moved into her sight line, rubbing my chin in thought. "I shall have to take a mistress to fulfill my voracious sexual needs."

She picked up a pillow and threw it at me. I palmed it away, laughing.

"Put that pecker anywhere but in my pussy, mister, and I'll take a sharp blade to it."

I winced. "Ouch. You're vicious."

"You have no idea." She climbed off the bed. I smacked her ass as she passed me by.

"No masturbating in that shower without me there to witness it."

"This might come as a surprise to you, but I don't masturbate every time I shower."

"What a shame."

She tapped her forefinger against her lip. "Hmm, wonder what the water pressure is like here."

I made a move. She squealed, darted into the bathroom, and locked the door. The sound of running water drowned out her laughter. I sat on the bed wearing the biggest smile, one that, these days, rarely vanished. In Lee, I'd found everything I'd ever wanted. The only blot on an idyllic future was the lack of progress in finding Samuel. One of these days, I'd have to face up to the fact that I might never find him and what had happened after his parents removed him from the school would remain a mystery.

A few months ago—hell, a few *weeks* ago—the thought of that would have sent me spiraling into depression. I'd connected finding Samuel alive and well with the quashing of my guilt. I braced for the dark tendrils to creep into my mind, pulling me under to that place I had to claw my way out of. My mind remained clear. I wanted to find Samuel, of course I did, but maybe, *just maybe*, my happiness wasn't tied to that outcome any longer.

Blaize had booked a table at a seafood restaurant right on the beach. He was sitting on the patio. With a woman. One I didn't recognize. No surprise to me. Blaize changed his liaisons so often that I'd given up trying to remember their names a long time ago.

"There's my baby brother." He drew me into a hug,

clapping me on the back. "Leesa. How lovely to see you again." He hugged Lee, too. "This is Penelope."

We shook hands with a woman I'd never see again after tonight. I held out Lee's seat for her. Blaize caught my attention and gave me an exaggerated wink. I rolled my eyes. It was going to be one of *those* nights.

"So, lovebirds, how was the wedding?"

"Oh," Penelope interjected. "You got married?"

"Not us," Lee explained. "My ex-fiancé."

Penelope wrinkled her nose. "Your ex-fiancé invited you to his wedding?"

"Yeah. It's a long story." Lee gestured dismissively. "And a boring one, too. How about some wine?" She picked up the bottle of red already on the table and topped off Penelope's glass. Lee had this ability to change the subject from one she wasn't interested in pursuing without hurting the other person's feelings. It was a skill I envied. She engaged Penelope in conversation, allowing me to edge closer to Blaize.

"Have you talked to Dad?"

He shook his head. "Why?"

"I think Lee's ex knows about Switzerland. Dad's looking into it."

Blaize's eyebrows shot up his forehead. "Fuck. Are you sure?"

"Not a hundred percent, no. That's why Dad's on the case."

"You okay, man?" Blaize touched my arm.

"Yeah." I glanced over at Lee. "I am now."

"Does she know?"

"Yep. I told her everything."

"And she's cool."

"Better than cool. She's amazing."

"What are you two boys in cahoots about?" Penelope nudged Blaize with her elbow.

"Nothing to concern you, lovely." Blaize tucked a strand of hair behind her ear, and Penelope almost swooned.

Make the most of it. If he weren't my brother, I'd have Lee warn her not to fall too deeply. But he was, and I'd never betray him like that. Bro code trumped everything else. Always had, always would.

We ordered lobster and crab and chatted about the business until both women emitted loud groans and begged us to stop. I liked Penelope. She'd be good for Blaize, but he wouldn't see it like that. He'd always been the same, scanning the horizon for the next obsession, which never lasted.

Lee excused herself to visit the restroom, and Penelope tagged along. Lee's hips swayed with every step she took, her pert ass filling the cream dress to perfection.

"Stop eye-fucking her and tell me about Switzerland. Leesa won't say anything, right?"

The two women disappeared into the ladies' room. I turned my attention to my brother. "No. I trust her with my life. She's been amazing. So supportive. Telling her was hell, but afterward..."

"Your eyes have misted over." He pressed a hand to his chest. "Aww, look at my baby brother, madly in love. So, afterward...?"

"Mind your business. How long is this one going to stick around?" I motioned to Penelope's vacated chair.

"Stop changing the subject."

"Fine." He wouldn't give in until I offered him something. "I fake-kissed her, twice, then Benedict dropped his truth bomb, I confessed, and one thing led to another."

He held up his wine glass, tapping it against mine. "I'm happy for you, man, seriously. She's terrific."

"Yeah, she is. She's—"

Leesa walked toward me, her face ashen, Penelope trailing a few feet behind. I dropped my napkin on the table and rose to greet her.

"What's wrong?"

"Ayesha... Ayesha... she's..."

She plunked into the chair. Crouching in front of her, I gripped both her knees. "What about Ayesha, babe?"

She blinked several times, absently wiping her mouth. Her eyes were glassy, as if she were looking through me rather than at me. "Kadon, she's dead."

My head snapped back. Dead? What the fuck? It'd only been two weeks since she'd stopped by our table in Dubai. I mean, she'd been horribly thin, but...

"How?"

"She... killed herself."

"Oh, Christ."

"Who's Ayesha?" Blaize mouthed at me. I shook my head. Now wasn't the time.

"Lee, do you want to go back to the hotel?" Her face was as pale as wax. Shock, most likely.

"Yes, please."

I curved an arm around her waist and took her purse from Penelope.

"Thanks."

"I'm so sorry to ruin the evening."

Blaize got up and came around our side of the table. He kissed Lee on the cheek and squeezed her hand. "You haven't ruined anything, sweetheart."

"We should pay the bill." She looked around, bewildered. "Where's my purse?"

"Forget the bill. Blaize will sort it out. I've got your purse."

Even though she and Ayesha had been more enemies than friends, it couldn't be easy to hear that a woman you'd spoken with recently wasn't around any longer.

Suicide. A tremor hit me. I'd been there. I'd never told a soul. Not my parents or my brothers, and not Lee either. But sometimes in the weeks and months that had followed Henry's death, I'd thought about ending it all. The only thing that had stopped me was knowing the disastrous effect my decision would have on my family. It was the one thing I clung to, to see me through the darkest of days.

"Call me," Blaize said.

"I will."

Settling Lee in the back of the car, I jumped into the other side and instructed the driver to take us to the hotel. Lee didn't say a word during the entire journey. She clutched her purse, bit her nails, stared out the window, but she didn't give me any more information on how she'd found out about Ayesha or what had happened. Although, these things often took weeks to unravel, and answers weren't always forthcoming.

She leaned against me as we took the elevator up to the top floor and flopped onto the sofa seconds after we entered our suite.

"Do you want to talk?"

She lifted her head, eyes bleak. "I can't take it in. I've never known anyone who's killed themselves before."

I brought her a glass of water, and a beer for me. She took the glass from me and guzzled half, setting the rest on the coffee table. I sat beside her. She tucked her legs underneath her and curled into my side.

"How did you find out?"

"I bumped into a mutual acquaintance in the ladies' room. She told me. It's been on the news, apparently. I missed it. How did I miss it?"

"We've had a busy couple of weeks."

"Yeah, I guess." She rubbed her forehead and pursed her lips, letting out a stream of air. "My mind won't stop spinning. I mean, we weren't friends. Far from it. She hated me, and I wasn't all that keen on her, either. But still... how lonely she must have been. How desperate."

"Did she leave a note?"

"Yeah. Splashed all over the internet, apparently. Her poor family."

"Did it give a clue as to why?"

"I'm not sure. I haven't looked, and I don't intend to. Elly, the woman who told me, said that it referred to the pressure. The constant coercion to get thinner, thinner, thinner. The work Daniel committed her to. The relentlessness of it all. I mean, you saw her in Dubai. There was nothing left of her." She leaned forward, clutching her stomach. "I think I'm going to be sick."

She launched off the couch and ran to the bathroom. I followed. Crouching beside her, I held her hair, then passed her a box of tissues when she'd emptied the contents of dinner into the toilet. Flopping onto the cool tile, she rested her head against the wall.

"Do you want more water?"

"Please."

I retreated to the living area and refilled the glass. Lee was brushing her teeth when I returned to the bathroom. I waited for her to finish. "Here." I handed her the glass of water.

"Thanks." Sidling past me, she made her way to the couch. I trailed after her.

"I can't believe you saw me throw up. We're way too early in our relationship for such a delight."

I chuckled. "You think, after all these months of secretly loving you, I'd care a jot about a bit of puke?"

"Even so. A girl wants to show herself in the best light."

"Lee, I want every part of you. The good, the bad, the happy, the sad. They're all you, and I love them all."

She rested her head on my shoulder. We didn't speak. Not that I cared. I'd sit here all night if that was what Lee needed to process a momentous event. Something was on my mind, though. I didn't want to upset her by raising it, but Lee and I had always been honest. No reason to stop now.

"I'm surprised it hit you so hard. Especially since, like you said, Ayesha was a bitch to you."

"Me, too. And I'm not sure I fully understand why. I guess a part of me thinks that, in another life, it could have been me. Not that I was ever suicidal, but the relentless demands take their toll, you know? And I can't shake how ill she looked when we bumped into her in Dubai. I keep wondering whether I could have done something to help her."

"Like what?"

"I don't know. It's a nonsensical reaction. I couldn't have known she was so close to rock bottom, and even if I had, Ayesha wouldn't have listened to me anyway."

She took a sip of water. "Remember how I've been trying to figure out what to do with the rest of my life?"

"Yeah."

"I think I know. But I'm not sure where to begin."

"Can I help?"

"Possibly." She shifted her position to face me, crossing her legs. "I keep coming back to the terrible pressure put on models to be the thinnest, the prettiest, to eat less, to go under the knife again and again, all in the name of the 'perfect look.' I mostly resisted." She pointed to her nose and her chin. "Apart from these."

My eyes ballooned. I had no idea Lee had gone under the knife.

"You've never mentioned that."

"I don't like to talk about it. I regretted having it done for a long time, but the browbeating is constant and hard to resist. On the whole, though, I fought my corner pretty well. It's women like Ayesha, who crave the limelight to an unhealthy extent, that are easy to take advantage of, to push beyond their limits. Not for their sake, but for the whole fucking industry, many of whom see it as a way to make a lot of money from someone else's face and body and hard work."

"It sounds toxic as hell."

"It can be. There are good people in the business, but

there are a lot of bad ones, too. Exploitative arseholes who gaslight vulnerable women all in the name of the mighty dollar."

"So what is it you want to do?"

Right before my eyes, she blossomed, like a flower fed the right amount of water and sunlight. Whatever she'd decided upon, I'd move mountains to ensure she fulfilled her dream.

"I want to start a modeling agency, but not like most of the others. Mine will focus on body positivity, showcasing all kinds of people, both young and old, tall and short, figures of all shapes and sizes." Her eyes shone, her jaw set in determination. "It'll be epic."

"It's a terrific idea, and with you at the helm, I wouldn't doubt its success for a second." I tucked her hair behind her ear. "I can help."

She shook her head. "If I need help, I'll ask. But I want to try to do this on my own. It's scary and I might fail, but at least I'll have given it a go and attempted to do some good. It's better than sitting back and doing nothing."

Her determination to launch this business by herself didn't surprise me. Given her misbelief—echoed by her mother—that she had no worth outside her physical appearance, I understood, and supported, the need to go it alone.

"I'm proud of you."

"I haven't done anything yet."

"No, but you will. You'll do great things, Lee. It's your destiny."

Chapter 24

Kadon

I'm not ready for this.

"Home sweet home." I set down Dash's cat carrier. He hissed at me. "Love you, too, Dash, you little shit."

"He blames you for keeping me away from him for so long."

"He'd better get used to it. You're mine now."

Lee chuckled. "Try telling him that."

I peered through the bars of his cage, eyeing him warily. He hissed again, pawing at the door. I crouched down. "If I let you out and you draw a drop of blood, you'll be sorry."

He licked his paws, but his eyes were on me. Watching. Waiting. Ready to pounce if he saw an opportunity. I opened the door, snapping my hand back in case he led with his talons. He barged through, scampering across the kitchen floor and into the living room.

"Lucky escape."

"Yeah, for him."

Lee laughed. "Oh, my. You've got a lot to learn about cats."

"He's got a lot to learn about me."

"Hmm." Lee tapped her finger against her lips. "If I had to place a bet, the cat will come out on top. Every time."

"I'm offended you think I can't outsmart a cat. Besides, if he doesn't behave, he won't get to tag along."

She frowned. "Tag along where?"

I tapped my nose. "Aha. Now you're intrigued."

"I'm also jet-lagged, so if you're planning on whisking me off to Australia or something, I'm about to disappoint you."

Resting both hands on her hips, I dropped the teasing act. Dark circles, almost like bruises, framed her eyes, more prominent in natural light.

"How are you feeling about it all now that you've had some time to process?"

She sighed. "One second, I'm fine. The next, it hits me out of nowhere."

"It's not all that surprising. Hell, I've struggled to comprehend the odd celebrity who took their own life. You knew Ayesha. You worked with her. That's gonna hit hard. Need to give yourself space and time to reconcile it. Not that something so awful is easy to reconcile."

"You're pretty smart for a pretty boy, Kingcaid."

I squeezed her hips. "And my fabulous, amazing, sarcastic woman is back in the room."

Standing on tiptoes, she pecked my lips. "Right, spill. What are you planning?"

Skimming her sides, I tucked her hair behind her ears. "I want to take you away for a week or so, but it's in France. And we don't leave for nine days. That's plenty of time for you to rest and recharge."

"That's also only five days before Christmas."

"Yep."

She canted her head. "Won't you want to see your folks at Christmas?"

"I've already told them we'll fly out early in the new year."

"We?"

"You don't think I'm leaving you here, do you?"

"You want me to meet your parents?"

A look of fear mingled with curiosity inched across her face, almost as if I'd told her she had to stick her hand in a basket filled with poisonous snakes and she couldn't help but wonder if they would bite her or if she'd escape unscathed.

"Yeah. You're my girlfriend, and I want to show you off."

"What if I show you up?"

"You won't."

"I did the first time I met Benedict's parents."

I clenched my jaw at the mention of that jerk. Dad hadn't yet uncovered what Benedict knew, or thought he knew. As time passed, I did wonder whether he'd been fishing for information after all. It seemed far too coincidental for me, but stranger things had happened.

Either way, he hadn't made the information public, although that meant little with a man like Benedict. Not that blabbing about something that had happened nine years ago would cause me any harm. The authorities had given me the all-clear, but I hated the idea of bringing bad press to the family firm. Conglomerates like ours had enough enemies without me adding to the pile.

Despite my antipathy toward Benedict, curiosity got the better of me. "What did you do?"

"I choked on a piece of steak. His father got up and thumped me on the back. The chewed-up morsel shot out of my mouth and right into his mother's lap. Oh, but not before slapping her in the face first."

I burst out laughing. "You're kidding?"

"Nope. A hundred percent fact."

"Oh my God." I got out my cell and tapped the screen.

"What are you doing?"

"Telling Mom to leave steak off the menu unless she wants to wear it first."

Her eyes popped. "You didn't."

I turned the screen toward her. On it I'd typed "Gotcha."

"I hate you."

"You love me."

A growl rumbled through her chest. My dick stood at attention.

I snagged her around the waist. "Make that noise again."

"No. You obviously like it, and I'm trying to punish you, not reward you."

I faked a full-body shudder. "Baby, you can punish me any time you like."

Rolling her eyes, she wriggled out of my hold and flicked on the kettle. "Where *are* you taking me, anyway?"

"Val d'Isère."

Her eyes widened. "Skiing?"

"Yep. I own a lodge there."

"You're an expert skier, then?"

"Learned as a child."

"Great." Sarcasm laced her tone.

"You've never been skiing?"

"Affirmative."

"I'll teach you."

"I envision spending more time on my arse than on my feet."

"Don't worry. I'll kiss every bruise."

"You're just looking for excuses to get me naked."

I took the packet of tea bags out of her hand and set them on the counter. Encircling her waist, I pulled her close. "I don't need any excuses to get you naked."

"Confidence comes before a fall."

"You mean pride."

"That, too."

I laughed. "We'll have fun. I guarantee it. The resort is beautiful, and the lodge has a real fire we can curl up in front of."

"Does it have a bearskin rug on the floor, too, where we can make love while our legs char in front of the flames?"

I laughed again. "It does have a rug, although no

animals were harmed in production. A few sheep might've been sheared, but that's about it."

"Okay, but if I'm rubbish at this skiing thing—"

"You won't be."

"Famous last words."

K

"Kadon! Look at me! I'm upright." Lee brandished her ski pole in the air.

Big mistake.

She lost her balance and landed on freshly fallen snow. "Oof."

I skied over to her. "You almost had it." Holding out my hand, I pulled her up.

"Aww, look at you talking shit to make me feel better."

"I speak only the truth."

"It doesn't matter anyway. I might be rubbish, but I'm enjoying myself."

"You'll improve each time you do it. We're only on day three."

"Aren't you bored, though? Hanging around with me on the nursery slopes?"

"Hanging around with you is the only place I want to be." I dropped my poles, moving in for a kiss.

"This skiwear isn't the sexiest."

I dragged my gaze over her body. "It's okay. I know what lies beneath. All I have to do is close my eyes." I closed them. "Ohh, yeah. What a body. Those legs. That ass. Tits that fit my hands perfectly." I made a squeezing motion as if I was helping myself to a handful of her best assets.

Correction. One of her best assets.

She had a ton of them.

"Kadon!" She palmed my shoulder. I barely felt it through the padding in my jacket.

"What?" I blinked, the picture of innocence.

"You're insatiable."

I hooked my leg around the back of her knee. She lost her balance, as I'd intended, and we tumbled to the ground, her on top so I could cushion the blow.

"Kadon. We're in public."

"So? Kiss me."

"What if someone recognizes me? What if they take pictures and sell them to the highest bidder?"

"I'm asking for a kiss, not for you to bounce on my dick. Besides, who cares if they take their stupid pictures? We're in love. I want the fucking world to know."

Her lips took mine. Usually, I set the pace, but on this occasion, I forfeited control.

The whoosh of passing skiers faded into the background, as did the grind of the ski lift carrying people farther up the mountain. Her tongue slipped inside my mouth, gentle at first, then intense, fierce, *needy*. Fingers tangled in my hair, tugging on the roots. My body merged into hers. In my mind, the bulky barrier of winter clothing melted away. I could almost *feel* her nakedness pressing against mine.

My dick throbbed, blood racing through my veins. I didn't care that we were lying in the freezing snow surrounded by tourists or that my ass and back were already numb from the icy temperatures. All I cared about was Lee, her weight pressing down on me, her lips hot despite the cold. I inhaled her scent, my heart galloping, the beats rapid, increasing in speed with every sweep of her tongue.

"Get a room!" someone hollered.

Lee faltered, about to pull away. I tightened my arms around her, taking back control, anchoring her head as I ravaged and pillaged and stole her breath. She was giving me everything she had, and it wasn't enough.

Not nearly enough.

I yearned to crawl inside her skin and live there for eternity.

"Kadon," she murmured against my lips.

"Don't say *stop*. I'm not ready to stop."

"People are staring."

"Let them stare."

She wriggled against me. Reluctantly, I loosened my grip. She climbed to her feet, holding out a hand for me to hoist myself upright. We gazed into each other's eyes, our chests heaving, fast at first, then slower.

"My legs are wobbly," she whispered. "That was some kiss."

"Get your poles," I rasped. "Skiing lessons are over for today."

Her eyes sparkled like the north star on a clear night. "Whatever will we do instead?"

"I'm sure we'll think of something."

It took us a while to return to the lodge. Lee kept losing her balance. I half considered dumping her skis and carrying her over my shoulder back to my lair, like a Neanderthal.

The chalet maid had visited while we'd been gone. A roaring fire burned in the grate, and the delicious smell of a casserole wafted through from the kitchen. I helped Lee out of her ski jacket, her boots, and her salopettes before removing mine.

She collapsed onto the sofa with a sigh. "If you want sex, you're going to need to do all the work. I'm exhausted. And freezing."

I laughed, hauling her upright. "Go get in the shower. That'll warm you up. I'll check on lunch and put some bread in the oven."

"I thought you'd pin me to the wall the second we walked through the door."

"Believe me, I was tempted." I pointed toward the nearest bathroom. "But sex in a hot shower sounds far more appealing. Go. I'll be in shortly."

"Yes, sir." She saluted.

I groaned. That woman would be the death of me.

I turned the oven on and stuck my nose in the Crockpot. My stomach grumbled at the smell of beef and ale casserole. I rubbed it.

You'll have to wait, buddy.

I put the lid back on, catching sight of Dash sitting on the window ledge. He had an evil glint in his eye.

"Whatever you're planning, you little fucker, save it."

I picked up my cell phone and checked my messages. Nothing urgent. I scanned my emails, deleting a few junk ones and filing a couple of work-related messages to review later after Lee went to sleep.

A new message appeared right when I was about to put down my phone and go join Lee in the shower.

My heart stopped.

My legs quaked.

I braced a hand on the kitchen table for support.

I looked again at the message from Joseph, the private investigator I'd hired to find Samuel.

The subject line gave me palpitations.

Every single email he'd sent until now had the same subject line: Update.

This one said, "You'll want to read this."

My mouth dried up. I folded an arm across my stomach.

Breathe.

Only one explanation made sense for the change: he'd found Samuel.

Or, at least, he'd uncovered information *about* Samuel.

What if he was dead?

What if, like Ayesha, he'd taken his own life, the horrors of what had occurred at that school haunting him until he couldn't take it anymore?

Or he was on his seventh marriage because he couldn't get over what happened?

Oh God. What if he's in prison because he abused others?

I'd read about such things. Abused kids, in adulthood, inflicting their own trauma on others.

My finger hovered over the screen.

No. I couldn't do it.

If it was bad news, it'd ruin Christmas with Lee, and I

refused to drag her down with me. She had her own troubles, and I wouldn't add to them.

I filed the email away in the *For Action* folder.

If only it was that easy to file away the knowledge that it was sitting there, waiting for me to find the courage to open it.

Chapter 25

Leesa

The universe fucking hates me.

THE EMBERS OF LAST NIGHT'S ROARING FIRE flickered in the grate, a last attempt to cling to life that would ultimately end in failure. I pulled my robe around me, shivering. Stuffing my feet into furry slippers I'd had the foresight to leave beside the hearth, I trudged into the kitchen and filled the kettle.

While I'd slept, fresh snow had fallen, the blanket of white pristine in the early morning light. It wouldn't last long. All too soon, skiers would emerge from their cabins and hotel rooms and ruin nature's perfection. On Christmas Day, too. Heathens.

But not us.

Not today.

Our plans comprised opening our gifts, cooking a

hearty breakfast, and curling up by a fire I hoped Kadon either knew how to make or had someone coming in to make. I'd brought a book to read that, so far, remained unopened. I hadn't expected skiing to exhaust me so much. It had to be all this fresh mountain air. Or the fact that I was so dreadful at this skiing lark I spent most of my day falling over and having to get back up again.

What was it Kadon had said before we'd left? You'll nail it. No problem.

I had news for him. It was a big fucking problem.

Dash curled around my legs, purring. I crouched to pick him up, snuggling against his cute little face.

"You hungry?" I grabbed a pouch of his favorite food and squeezed it into a bowl, setting it and him on the floor. "Happy Christmas, puss."

His tail swished as he ate. Gratitude? Unlikely. Cats didn't have the gratitude gene. I left him to his breakfast and made a cup of tea. I ventured into the snug at the back of the lodge, putting my hand on the radiator as I passed. Warm. Good. The central heating would soon heat the lodge in the absence of a real fire. I did like the fire, but it was a ball-ache first thing in the morning.

Curling up on a squishy chair, I sipped my tea and drank in the view. Val d'Isère might be the most beautiful place on earth, and Kadon's lodge made the most of the vista. The sun glinted off the rooftops and shone down into the valley. I wished I were a painter and could capture the scene on canvas. Maybe the local town had an art gallery and I could pick up a painting before we left.

"You should have woken me." Kadon leaned over the chair and kissed me. "Merry Christmas, beautiful." He ruffled his already tousled hair. Another couple of months and it'd be back to his preferred length. Squeezing into the small space beside me, he hoisted me onto his lap.

"Merry Christmas to you. What a view, huh?"

Peering into the gap in my robe, he nodded. "Yeah. Pretty damn fine."

"You are so predictable."

He buried his face in my cleavage. "That's me set for the day."

"You won't want your gift, then?"

"Got the best gift ever right here."

"If only I'd known. I could have saved myself the expense."

He tugged down my camisole top, sucking my nipple into his mouth. Everything clenched. Stomach, toes, hands, thighs. I arched my back, groaning.

"All day," he murmured. "You're at my mercy all day. And I'm going to—"

Dash jumped in between us, a ball of black fur and smelling of fish from his breakfast. He shoved his backside in Kadon's face and nuzzled mine. Talk about staking your claim.

"Christ, cat!"

Kadon tried to shove Dash away and received a deep scratch on his arm for his troubles. He growled—Kadon, not the cat—and rubbed at the angry mark.

"I swear, one of these days, I'll... I'll..."

"Realize he rules the house and accept your place at the bottom of the hierarchy."

"I refuse to capitulate."

Kadon scooped him up and plunked him on the floor.

Dash side-eyed him, already plotting revenge. It would come, when Kadon least expected it. I should stock some popcorn for the occasion. A show not to be missed.

Swishing his tail several times—his version of flipping the bird—Dash sauntered out of the room.

"You're in deep shit."

Kadon snorted. "I can handle a cat."

"We'll see."

He resumed nuzzling my boobs, his large hands firm on my hips. "Let's go back to bed." His tongue flicked my nipple. "I'll make it worth your while. Promise."

Divine pleasure uncoiled within me. I gripped the back of Kadon's head, urging him on. His teeth against my sensitive flesh pulled a gasp from me.

"I'll take that as a yes." He gathered me up and got to his feet, striding into the bedroom. Kicking the door closed, he set me on the bed and lay down beside me. "That'll keep the little shit out."

"Poor Dash."

He snorted again. "There's nothing poor about that cat. His problem is he thinks he's regal. 'Bout time he learned there's only one king around here, and it isn't him."

"Look at you." I giggled. "Delusions of grandeur."

Tugging on the belt around my middle, he parted the two sides of my robe. His hand burrowed inside my lace shorts. "A queen deserves a king, don't you think?"

"Is that what I am?" I sucked in a breath as he pushed two fingers inside me. "A queen?"

"You're my fucking queen." He pressed his thumb against my clit, rubbing in circles while his fingers massaged me on the inside. His soft lips explored my neck, journeying along my collarbone. Ever since the first time we'd slept together, I'd wondered how Kadon seemed to know instinctively how I liked to be touched, the fastest way to bring me to orgasm, or, conversely, how to slow me down when my body sprinted to the finish line.

"Keep going like that and I won't last ten seconds." He curled his fingers and sucked on my neck. I gasped again. "Make that five."

His mouth closed over mine, a deep, drawn-out, lazy kiss. My lower abdomen grew heavy, my climax approaching too fast for me to hold on. I came, crying into Kadon's mouth. My calves tightened. I curled my toes and fisted the sheets, my body in control, my mind chaotic. Joy and lust and pleasure tore through me. Tears leaked from my eyes. Not sad tears but a physical reaction to a spiritual experience. Kadon wasn't a king; he was a god. Between the sheets, at least.

And *that* was a thought I'd take to my grave.

He tugged my shorts down my legs and tossed them off the side of the bed. His T-shirt and boxers followed. Settling between my legs, he lined himself up.

"Stop. Don't move."

He paused, the head of his cock nudging at my entrance. "Are you okay?"

"I am. But you might not be in a second."

His dark brows drew inward. "I'm lost."

I pointed behind him. Kadon twisted. "Ah, fuck."

Dash stood beside the bed, claws drawn, coiled and ready to spring.

"What do I do?"

I grinned. "Pray."

"If that bastard digs his claws into my balls, or any other precious part of my anatomy, he'd better prepare to sleep in the snow." Kadon glared at Dash. Dash glared right back. "Want to stake your claim to your mistress, do you, little shit?" Dash's back arched. "Too bad. I've already staked mine."

Kadon thrust his hips. I cried out as he filled me, suddenly, completely. The man was either brave or stupid. A risk-taker. I considered cupping his balls if only to provide some protection from Dash, should he choose to strike. I caught my cat's eye, sending him a silent warning. *Don't even think about it.*

"Is he in retreat?"

"No."

"Fuck's sake. I refuse to be cockblocked by a goddamn cat." He thrust again. Dash hissed. "Right, that's it."

Kadon pulled out of me. He rolled off the bed, his cock bobbing as he made a move toward Dash.

"I told you he was plotting something evil."

Kadon went for Dash. Too slow. Dash darted past him and jumped up onto the bed. He took up position between my spread thighs, facing Kadon. Dash's message was crystal clear: *You want that pussy? Well, you have to get past* this *pussy first.*

I burst out laughing. "This is like a comedy sketch for porn channels." Scooping Dash into my arms, I put him outside the door. "Sorry, little man, but as much as you'd like to slice open Kadon's balls with those talons of yours, I can't let you do it."

If Dash could talk, I'd have sworn he'd have called me a spoilsport. He stomped off—if cats could stomp—in a huff and disappeared into the living room. I closed the door and crooked my finger at Kadon.

"Now, where were we?"

K

I removed the diamond teardrop earrings Kadon had bought me for Christmas and set them on the dresser. We were going skiing again today, and I couldn't risk losing them. They were far too beautiful. And expensive. He refused to tell me how much they'd cost, but I'd been draped in enough diamonds at modeling shoots over the years to know these cost a pretty penny. It made my gift of a customized surfer watch that connected to this neat app, which would allow Kadon to see all his recorded waves, look cheap. It hadn't been, but I'd definitely not spent as much as Kadon.

"Ready?" Kadon zipped up my ski jacket.

"I suppose so."

He clipped me under the chin. "Today is the day it's all going to come together. I guarantee it."

"With my performance so far, you can't guarantee anything."

"Want to bet?" He tapped the side of his nose. "I have a sixth sense for these things. You're not the first person I've taught to ski, and from what I saw on Christmas Eve, you're right on the cusp of cracking it."

"More like cracking up," I muttered.

"Stop being dramatic." He zipped up his own jacket, and we stepped outside into the crisp air. Kadon grabbed our skis from the outbuilding, carrying mine and his to the slopes, despite my grumbles about capability and not needing anyone to take care of me. Which he ignored. Funny thing was, I liked it when he coddled me. It showed he cared.

The nursery slopes were busier than I'd expected, but Kadon found a quiet spot for me to practice. And, bugger me, I stayed upright, even managing a couple of turns. The more I kept my balance, the greater my confidence grew. An hour passed, and I hadn't fallen over once.

"See," Kadon said, not even bothering to hide his smugness. "What did I say? I told you today was the day."

"No one likes a know-it-all," I groused.

He smirked. "Want to take the lift up to the next level?"

"Do you think I'm capable?"

"More than capable. Besides, I'll be there. I won't let you hurt yourself." He motioned for me to go first. I set off, digging my poles into the ground and internally high-fiving myself when I steered around a group of teenagers messing about in the snow. We lined up behind several skiers waiting for the next available chair lift. Everyone except me seemed highly capable, hopping onto the moving lift with ease.

"I'm going to make a tit of myself, aren't I?"

Kadon chuckled. "If you struggle, I'll pick you up."

"That won't be embarrassing at all."

"You're far more capable than you give yourself credit for. You're a few days into your first-ever ski trip. Give yourself a break."

"You're too nice to me." I pulled his mouth down to mine, the kiss all too brief.

"Only because I want to—"

"Annaleesa?"

My eyes ballooned wide. *You have got to be kidding me.* Pivoting slowly, partly to keep my balance and partly because I didn't believe the universe could be that shitty. Except it was.

"Benedict. Fenella. What a surprise."

Kadon took my hand, squeezing it, his presence solid at my back.

"I never took you for a skier, Leesa," Fenella said.

"I'm not. But I'm learning." I gazed up at Kadon, who'd moved to my side. "I have the best teacher."

"I have to say that when you arrived for our wedding, I thought you two were faking it to help you save face, Leesa." Fenella giggled. "Looks as if I was wrong. You're a couple of lovebirds."

Hidden beneath the layers of skiwear, heat crept up my neck. If it edged to my face, the game was up. Fenella would take that blush as evidence of the truth she'd inadvertently stumbled upon. And here I was thinking we'd fooled everyone.

Benedict turned his attention to Kadon and dipped his chin. "Kingcaid."

Kadon's eyes flashed, his thoughts about Benedict in plain view. He said nothing. No greeting, no nodding, no acknowledgment that Benedict had uttered a word.

"You left the manor in rather a hurry." Benedict pulled himself upright. Bless. He kept trying to look like he was a match for Kadon's superiority. "Running from something?"

Kadon tightened his grip around his ski poles. I gently pressed a hand to his back. *Don't do it. Don't react. It's what he wants.* Evidently, Benedict didn't plan to let this drop, but if he was going to do something about it, he'd have done it by now. I stood by my belief that whatever he thought he knew about Kadon's past and the troubles in Switzerland wasn't enough for him to cause bother.

"We had a flight to catch," I explained.

"To where?" Benedict smirked. "Switzerland."

Kadon dropped his ski poles. I darted in between them, reaching behind me in warning. "Dubai, actually."

Groups of people edged around us when it became clear we weren't planning to move.

"Ah, your old stomping ground. Going back to modeling?"

"No."

"Then what *are* you planning to do with the rest of your life? Help him hide the bodies?"

"You fucker."

"Don't." I made a grab for Kadon. Too late. His large hand clamped around Benedict's throat. Fenella squealed. Other skiers gasped, jostling each other to get a better view of the brewing altercation.

"Leesa, do something!" Fenella hollered.

Benedict's face reddened, his eyes bulging. He clawed at Kadon's hand.

"Let go of me, Kingcaid," he rasped.

"Kadon. Stop. Let him go."

He mashed his forehead against Benedict's, like boxers did before a big fight.

"Do your fucking worst, Oberon. You think you've got

something on me? You think you fucking know me? You don't know shit. You're a miserable, useless loser whose only claim to fame is being a cheating asshole and throwing away the best thing you ever had."

"Kadon, please."

"Well, she's mine now. She's fucking mine. You chose, you douche. You chose and you lost."

"He can't breathe!" Fenella screamed. "Someone get help. Call the police."

Shit. I put my hand over Kadon's, trying to peel his fingers away from Benedict's throat. "Let him go, Kadon. Do it for me."

As if my words were the key to breaking through his rage, he dropped his hand. Benedict braced his hands on his knees, gasping and coughing. Fenella glared at Kadon.

"You could have killed him."

"Oh, stop being so dramatic, Fenella," I scoffed, even though my knees shook and my stomach roiled. It didn't cross my mind for a second that Kadon would seriously hurt Benedict. Scare the shit out of him, perhaps, but nothing more than that. No, what concerned me far more was the effect this might have on Kadon. The last thing I wanted was for him to take a backward step, especially as confessing to me seemed to have given him some peace.

"You're making a big mistake, Annaleesa," Benedict wheezed. "He's crazy. You'll live to regret the day you rejected me."

A flicker of a frown darkened Fenella's features. She narrowed her eyes at Benedict. "Rejected you? Don't you mean you rejected her?"

Benedict rubbed the back of his neck, his expression

pained. I crossed my arms over my bulky ski jacket. *Get out of that one, twat.*

"I-I mean—"

"He means that on your wedding night, he cornered Lee and asked her—no, begged her—to take him back. As his mistress, of course. I mean, our Benny here likes to have his cake and eat it, too."

Oooh, Kadon. Revenge truly was a dish best served cold. A part of me felt sorry for Fenella, but like I'd said to her that weekend, men who cheated, even once, were likely to reoffend.

"Benedict?" Fenella's chin trembled. "Is this true?"

"No. I mean... no. Of course it's not true."

"A cheat *and* a liar." Kadon barked a laugh. "What a catch you are, Oberon."

Like a wounded animal, Benedict screeched. He threw himself at Kadon, fists flying. Kadon, an expert skier, swished out of the way. Benedict lost his footing and sprawled facedown in the snow.

Don't laugh. Do. Not. Laugh.

I laughed. Heartily. I shouldn't have, but God, it felt good. Like an exorcism. Benedict's final humiliation. He'd taken on an adversary far more powerful and competent than he, and he'd lost. Served him right.

"You know what?" I linked my arm through Kadon's. "I've had enough for one day. Shall we go home?"

"Sounds good to me."

I detected a slight tremor in Kadon's voice. Adrenaline, probably. The altercation must have affected him far more than he'd like to let on. He picked up his poles, and we skied back to the lodge in silence, neither one of us glancing behind us. Benedict could lie in the snow for the rest of the day, for all I cared.

Kadon helped me out of my ski clothes, then removed his own. He put a few logs on the fire and lit it, all the while saying nothing. I left him to his thoughts and went into the kitchen to put the kettle on. It wasn't long before he appeared, propping his shoulder against the door frame, his eyes tracking me as I moved between the fridge and the kitchen counter.

"Aren't you going to say anything?"

The kettle popped. I filled the teapot with hot water. "What do you want me to say?"

"Are you angry?"

Both eyebrows flew up my forehead. I put the lid on the teapot and left the tea to brew. "Angry? Why would I be angry?"

"Because I reacted when I shouldn't have."

I pulled out a chair and sat down, waiting for Kadon to join me. He slumped into one on the other side of the table, all the earlier fight knocked out of him. I couldn't read minds, but I was close enough to the man sitting opposite to guess where his mind had gone. A delicate situation like this needed careful handling. I hoped I was up to the task.

"What are you afraid of?"

The comprehension in his eyes meant my question needed no further explanation. He reached for my hand. I gave it to him. His thumb traced my knuckles. It took a few seconds before he looked at me.

"Letting my anger get the better of me and killing someone else."

I knew it. "I understand why you'd think that, but you

285

know what's different between that situation and this one?"

He rubbed his lips together. "No."

"You're older. Wiser. You're in control. You understand the consequences of your actions. And I stand by what I've said all along. What happened in Switzerland was an accident. You were a seventeen-year-old boy faced with a horrific situation, and you acted on instinct. All you wanted was to make what Henry was doing to Samuel stop." I put my hand over the top of his. "You'd never have hurt Benedict. Not really." I grinned. "Other than his pride, that is."

"You sound pretty sure of yourself."

"That's because I am." My grin spread. "Can you imagine the conversation he and Fenella are having right now?"

"Divorced in three months?"

"Fenella's father is pretty powerful. I'm sure he can fast-track it through the courts in less time than that."

"Serves him right."

"I agree." I poured two cups of tea, pushing one across the oak table toward him. "Can I ask you a favor?"

"Always."

"Do you mind if we head home tomorrow?" Although I doubted we'd bump into Benedict and Fenella again, especially as she was probably packing her suitcase right this second, I didn't want to risk it. Benedict was enough of a smooth talker to wriggle his way out of this mess if he chose to, and the thought of having to constantly look over my shoulder didn't appeal to me.

"I was going to suggest the same thing."

Dash jumped onto Kadon's lap and curled up, purring. Kadon's mouth fell open. "Jesus. Is this your way of apologizing for threatening my balls, Dash?"

"No. I think it's his way of saying he's ready to go home, too."

Chapter 26

Kadon

Anything but the devil cat.

I HEAVED THE LAST SUITCASE INTO THE CAR AND slammed the trunk. Lee appeared with Dash in his cat carrier. His expression couldn't have been more pissed off. I laughed.

"He's in a joyous mood."

Lee held up her hand. "Little sod scratched me as I was putting him in."

"He hates that thing."

"I know. But we can't exactly let him roam freely around the car when you're driving."

She opened the back door of the four-wheel-drive SUV I'd rented especially for the trip and put him on the back seat. I only owned one vehicle, my beloved Aston Martin, but the roads up here were far too treacherous for a sports car. I didn't see the point in owning several cars. I could only drive one at a time. The Aston suited me, and when it wasn't suitable, I rented.

"We could put him in the trunk with the luggage. Let him roam in there to his heart's content."

"Try that, and the first chance he gets, he'll rip your balls right off."

I believed he would, too.

"Have you got everything?"

"I think so. Let me have a final scoot around to check."

She disappeared inside. I followed, waiting in the entranceway while Lee opened drawers we hadn't used and checked under the sofa for... who the fuck knew? Satisfied that she'd left nothing behind, she made her way outside. I locked up, checked the outbuilding where I kept my skiing gear, and then climbed into the driver's side.

"Ready to hit the road?"

"Yeah. Nine hours. Ugh."

"The scenery is nice, though. You'd miss all that if we'd flown." I always drove from Saint Tropez to my place here. The views were too gorgeous to pass up.

"True. Can we stop at that little bistro for lunch? The same one we visited on the way here?"

"Sure. It's about halfway, so a good time to stop."

With a final look back at the lodge, I pulled away. Tires crunched on the snow, the chains digging in and providing the traction needed to navigate the mountainous terrain. Once we reached the highway, I'd pull over and remove them.

We hadn't traveled far when my dad called. I'd dropped him a line last night after my altercation with

Oberon to update him on the situation. He'd told me then he might have an answer for me regarding Oberon's source, or otherwise. Looked as if this was it.

I pressed the button on the steering wheel to answer the call. "Hey, Dad. You're on speakerphone, and I've got Lee in the car with me, so behave yourself."

Dad chuckled. "You can talk. Hi there, sweetheart. I hope my son is treating you right."

"Like a queen," I responded, before Lee could.

"I wasn't asking you," Dad said. "You're going to paint a pretty picture. I'd rather hear from the lady."

Lee grinned. "He's been great, Mr. Kingcaid."

"Jameson, please. And I'm glad to hear it. His mom and I are looking forward to meeting you in the new year."

"Thank you, sir. Mr. Jameson... I mean, Jameson. No 'Mr.' Just Jameson." Her ears went pink, and her cheeks bloomed red. She mouthed, "I told you so," at me.

Laughing, I squeezed her knee. "We can't wait to visit. I'm presuming that's not why you called."

"No." He paused. "Do you know someone called Barry Sanderson?"

I screwed up my nose. "I don't think so. Name doesn't ring a bell. Why?"

"He said he knows you. Or rather, he met you once. At Oberon's wedding."

"Oh!" Lee nodded furiously. "I remember him. He was that jerk reporter who needled me about Benedict breaking off our engagement."

"Oh, yeah. The guy in the blue tux."

"That's him."

"Who wears a blue tux?" Dad queried.

"That's what I thought. What's he got to do with this anyway?"

"He's the one who told Oberon about Switzerland."

My jaw dropped. "How the fuck does he know?"

"Turns out he worked for a European newspaper when... when it happened. My lawyers slapped a gag order on several media outlets at the time, preventing them from publishing a single detail."

"Yet Sanderson told Oberon." I gripped the steering wheel.

"Yes."

"Why would he risk breaking the NDA? I know they're pretty toothless, as suing would mean taking the issue to court and then the whole reason for the NDA becomes moot, but still. Most people abide by them."

"Sanderson is a gambler. He ran up a raft of debts with the wrong people. He needed to get his hands on fast cash, and Oberon was only too happy to pay for the intel Sanderson had."

"Great." I breathed out through my nose. "What can we do to quash this? To stop Sanderson from telling anyone else the next time he runs up a gambling debt he can't pay, and Oberon from dangling it in front of my face like a fucking noose."

"Already done."

I loved my dad. He was my hero. "How?"

"Sanderson was no problem. He's freelance, so he relies on his reputation for work, and to keep feeding his gambling habit. I told him that if he broke the NDA a second time, I'd make sure he never worked again. Man's a coward. He capitulated easily."

"And Oberon."

"Ah. Mr. Oberon. You won't have any more trouble with him."

"How can you be so sure?"

"Darren Grange and I have a mutual friend in the British Government. He put us in touch, and Mr. Grange and I had a very fruitful conversation. If Oberon wants to both stay married to Grange's daughter and have any chance of a political career, he'll do well to keep his opinions to himself. If that fails, I've got a little insurance policy as backup."

"What insurance policy?"

"Nothing for you to be concerned about."

I'd grown up hearing that tone from Dad. It meant you could ask as much as you liked, but you wouldn't get anywhere. I'd long since given up pushing him whenever he used it.

"His marriage might be over anyway, given what I told his wife yesterday."

"True. Either way, he won't give you any more trouble."

"I hope not. Thanks, Dad. I owe you."

"That's what fathers are for. Love you, son. Bye, Leesa. See you in a few weeks."

In true Dad style, he hung up without waiting for a goodbye.

"Your dad sounds lovely."

"Yeah, I'm lucky."

Her face pinched, almost a wince. I grazed a hand over her cheek. "You'll find a way to make up with your parents."

She picked at a fingernail. "Wonder what's in that insurance policy?"

The change of subject didn't surprise me. Lee was in avoidance mode in relation to her parents. I hoped that would change one day. For her sake as well as theirs. Her estrangement from them was clearly a sore point for her, but not sore enough to get past the hurt their judgment of her had caused.

"We'll never know. Dad used his 'mind your business' tone."

She put her hands up to her face. "I came across like an idiot. I told you I was useless with parents."

"You were fine. Stop worrying. Dad doesn't care."

"*I* care. What if I behave like that when I come face-to-face with them?"

"What if you do? They won't give two shits. Promise. My parents—my whole family, in fact—are some of the most down-to-earth people you will ever come into contact with. They just want to meet you." I captured her hand and kissed her fingertips. "The woman who's stolen my heart."

"Christ, you'd better not introduce me like that. I'll set Dash on you if you do."

"Dear God, not that. Anything but the devil cat."

She twisted in her seat. "Dash, put your paws over your ears."

As she turned to face the front again, I braked to prepare for a sharp bend in the road. My foot went right to the floor.

The car didn't slow.

The fucking car did not slow down.

"Shit." I pumped the brake pedal.

Nothing.

The corner approached. Too fast. Too fucking fast.

"Kadon." Lee's voice trembled with fear. She gripped the handle above the door with one hand and grabbed the edge of her seat with the other.

"Hold on."

Fuck. Fuck, fuck, fuck.

I wrenched the steering wheel to the left. The back end stepped out. The car spun.

"Kadon!"

I can't stop it. I can't stop. I can't—

We plunged over the edge, Lee's screams piercing my ears.

Chapter 27

Kadon

This is the butterfly effect, in all its horrifying glory.

MY FACE WAS WET. WAS IT RAINING? I LIFTED MY arm. Pain shot through my shoulder. I cried out. Christ, that hurt. Where was I? I blinked. Dazzling light pierced my retinas. Squeezing my eyes shut, I reached for my face a second time.

Wet.

Forcing my lids open, I squinted. My fingertips were red. Rain didn't have a color. Why were my fingers red? An iron-like smell filled my nostrils. I licked my fingers. Blood. Groaning, I turned my head.

"Lee." I reached across the center console. Cold. She was so cold. "Lee. Can you hear me?"

No response. I shifted in my seat. "Argh." My shoulder was killing me. Was it dislocated? The material of my jacket was torn from elbow to wrist. I blinked again, my vision clearing. Lee's eyes were closed. She looked as if she was sleeping. Blood coated her chin, and a jagged piece of metal protruded from her right cheek.

What had happened came back to me in a blinding flash. Brakes failing. Car spinning. Careering over the side of the mountain, bouncing over tufts of grass and rocks. Blackness.

Fuck. We'd crashed.

"Lee. Wake up." I shifted again, gritting my teeth through the agony ripping through my shoulder. "Christ." I squeezed her icy fingers. "If you can hear me, squeeze me back."

Nothing. Cell phone. We needed help. I patted my jacket pocket. No phone. Where was my phone? Shit. Shit, shit, shit.

"Lee, hold on. Help's coming." I touched my fingertips to her neck. A steady pulse. Good. That was a positive sign. "That's it, baby. Stay with me." She muttered something incoherent, and her arm twitched. "Don't move, baby."

A meowing sound came from the back seat. I somehow twisted enough to check it out. Dash's piercing blue eyes stared back at me from behind the wire of his cage. From this vantage point, he looked unhurt.

"Relax, buddy. Your mom's going to be fine."

I returned to my previous position. Nausea rolled through my stomach as the pain kicked in again. I breathed through my nose "Don't throw up. Don't throw up." I unclipped my seat belt. The front of the SUV had crumpled, leaving me little space in the footwell. I strained, searching the floor for my cell. Where the fuck was it?

"Lee. I got you, baby. I got you."

Exhausted, I sank back against the seat. My heart raced as if I'd run a flat-out sprint. *Calm down.* If I lost my shit, we really were fucked. I tried the door. It opened. Cold, mountain air rushed into the cabin. I stumbled outside, my feet sliding on ice. I gripped the top of the door for support. Falling to my knees, I felt around inside the car for my phone. It wasn't there.

It wasn't there!

Staggering upright, I shielded my eyes from the too-bright sun and checked out our surroundings. We'd caught a break, if this disaster could be described as such. We'd fallen about ten or so meters, the car stopped by a sizable piece of rock jutting out from the mountainside. If that hadn't been there, we'd have careered to the bottom and been killed outright.

Would any passing cars see us from the road? I doubted it. Without my phone, the only option left was to somehow haul myself up the mountain. With a busted-up shoulder.

But Lee... Lee was in worse shape. She could have internal injuries.

I didn't want to leave her.

I had to leave her.

Big picture. Get to the top. Flag down a car. Call for help.

"Don't move, baby," I repeated, squeezing her arm. "I'm going to get help."

She muttered again, but her eyes didn't open.

My feet slid with every step I took. My shoes had some tread, but not nearly enough for a mountain covered in a thick layer of snow and ice. Several times, I fell. Each time, I got up and kept going.

How long had I been out? How long had it been since we'd crashed? An hour? More? Every second counted.

An eagle soared above me, dipping its wings, circling. Looking for prey. At least it wasn't a vulture. Then I'd know for sure we were well and truly fucked.

Lee was a survivor. She'd come through this. She had to. I couldn't have another death on my hands. Not another one. Not this one.

Not her.

This was my fault. I was responsible. I'd been the one driving. I'd lost control.

Dear God, if you require a sacrifice, let it be me.

I slipped again. Got up. Slipped. Got up. One foot in front of the other.

I paused. Wait. Was that... was that...?

The faint whir of sirens in the distance reached me. My knees buckled, hands clawing at the snow. *Please, God, let them be coming for us.* I took off my jacket. They might not see me, but I had to try. I was still five or six meters from the roadside. I waved the jacket over my head. The sirens grew louder, the unmistakable sound of tires on asphalt approaching. Getting slower. Slower.

"We're here!"

I couldn't stop myself from yelling, even though they'd never hear me over that racket.

The sight of a bright yellow ambulance coming into

view sent me to my knees again. It stopped right above me. Seconds later, an EMT peered over the side.

"Here!" I cried. "Thank God."

The fire service winched Lee up first. She'd regained consciousness for a few seconds, but nothing she said made any sense. I kissed her forehead. It killed me to let her go, but what use was I? She needed medics, not me.

A second ambulance arrived for me and for Dash, although they weren't too happy about transporting a cat. Too bad. We came as a package. Lee would never forgive me if I left Dash out here. Shivering, I sat in the back, refusing to lie down on the gurney. The EMT put a blanket around my shoulders. Even that hurt. He cleaned me up, dressed my wounds, and put my shoulder in a sling.

I didn't care about me. All I cared about was Lee. Why her? *Why did she have to be with me when I crashed the fucking car? I should've been alone.* She didn't deserve this.

I didn't deserve her.

Why hadn't I pulled the emergency brake? That was its whole fucking purpose. I should have tried something, *anything*. Instead, I froze.

Lee's injuries were my punishment for Henry. I'd never paid through the courts. The Swiss authorities had declared it an accident, but I'd always believed Dad had paid a handsome price for my freedom. If I had gone to prison, would life have been different? Would this guilt be easier to bear?

I knew one thing: Lee would be safe in her bed rather than in an ambulance on her way to the hospital. This was the butterfly effect in full flow. Everything we did impacted the universe around us. Each action left a footprint, the effects of which we might not see for years. But when the ripples reached their destination, the consequences could be devastating.

I was living proof of how devastating.

"Do you want some pain relief, monsieur?"

I shook my head. I needed to feel the pain. Every agonizing bit of it. "How did you find us?"

"Your vehicle had an SOS feature. As soon as you crashed, it called the emergency services, and we were dispatched to your location."

Thank Christ for modern technology. All that time searching for my cell, and the car had already made the life-saving call.

Dash meowed. I stuck my finger through the bars. He licked me as if to say, "We're in this together." Maybe this was how we finally bonded. Except I'd rather live under the threat of losing precious parts of my anatomy and have Lee safe and well.

We arrived at the hospital, where they insisted that I sit in a wheelchair, even though I could walk perfectly well. Procedure, apparently. I asked the nurse taking care of me about Lee, but she had no information.

A doctor examined my injuries. Much to my surprise, my shoulder wasn't dislocated, but it was strained. Instructing me to rest it and apply ice regularly, he signed my discharge forms. Picking up Dash, I set off to find Lee.

It took an age to locate a member of staff who had any

information, and even then, they weren't keen on telling me anything useful. Apparently, boyfriends didn't count as next of kin. In the end, a nurse took pity on me and told me they were operating on her, but when I pushed for more details, she clammed up. She told me which operating room Lee was in, though. I dashed up to the fourth floor, found the waiting room, and collapsed into a chair.

People came and went, visitors and staff alike. Dash grew restless. He must be thirsty, and hungry, too. I should call a local vet and ask them to take him, but I couldn't bear to let him go off with strangers. Lee wouldn't like that.

My chest vibrated. Jesus Christ, my cell. It was in my jacket pocket all along. I reached inside and removed it. The call log showed a couple of missed calls from numbers that weren't in my contacts list. Junk, most likely. I should call my parents in case they somehow found out about the accident. I'd do it later. Once I had confirmation that Lee was okay.

Dash whined and clawed at his cage. I couldn't keep him here with me. I might be here for hours, days even.

Audrey!

She'd take him. Plus, he was familiar with her. He loved her. He'd taken over her house when Lee and I were traveling.

God, had that been only a couple of weeks ago? It felt like another lifetime.

I made the call. Audrey was only too happy to look after Dash, and as luck would have it, she had a friend who lived close to the hospital who, she said, would be happy to pick him up and take him to Audrey's.

People's kindness in times of adversity humbled me.

An hour later, I handed Dash over to Audrey's friend, giving her my number in case she had any problems. Letting him go was harder than I'd thought it would be. He was my connection to Lee. He loved her. I loved her.

A volunteer came through the waiting area, offering hot drinks and sandwiches. I refused the food but accepted a coffee.

How much longer was she going to be in there?

Every minute worried me more. I prayed. I prayed like I'd never prayed before.

Please don't die. Please live. I'll do anything. I'll give you up. If that's my penance for your life, I'll do it.

I checked my watch. Five in the afternoon. What time was it when the ambulance had brought us in? I couldn't remember. I should prepare for bad news, but I couldn't. It felt too much like giving up, giving in.

A doctor wearing blue scrubs emerged from the operating room. He slipped the paper cap off his head and screwed it into a ball. I launched from the chair.

"Annaleesa Alarie? Do you know how she is? I'm her boyfriend. I was in the car with her when she... when she..."

"Ah, Mr. Kingcaid."

My eyes widened. I hadn't expected him to know me. "How is she?"

He gestured to a room off the main waiting area. "Let's go somewhere more private."

My heart plummeted. Private meant bad news. Doctors never gave people bad news in public. They didn't want to have to manage the bereaved relative causing a scene.

I wasn't prepared for this. I'd *never* be prepared for this.

"She's dead, isn't she?" I blurted, tears pricking my eyes. "She's dead and it's all my fault."

"Not at all, Mr. Kingcaid." He smiled, empathy reflected in his gray eyes. "Please. Come with me."

He led me to a windowless room with four chairs, a scratched table, and a water fountain tucked in the corner. One chair was askew. I chose that one, wincing as I sat.

"Are you in pain?" He jerked his chin at my shoulder. "I can have a nurse bring you something to take the edge off."

"I'm fine. Please, tell me how she is."

He grimaced. I braced myself. Just because he'd said she was alive didn't mean her situation wasn't dire.

"We had to perform a splenectomy, but she'll recover from that pretty quickly. She also had a deep laceration to her face, and she's heavily concussed."

"But she's okay?" I couldn't give two shits about spleens and facial injuries. "She'll be okay?"

"Absolutely. The liver takes over some functions of the spleen. Lack of one leaves a slight risk that infections such as pneumonia and meningitis can spread quickly, but as long as she reaches out for medical help should the situation arise, I expect her to live a normal life."

My shoulders sagged. "Thank God. Can I see her?"

"In a little while. If you wait in here, I'll have someone take you to her room once she's had some rest." He patted my uninjured shoulder and left the room.

The door clicked shut. I put a hand over my face and cried.

Chapter 28

Leesa

Well, you got what you always wanted.

SOMETHING BRUSHED MY SKIN.

Itchy.

Irritating.

I lifted my arm to scratch it. Except nothing happened. My arm didn't move. Frowning, I opened my eyes.

Harsh strip lighting greeted me.

Where am I?

Argh. That goddamn itch.

I tried once again to scratch it. So heavy. My arm was so heavy. I groaned. My head pounded.

Thump, thump, thump.

"Ah, you're awake. How are you feeling, Annaleesa?"

I squinted. A nurse? Was I in the hospital? What happened?

Thirsty.

I licked my lips and swallowed.

"Where am I?"

I answered her in French. Or I thought I did. It didn't sound like me. It sounded like Kathleen Turner as Chandler Bing's dad. Speaking French.

Have I lost my mind?

"Saint Genevieve Hospital. You were brought in earlier today. Car crash." She touched my wrist, her gaze on her watch. Her fingers were cool against my skin. "Do you mind if I take your blood pressure?"

Car crash?

What car crash?

I strained to remember.

My memory came back faster than a raging river after a month of rainfall.

I remembered now.

We hurtled toward the bend in the road. The car didn't slow down. Spinning. We went over the mountainside.

We went over the mountainside.

"Kadon." I tried to sit up. She put her hand on my shoulder, pressing me back into the mattress. I swatted at her. "Where's Kadon?"

"There's a gentleman sitting outside. He's been there a while. I can see if that's him if you like."

It'd be him. I didn't need confirmation. "No, it's okay."

Why had I said that? Didn't I want to see Kadon?

No.

Shock hit me in the chest, confusion and fear weighing me down.

Why wouldn't I want to see Kadon?

"Does he have a cat with him?" Dash. My poor kitty. I couldn't stand it if he hadn't made it.

Her eyebrows dipped in the middle, and I could have sworn I read her mind.

She's losing it. This is a hospital for humans, not animals.

"No."

"Okay." I lifted my arm. This time it worked. I touched my face "What's this?" I pressed against a thick wad of what felt like cotton wool. Spongy. Soft.

"It's a dressing." She moved my arm back to the bed. "Try not to touch it. We don't want it getting infected."

"A dressing? What dressing?"

"To protect the stitches."

Stitches?

I had stitches? In my face?

"You had a deep cut to your cheek. And you've had your spleen removed." She held my hand. "You're also concussed. Are you sure you don't want me to get the young man? It's a lot to take in."

I shook my head. "I'd like to use the bathroom."

"I can get you a bedpan." The horror must've shown on my face because she laughed. "Okay, no bedpan. But you'll need to take it steady. We don't want you to fall."

Easing back the covers, she helped me upright. My midsection protested, a sharp pain sucking the air from my lungs.

I hissed, clutching at my middle. "Christ, that hurts."

"It will for a week or so. But you'll soon recover. A fast recovery is one of the benefits of keyhole surgery. Plus,

you're young and fit. You'll be back to normal in no time."
She placed my feet on the floor. "Sit there for a minute. Let
your blood pressure equalize. It'll drop if you stand up too
quickly, and that'll make you feel nauseous and light-
headed."

I took several deep breaths and, with the nurse's help,
stood without my legs giving way. The IV line was
attached to a pole with what I guessed was a saline solution
giving me fluids. I gripped the pole with one hand and the
nurse with the other and made it to the attached bathroom
without incident.

"I'll give you some privacy," she said. "Pull on that red
cord if you need me. And don't lock the door."

Nodding, I shut myself inside. Bracing my hands on
the sink, I steeled myself for what I was about to see.
Stitches in my face meant only one thing.

A permanent scar.

Even the most proficient plastic surgeon couldn't
entirely remove a scar.

The question was, how bad was it?

Only one way to find out.

I picked at the edge of the white tape and slowly
peeled the thick wad of gauze away from my right
cheekbone.

My lungs expelled a gasp of air.

That wasn't me.

It couldn't be me.

It was the ugliest thing I'd ever seen.

I was the ugliest thing I'd ever seen.

My nostrils flared, sweat breaking out on my skin. I
closed my eyes.

Go away. Go away. Go away.

I opened them. Nothing had changed.

Nothing. Had. Changed.

The black stitches taunted me. *Haunted me.* I pounded my fists against my thighs.

Well, Leesa. You got what you wanted. No one will ever call you pretty again. Happy now?

A laugh burst out of me. I thrust my hands into my hair, pulling, tearing. Hysteria. I edged on the right side of sanity to recognize it. The muscles in my legs went limp. I caught the edge of the sink in time to cushion my fall. Hugging my knees to my chest, I let the tears come.

"Oh, chérie."

The nurse crouched beside me. Hooking her hands underneath my armpits, she helped me to stand. She stuck the gauze back in place, pressing on the sticky part until it stayed there.

"Let's get you back in bed, shall we?"

She posed it as a question, but it wasn't one. Not really. I did as I was told. No point in fighting. What was I fighting for? The person I'd been? The one I'd wished others would see for more than her looks?

I'd lived almost my entire life under the spotlight, surrounded by people who gushed over my physical appearance. Now, I imagined they'd turn away. Disgusted. Horrified, even. The funny thing was, I'd guarantee I'd still get judged for my looks, but for different reasons.

Ugly as opposed to beautiful.

I turned to the window. It was snowing. Huge blobs of the white stuff. So pretty. So perfect. I squeezed my eyes closed. I couldn't stand to see the beauty in nature.

"I'll leave you in peace. Call me if you need anything."

I didn't react, didn't acknowledge that I'd heard her at all.

Manners, Annaleesa, Maman would scold if she were here.

My eyes burned behind my closed lids. I craved to see her, to feel her lips press to my forehead, to hear her voice and smell her perfume. Floral, like lavender but subtler. Yet even now, after a near-death experience, missing a body part, and with my face in tatters, I couldn't bring myself to call them.

What the hell was wrong with me?

A single rap sounded on the door. I didn't even bother to open my eyes to see who it was.

"Lee."

Kadon's warm hand closed over mine. He must've gotten frustrated waiting for permission to see me and took matters into his own hands. Unless the nurse had told him that if he was waiting for me to approve his visit, he'd wait forever.

I kept my eyes shut. "Where's Dash?"

Please let him be alive. I couldn't take it if he hadn't made it. My poor innocent cat.

"Audrey's got him."

A breath whooshed out of me. *Dash is alive.*

"Is he okay?"

I couldn't bring myself to open my eyes and look at Kadon. If I saw pity, it would kill me. Fingers of depression were already reaching out, like black souls, all too ready to suck me into the darkness of their world. I didn't need a shove over the edge.

"He's fine."

Silence. Five seconds passed, then ten. I should say something. What, though? Kadon wasn't the one lying in a hospital bed, so he must've escaped the accident unscathed. Lucky him.

"Lee." He applied pressure to my hand. "Look at me, please."

The desperation in his voice got to me. I opened my eyes.

"I'm so sorry, Lee. This is all my fault." He held my forearm in a tender grip. "I don't know what happened. I lost control. Forgive me, please."

"Do you want to see it?" The words spewed out of me in raw, bitter tones. I pointed at the dressing covering up the hideous stitches that, after removal, would leave an even more hideous scar.

"You should probably leave the dressing in place. Let it heal."

Right. Of course he didn't want to see it. Why would he? Bad enough that I'd almost puked when I'd seen it. When I got home, I'd smash every mirror in my house so I never had to look at myself ever again.

"I'm tired, Kadon. You should go."

His head snapped back as if on a piece of elastic. "Go? I'm not leaving you."

"I don't want you here."

His face crumpled. I should feel something. Sympathy, sorrow, contrition for the pain I'd caused.

I felt none of those things.

Despair streamed shapelessly through my mind, a

cancer eroding everything it touched. Life as I'd known it had ended the moment we'd crashed.

Ugh. *Stop being overdramatic.* So what if my face had a scar that I'd have to live with for the rest of my life? I was alive. I'd survived a plunge down a mountain. Things could be so much worse.

Right now, though, none of that mattered. Maybe it would in a few days when I'd had time to come to terms with the gash that ran the length of my cheekbone, but for now, I deserved to wallow in misery. Didn't I?

"Lee, you're killing me. I need you to forgive me. I can't... I can't—"

"I can't deal with your issues and my own, Kadon. You'll have to figure out a way to manage your guilt. It's not like you're new at it."

It was a low blow. Even through numbness that had invaded my body, I winced.

"I'll come and see you tomorrow."

"Don't bother."

Air whistled through his teeth. "You don't mean that."

I said nothing in response. Partly because he had a point and partly because every time I opened my mouth, the cruelty I found myself capable of stunned me. This wasn't like me at all. I loved Kadon. Deeply. And he loved me.

Until he sees that ugly gash on your face. He won't love you then.

I faced away from him. If that didn't send a message, nothing would. A soft sigh feathered over me. He laid a hand on my shoulder.

"Love you, Lee."

Seconds later, the door clicked shut. I rolled onto my side, burrowed my hands underneath the pillow, and let the tears come.

Chapter 29

Leesa

The good, the bad, and the ugly.

THE DEWY GRASS COOLED MY FEET AS I SCAMPERED down the hillside, and fresh mountain air filled my nostrils. Spring flowers bloomed, dotting the landscape with yellows and blues and the brightest pinks. Sheep grazed in a paddock nearby, and I paused for a few moments to watch the lambs frolic, their joy at being alive contagious.

A broad smile crossed my face. "There you are." I ran to him, my fingers burrowing into his silky locks, his lips searing hot as he kissed me. We tumbled to the ground, laughing with abandon, his body fusing with mine until I lost where he ended and I began.

"I love you," I murmured, refusing to break our kiss to tell him that.

"I'm sorry," he replied, the love in his eyes fading so fast I wasn't sure it'd been there at all.

"Sorry for what?"

"For leaving you."

The grass turned white. The lambs vanished. Clouds moved in, their gloom sucking all the joy from the air. Dampness seeped through my thin blouse, soaking me in seconds.

Cold. *I'm so cold.*

"Don't go." I stretched my arms toward him. "You can't leave."

"You're wrong," he replied. "I can't stay. Not now. Not after this."

He edged away. I crawled on my hands and knees toward him, my fingers growing numb as I clawed my way through the snow. "Kadon, please. I need you."

Tires screeched. Spinning. Blind panic. Fear.

"Kadon!" I screamed. "Don't leave me!"

"I have to. I'm no good for you. Next time, you won't get off so lightly."

I sat bolt upright, my chest heaving, heart almost hacking its way through my rib cage. Scrunching the bedclothes in my fists, I fought for breath, the dream lurking at the edges of my mind.

"Annaleesa?"

Maman.

I whipped my head toward the voice. The same voice I'd last heard in anger. Maman hovered over me, tears streaming down her face, wisps of graying hair escaping the chignon she always wore. Beside her stood Papa, more salt-and-pepper flakes at his temples than when I'd last seen him, but with the same soft brown eyes and thick, bushy eyebrows.

"Oh, Maman."

She scooped me up into her arms. I collapsed, physically and emotionally, my body racked with sobs I couldn't hold back. Maman cried, too. Even Papa, a man who held his emotions in check, sniffled and blew his nose on the handkerchief he insisted on carrying.

"Here." Maman handed me a tissue and took a fresh one from the packet for herself. I wiped my eyes and blew my nose.

"How did you know I was here?"

"We saw it on the news," Papa said. "We got the first flight out."

Laughter crawled into my throat where it died on my tongue. Even after all these months away from the glare of publicity that modeling had brought to my life, I still made the news.

"My baby." Maman's eyes drifted to the thick dressing covering the grotesque scar. She lifted her hand, then must have thought better of it. Her arm dropped back to her sides. Bitterness flooded me. She didn't need to say a word. I could read her as easily as a large-print book. Nothing had changed. She only cared about one thing: my physical appearance.

I peeled away the sticky tape holding the dressing in place. "Here. Have a good look at my ruined face. There's no going back to modeling now. How disappointed you must be."

Maman's face crumpled. "Oh, Annaleesa. Is that what you think?"

"Actions speak louder than words." A cruel laugh spilled out of me. "Although, you said plenty of words, too."

Her eyes glistened, and she pressed a hand to her throat. "I'm sorry for all those things I said. I was worried about you. About what you'd do if you gave up modeling."

My throat burned with suppressed anger. I snorted. "Isn't that peachy? Even my own mother doesn't think me capable of anything other than looking pretty for the cameras. What was it you said? I'm not clever enough... no, not bright enough to do anything else."

Big fat tears plopped onto her cheeks. "Darling, that isn't—"

"You probably don't know this, Maman, but I've always believed myself worthless outside of modeling. And when you said those things after I told you I wanted out, all you did was reaffirm that belief."

"I-I... I never meant to hurt you or for you to think you couldn't do anything you set your mind to. I shouldn't have said those things. I didn't mean them. Not a single one." She reached for Papa's hand. "Tell her, Francois."

"We've only ever cared about your happiness," Papa said, his hand resting lightly on Maman's shoulder.

"That's a lie. If you'd only cared about my happiness, you'd have supported me in my decision. Instead, you stood by while Maman judged me and berated me."

I shifted my gaze to her. She let out a whimper, her body shriveling in on itself.

"I want you to leave."

"But we only just got here," Maman exclaimed. "We want to be with you, look after you."

"I can take care of myself." I looked away. "I've managed just fine without you. I don't need you. I don't need anyone."

"But—"

"Olivia, let her get some rest. She's been through a lot."

Papa sounded weary. He wasn't the only one. My chest hurt, my insides felt as if someone was ripping me apart, and my eyes stung with tears that wouldn't fall.

"We'll be here tomorrow, ma chérie." Papa kissed my temple. "It doesn't matter how many times you push us away, we'll keep coming back. There are things that need to be said, but now isn't the time." He picked up my hand and squeezed it. "We love you deeply. Never doubt that."

I said nothing, simply let my hand lie limp in his. A few seconds later, the door clicked shut.

My tears came then. I wasn't sure they'd ever stop.

True to their word, my parents visited the following day.

Kadon did not.

How could I blame him when I'd told him not to bother? All he was doing was taking me at my word, respecting my wishes. I seesawed between this fervent need to see him and a profound belief that I was better off alone. I couldn't bear to face his reaction when he saw how badly disfigured the car accident had left me. Even if he clouded his disgust, I'd know. He couldn't hide from me. We were too connected.

When I refused to engage in conversation with

Maman and Papa, they left with the same promise they'd made yesterday. "We'll be back tomorrow." What they didn't know was, if my vitals remained stable, the doctor had said they might release me in the morning. With any luck, I'd be discharged and on my way home before they arrived.

Now that they'd made the first move, the long-overdue talk would happen. But not here in this sterile, impersonal hospital with the risk of interruption by a nurse wanting to take my blood pressure or a care assistant asking if I wanted something to eat or drink.

The thought made me nauseous. I'd never handled conflict well, preferring to keep the peace. That didn't mean I let people walk all over me. Far from it. But I always looked for consensus, common ground, a peaceful solution. I couldn't do that anymore. It was time to put my needs first. And I needed to tell them, Maman especially, how much she'd hurt me when she'd put my modeling career ahead of my happiness.

After lunch, I went for a walk. A touch unsteady on my feet—normal in cases of severe concussion, apparently—I stayed close to the wall, ready to brace myself if my legs buckled. I found myself on the seventh floor outside the restaurant. I ordered a coffee and sat by the window. The snow had stopped, and the temperatures must've increased because instead of pristine snow, gray slush covered the ground. I preferred that. A blanket of fresh snowfall was too perfect, too much of a reminder of what I'd had. What I'd lost.

I let out a short laugh. This wallowing in self-pity had to stop. I was alive, healthy, rich enough that I didn't need to worry about paying the bills even without a regular income. So what if I'd probably scare young children on the streets or have to suffer people gawking at me without an ounce of shame? I'd lived my whole life with people staring at me. Except now, they'd stare in disgust or horror, or pity.

Fuck them.

Fuck them all.

I didn't need anyone.

Dumping my half-full cup in the trash, I made my way back to my room. I opened the door. For a split second, my heart soared. Kadon. He'd come. Then I caught it. The flick of his gaze to my cheek. The wince he tried so hard not to show, yet failing miserably. The way he wrung his hands and fidgeted.

I flattened my lips. "What are you doing here?"

"I came to see you."

"I told you not to bother."

Swallowing, he ran his tongue along the inside of his mouth. "I won't stay long." He stuffed his hands deep into the pocket of his jeans, his hair falling over his forehead as he stared at his feet.

"Good. I'm tired." I peeled back the covers and climbed into the hospital bed, laying my head on the pillow, my eyes on a deep crack in the ceiling. They really should fix that before it worsened.

"Have they said when they plan to release you?"

"No." The lie tripped so easily off my tongue. I no more wanted Kadon to know when I might get out of here than my parents. I yearned to go home, pick up Dash, and lock myself away until I figured out how to live with this new version of me.

"Let me know when they do. I'll have a car drive you home."

Not "I'll drive you home," but "I'll have a car drive you." *I get the message, Kadon. Loud and fucking clear.*

"Thanks." Easier to accept than to argue over something so pointless. He'd made his decision, and I couldn't be bothered to try to change his mind.

"I'm sorry, Lee."

"So you said yesterday."

"I've gone over and over this in my mind. There isn't an easy way to say this." He ran a hand through his hair. "This... what happened to you, it's my fault. I'm responsible. I killed Henry, and I almost killed you. There's something about me that's poison. Everything I touch, I ruin. You're better off without me."

I sneered, my lip curling. I'd read him right. He was here to formally break up with me, but even I hadn't expected this approach. "So that's your play."

Fake confusion wrinkled his forehead. "Play? What play?"

"The self-flagellation, self-blame, self-pity, or any other self 'add adjective here to suit.' I'm no longer the flawless beauty, but instead of owning up to that, you hide behind the 'it's all my fault' bullshit. The 'I'm doing this for you' crap." I pointed two fingers at my eyes, then swiveled them in his direction. "I see you, Kadon. Be honest. You can't bear to look at me anymore, can you?"

He paled, his eyes bulging. "I can't believe you'd say

that." His voice shook, as did his hands. "This isn't to do with you, Lee." He punched his chest. "It's me. I'm toxic."

"Yeah, you are." I poured myself a glass of water, sipping it, the coolness a soothing balm to the fire in my throat, the charred embers of my heart floating around my chest. "So go. Get out of here. I don't need you. I'm better off alone."

He stayed where he was, his face frozen in stunned disbelief. Ah, he'd expected me to beg him to change his mind, to crawl on my hands and knees and plead with him not to leave me. Exactly as I had in my dream. Well, too bad. I'd beg no man. Not even him.

And dreams were just that. Make-believe.

"Get out!" I screamed.

The nurse burst into my room. Half the hospital had probably heard me. She planted one hand on her hip, the other she used to gesture to Kadon.

"Monsieur, I think it's best if you leave now."

He glanced at me. I turned away.

"I love you, Lee. I want you to know that. But I can't be with you. One day, soon, you'll find someone who's worthy of you. I'm only sorry that man isn't me."

I pinched my lips shut. Whatever. The sooner he left, the better off I'd be.

Seconds later, I got my wish. Or half of it, at least. He left.

And I had to face up to the fact that I'd never been poorer in my entire life.

Chapter 30

Leesa

As one void closes, another opens.

WINCING AS I CLIMBED OUT OF THE CAB, I GINGERLY cradled my stomach and made my way up the paved path to Audrey's house. If I walked too fast, I jarred the incisions the surgeons had made to remove my spleen. If I walked too slow, my impatience gene kicked in.

I was in a no win situation.

Audrey greeted me at the door before I'd knocked. Dash was already in his cat carrier at her feet, purring.

"He's missed you."

I gingerly dropped into a crouch and stuck my fingers through the gaps in the bars. "Hey, puss puss. I missed you, too."

He licked my finger, his spiky tongue tickling me. I'd missed him more than I could find the words for.

Not as much as I missed Kadon, though.

Rising to my feet, I put my hand on Audrey's arm. "Thank you so much for taking him in at such short notice. I don't know what I'd have done if you hadn't."

"It's my pleasure. I love having him. You know this."

She canted her head. I braced, readying myself to be gracious if she pulled out the pity card. Audrey was a lovely woman. She deserved my undying gratitude. I could stomach a few seconds of empathy.

"How's the pain?" She pointed her chin at my midsection. "I saw you wince as you got out of the taxi."

"It's not too bad. Doctors say I'll be good as new in a week or two." I twisted my lips. "Well, not quite, but you know what I mean."

"I won't trot out platitudes about beauty being on the inside, or in the beholder's eye." She took hold of both my arms and rubbed up and down. "Scars don't define you, sweetheart. You'll always be a stunner."

I mustered the merest hint of a smile. "I'd better go. You know what French cab drivers are like. He'll either disappear or charge me double if I don't get moving." Picking up Dash's cage and hiding another wince in case it brought on more sympathy I couldn't handle, I kissed Audrey's soft cheek. "Thanks again. You're a lifesaver."

She stood by the door as the cab pulled away, waving until we drove around the corner at the end of her street. Dash curled into a ball, his chest vibrating in a contented purr.

"Almost home, puss." I rested my head against the back of the seat and closed my eyes.

Lucky for me, the cabbie wasn't the chatty sort.

Or perhaps that was lucky for him. I wasn't in a talkative mood.

By now, my parents would have likely turned up at the hospital to find me gone. I'd never given them my address here in Saint Tropez, but it wouldn't take much effort to find me if they were of a mind to.

I fully expected them to turn up at some point. If not today, then tomorrow. And when they did, this time, I wouldn't push them away. Being surrounded by familiar things would help equip me to handle the difficult conversation.

As for Kadon...

My chest tightened, grief sweeping through me like a virus. I hadn't only lost my lover, but my best friend, too.

My *only* friend.

I sighed. I never did get Pippa's phone number.

The cab driver took pity on me and carried Dash's cage to the front door, putting up with my irascible cat without a murmur of dissent. I had no other luggage. The suitcase Kadon had slung into the back of his rented SUV a few short days ago as we left Val d'Isère had never made it to me at the hospital. For all I knew, it was still halfway down that mountain. Not that I wanted to see it, or the things inside, ever again. The reminders of what I'd almost had, and what I'd ultimately lost, were far too painful.

Did Kadon know the hospital had discharged me?

Had he ignored my bitter words for him to leave and never come back?

Was there a chance he'd change his mind and fight for me?

Did I even want him to?

Ah, wasn't that the six-million-dollar question?

I put down food and water for Dash and changed out of the dress I'd bought at the charity shop at the hospital. Being in my own clothes made me feel better.

A shiver ran through me. I put the heating on and made a cup of tea. For once, Dash had left the chair by the window free. He might have picked up on my sadness and decided to cut me a break.

The moment I sat down, he jumped up beside me, curling in my lap. I sipped my tea, absentmindedly stroking him as my thoughts meandered.

Loneliness settled in my bones. I missed Kadon. His sense of humor, his easy laugh, the way his eyes sparkled when something amused him, the dimple in his chin, a twin to the one in his cheek.

The way he kissed me as if it wouldn't ever be enough.

His muscular arms holding me at night until I fell into a deep, dreamless sleep.

If we'd never gotten together, then he wouldn't have taken me skiing.

We'd never have been in that car, on that road.

I wouldn't have a vicious scar running the entire length of my cheek.

And I wouldn't have known what it was like to have a man like Kadon make love to me as if I was the most precious gift in the world, the center of his universe.

No matter how much this hurt, I'd never give that up. I'd spent almost nine months in the dark about his feelings toward me, but if I had my time again, I'd make exactly the same decisions.

The sun set, and still I hadn't moved from the chair.

My stomach rumbled. I ignored it. My body might be hungry, but the idea of food made me nauseous. A cup of warm milk might help.

I put Dash on the floor, grimacing as I straightened. The doctor had warned me I'd get some pain for a few days. I'd smiled and told him I understood when inside, I'd assumed he was overreacting.

He hadn't overreacted. It hurt far more than I cared to admit.

As I traipsed into the kitchen and swallowed two painkillers, the bell rang. My heart jumped into my throat. Only my parents or Kadon would be at the door. If I had to guess, I'd pick the former. Kadon and I were done.

Over.

Finished.

He'd made his choice, and it wasn't me.

Rubbing my chest, I answered the door. I'd guessed correctly.

"Maman, Papa." I stood back. "Come in."

I didn't ask how they'd found me. It wasn't important. Dash spied strangers and darted upstairs, his bushy tail stuck straight in the air. He'd hide under my bed until they left. Kadon and Audrey were the only two people Dash tolerated other than me.

"You always wanted a cat," Maman said.

"I did."

I refrained from saying that, growing up, I'd wanted a lot of things I couldn't have. If we were ever to put this difficult period behind us and move forward, then barbed comments weren't helpful.

"What's its name?"

"Dash. He's a boy." I led them into the kitchen. "Would you like some tea?"

"That'd be lovely." Maman removed her coat and draped it over a chair. "You have a beautiful home, Annaleesa."

"Thank you." Dear God, we were behaving like strangers. I reached up for the tea bags. Ouch. That hurt. "Earl Grey?"

"Let me." She bustled over, taking the box of tea bags from me. I didn't have the energy to argue.

"You didn't tell us they'd let you out," Papa said.

"No."

He nodded, grasping the meaning behind the singular word. Maman set three mugs of steaming tea on the kitchen table. The atmosphere hung heavy in the air. I'd never been all that good with silences, but as difficult as it was, I kept quiet, sipping my tea. I wouldn't make this easy for them. If that made me a bitch, then fine. So be it. Surviving a plunge down a mountainside, surgery to remove my spleen, losing the love of my life, and a smashed-up face to boot...

I'd earned my bitch status.

Papa gave Maman a nudge.

Ah, they'd strategized an approach.

"Darling." Maman leaned her arms on the table and curled her hands around her mug. "I've thought of nothing else but what you said in the hospital, and I've done a lot of soul-searching."

She let go of the mug and touched me instead, her fingers warm from the heat of the tea. "I thought I was helping you fulfill your dreams, but the truth is, I was fulfilling mine."

She glanced at Papa, who rubbed her back in what I guessed was encouragement.

"Growing up, I'd applied to hundreds of modeling agencies, but they weren't interested. There was always something wrong. I was too tall, too short, eyes too far apart or too narrow, too thin, too fat. Always something. In the end, I realized it was futile and applied to Oxford instead."

She gave Papa a secret smile, a smile lovers shared.

Kadon smiled at me like that.

Or rather, he had.

Not anymore.

"Then you came along. I hadn't intended to push you into modeling, but I was walking down the street with you one day and a woman approached me. She said she was from a child modeling agency and you were perfect for an advertising campaign she was recruiting for. She gave me her card, and the next day I took you along. They hired you on the spot, and that was that."

Her grip tightened on my arm. "Please believe me when I say that whatever I did, I thought I was doing for you. If only you'd told me how unhappy you were."

"I did. Several times. I remember as a teenager begging you to let me go to 'normal' school with 'normal' kids, but you brushed it aside. You always brushed it aside."

She bit her lip. "I don't remember that."

A snort came out of me, derisive and brimful of a deep-rooted hurt I'd carried inside me for far too long. "Of course you don't remember."

She flinched. "We tell ourselves lies all the time, Annaleesa. We convince ourselves that what we're seeing is the truth. I made mistakes, terrible mistakes, none more so than what I said after Benedict broke up with you and you told me you were quitting modeling."

This time, I flinched. "You hurt me."

Until the day I died, I'd never forget the look on Maman's face as those words came out of my mouth. If I'd taken a knife out of the block and stabbed her with it, the agony wouldn't have been as deep. Tears streamed down her face, yet she didn't make a sound. Papa resumed his back rub, round and round as if he were winding a child after dinner.

"Please let me make it up to you. I've missed you so much. My life is incomplete without you in it. I shouldn't have left it this long. I wrecked our relationship; it was on me to fix it." She shifted her chair and took both my hands in hers. "Give me a chance. I won't let you down. I love you so very much, Annaleesa."

The sincerity in those words, the love in her eyes, and the pain etched into her beautiful face broke the dam.

Tears streamed down my face.

I reached for her. We fell into each other's arms. Papa wrapped his around both of us.

Home. Finally, I was home.

K

Bubbles appeared on the surface of the milk pan. I stirred it, adding a little sugar. Every part of me ached as though I'd completed a five-hour workout in the gym. Having my parents back in my life had filled a void created all those months ago when I'd broken the news I was quitting the only career I'd ever known.

And Kadon leaving me had created another one.

Would I ever feel truly whole?

Footsteps shuffled behind me. I glanced over my shoulder, smiling at Papa trudging into the kitchen, rubbing his eyes.

"Can't sleep?"

He shook his head.

"Same. Want some warm milk?"

He flashed his teeth. "You've always loved warm milk."

"It soothes me."

"If there's enough in the pan, I'll take some. Would you like me to do it?"

I shook my head. "I can manage."

I poured two mugs, and we made our way through to the living room. Papa tugged a blanket off the back of the couch and put it over us both.

We sipped our milk, quiet with our thoughts. Being around Papa had always been easier than spending time with Maman. He was a cool river on a summer's day; she was a fiery volcano always on the edge of erupting. Yet I'd spent my life craving her approval.

Which was the reason, I guessed, why the things she'd said to me had cut me so deeply.

"So, this man you were in the car with when it crashed. Where's he?"

I closed my eyes. "He broke up with me."

Papa sucked in a lungful of air through clenched teeth. "Did he now?" Displeasure laced every word. I couldn't help but smile.

"It's complicated, Papa."

He ran his thumb over my stitched cheek, his touch so gentle it almost brought me to tears, and I'd cried enough already.

"Because of this?" His jaw flexed, a pulse thrumming in his cheek. I couldn't love him more.

"At first, I thought it might've been, yeah. But now that I've had time and space to think about it, I know that's wrong. It's not Kadon's style. He's one of the most honorable men I know." I nudged him. "Other than you."

"Then why isn't he here, supporting you when you need him?"

I couldn't give Papa a full explanation. It wasn't my secret to tell. But I'd thought about this a lot since getting home earlier today. Kadon leaving me had nothing to do with *me* and everything to do with *him*. He'd laid it out for me, plain as day, yet I'd not been in a place to truly listen.

"Kadon has some things he needs to work through. This accident brought up a lot of triggers for him. He's blaming himself for my injuries, but it goes deeper than that. I hope he figures it out, and we can somehow find our way back to each other."

"And if you don't?"

My insides twisted as though someone were wringing out my intestines. "Then, unlike you and Maman, I guess we weren't meant to be."

He held out his arms, and I snuggled against him. He kissed my hair. "Ma chérie," he murmured. "You'll always be my baby. Whatever you need, whatever you want, I'm here for you."

"Funny you should say that, Papa, because there is

something you can help me with." I shifted position. "Let me tell you about a girl called Ayesha."

Chapter 31

Kadon

That's what big brothers are for.

Raindrops peppered my jacket and dampened my hair, and my ass grew numb from sitting in the same position for hours. I should go inside and sleep off the copious amounts of brandy I'd drunk.

Except, I couldn't.

Every time I ordered my legs to move, they disobeyed me.

An explosion of fireworks lit up the sky, and the sound of revelers partying on the beach drifted over. New Year's Eve. I should be here with Lee, snuggled up underneath a cozy blanket on the third-floor balcony of my beachfront villa, enjoying the celebrations. Instead, here I was, alone like a storm-tossed wreck.

I was a wreck all right. A fucking useless wreck.

The same thought whizzed around my head, over and over. This was my fault.

My fault.

I'd been behind the wheel. I hadn't had the skills to stop the car from skidding and plunging down a mountainside. Lee's injuries were down to me.

Everything I touched, I ruined.

What was it she'd said at the hospital before she'd kicked me out that first day? Something about managing my guilt and not being new at it?

She wasn't wrong.

For more than nine years, I'd worn guilt like a second skin, and the car accident had buffed it up, given it a fresh coat of paint, so to speak. Except the paint was filled with lead, and the weight, this time, might crush me.

A woman squealed, her excitement ripping through the air as a man picked her up and ran into the sea. He dunked them both. They came up for air, laughing. The laughter stopped, and the kissing began.

I turned away, pain ripping through my chest. Lee and I should have remained friends. If I hadn't opened Pandora's box and suggested that stupid fake relationship, she'd still be here with me, celebrating New Year's snuggled and cozy and oblivious to my feelings.

And I wouldn't have this crushing guilt to deal with all over again.

Reaching down, I swiped the bottle of brandy off the wooden deck and gulped another mouthful. The alcohol burned as it trickled down my throat. Didn't matter how much I drank; the pain stayed the same. Raw, agonizing. Warranted.

She was better off without me. I'd always thought it, yet I'd dared to hope, dared to *dream* she could be mine. I didn't deserve her. Not then. Not now. Not ever.

Poison. Toxic. Ruinous.

Described me perfectly.

The all-consuming love I had for Lee, unrequited now, was my punishment. Living with this pain for the rest of my life was my destiny. I'd never meet another woman like her, and I didn't want to. I should spend my life alone. That way, I couldn't bring this noxious malignancy into someone else's life.

A cab pulled into my driveway. My heart leapt, my pulse juddering.

Stupid heart.

Stupid pulse.

It wouldn't be Lee. She had no reason to come here. She'd made her feelings clear when she'd left the hospital without taking up my offer of a ride home, a fact I'd discovered when I'd called to check on her. We might've broken up, but I'd never stop worrying about Lee, caring about her, praying for her happiness as I prayed for Samuel's.

Blaize stepped out of the cab. His gaze drifted up to me. He must've seen me sitting here from the back seat.

Here we go.

It didn't take a genius to work out the reason for my brother's uninvited visit. I'd spoken with Dad briefly after the accident to reassure him I wasn't hurt. Since then, he'd called several times. As had Blaize and Nolen. Even my cousin Johannes had left a voicemail. I'd answered none of them. Better to wallow in self-pity alone than drag my family into the mess I'd created.

Blaize must've drawn the short straw, sent across the Atlantic to deal with the wayward son.

The fuckup.

The failure.

The idiot trouble followed wherever I went.

Sighing, I set the brandy bottle on the ground and heaved my ass out of the chair. I braced myself against the wall of the house.

That's what a half bottle of brandy will do.

Worst of all, the alcohol hadn't numbed the pain. If anything, it'd accentuated my misery.

I answered the door with a glower. "I don't need a babysitter."

Shoving his overnight bag into my solar plexus, Blaize arched an eyebrow. "I beg to differ. Behave like a child, get treated as one."

Without waiting for an invite, he marched into my house, but not without giving me a sniff first.

"Take a shower, Kadon. You smell like shit."

"No, I smell like brandy."

"Cut the attitude. I've had a long flight. I'm up to my eyeballs with work, and I could do without this."

"So fuck off. I never asked you to come." I left the front door open, dropping his bag at my feet.

"No. *Dad* asked me to. If it were up to me, I'd leave you here, swimming in self-pity. We both know it's what you do best."

Ouch. "Low blow," I muttered.

Blaize gripped both my arms, and he wasn't gentle about it, either. "I refuse to let you sink back into that fucking hole you took years to claw your way out of. You can fight me. You can toss insults around, you can tell me you hate me. It won't make a difference. I'm here until I'm satisfied that you're okay."

Releasing me, he made his way to my kitchen. I picked up his bag, sighing, and kicked the front door closed.

Should've answered the fucking phone, dickhead. Pretended you were fine. Schoolboy error.

I winced. Fuck if I hadn't made the biggest one of those.

"Where's your coffee?" Blaize opened several cabinets. "Ah, here it is."

"I don't want coffee."

"You think I care? You and I need to have a serious conversation, and I can't talk to you when you're brimming with alcohol. The belligerence will piss me off."

He made a pot, standing with his back to me while it brewed, his shoulders bunched around his ears. A dart of shame shot through me. Blaize had bigger fish to fry than me. In a few short months, our new cruise ship would launch. Yet, rather than dealing with what was probably a crammed inbox, he was here, looking after my sorry ass.

The coffee came at me black, even though I hated taking it that way. Instead of complaining, I kept it zipped. I took a sip. Christ, that was bitter. Bitterer than me.

I laughed.

"What's so funny?" Blaize added cream to his cup.

"Nothing. Private joke."

A loud bang rent the air, followed by several fizzes and whistles. I checked my watch, raising my coffee at my brother. "Happy fucking New Year."

Blaize pulled out a chair at the breakfast bar, sitting. "I

gave up sex with the hottest bartender I've ever seen to come here. So sit down and talk to me."

"You were robbed." I flashed him a grin.

"Tell me about it." He tapped a fingernail against the granite. "I saw Leesa."

My head jerked back. "When?"

"Before I came here. When you wouldn't answer anyone's calls, I figured it had something to do with her."

"I broke it off." Pain lanced through my chest. I let it consume me.

"I know."

"I'm no good for her."

"Disagree."

"She doesn't."

He arched the same eyebrow as earlier. "Is that right?"

"I ruin everything I touch, Blaize."

"Don't exaggerate. The beach club business is thriving. You haven't ruined that."

"I ruin *people*. You're all better off without me."

He sighed, shaking his head. "Remember that old movie *It's A Wonderful Life*?"

"Don't tell me, you're Clarence." I gifted him another smile. I'd never tell him this, but by being here, he'd lifted my mood.

"We both know I'm going straight to hell." He returned my grin. "No angel wings in my future."

"Nor mine."

"That movie reminds me of you. Without you, all our lives would be so much poorer, yet it doesn't matter how often we tell you that; you remain trapped in Switzerland."

"Lee pulled me out. For a few short weeks, I escaped."

344

"Then what changed?"

Incredulous, I glared at him. "I almost fucking killed her. That's what changed."

"You told Dad the brakes failed."

"Yeah."

"How's that your fault?"

"I should have been able to control the car."

Blaize snorted. "A car traveling downhill, heading toward a sharp bend with no brakes? And you think you should've somehow been able to stop it? By what means?"

I thumped the countertop. "I don't fucking know. But it haunts me, Blaize. It fucking haunts me. Like that night." I poked myself in the temple. "It's so full in here I can't breathe."

"Have they recovered the car yet?"

"No idea. Why?"

"Because if those failed brakes are down to a mechanic somewhere not doing his fucking job, I'm out for blood."

Until that second, it hadn't occurred to me that it might be human error. A servicing fuckup or similar. Jesus. Then again, I hadn't exactly been thinking straight since it'd happened.

He drained his cup and set it in the sink. Yawning, he stretched. "I need to get some shut-eye. We'll talk more in the morning. I'll make some calls and see if I can locate the car and whoever is in charge of the investigation." He clapped me on the back. "Take some headache pills and drink a gallon of water."

His footsteps echoed up the stairs. The house fell silent.

For once in my life, I obeyed my brother. I took the pills, drank the water, and fell into bed.

The next morning, the smell of fatty bacon and strong coffee filled my nose as I made my way into the kitchen. Blaize arriving unannounced had pissed me off, yet with a clear head and a full night's sleep, I was glad he'd come. I didn't feel so alone with my brother in my corner.

"Don't burn mine to a crisp."

Blaize turned around, brandishing a spatula in the air. "For that, I'll make yours extra crispy."

"Jerk." I poured a cup of coffee, adding cream this time. "How long are you planning to stay?"

"As long as it takes me to pull your head out of your ass and stop with the crazy talk you greeted me with last night." He cracked eggs into a bowl and whisked them up. "And for you to call Mom and Dad. They don't deserve the silent treatment. You're their youngest son. They love you, and they're worried."

"As soon as it's morning in Seattle, I'll call."

"Good."

He poured the egg mixture into a pan. I pulled out a chair, using the time to check my emails. I hadn't looked at them since we'd left Val d'Isère. I replied to a few work-related messages, moving the actioned ones to the relevant folders. As I scrolled down my *For Action* folder, scanning for anything that needed immediate attention, a message caught my eye. One I'd completely forgotten about in the midst of everything else going on.

"Shit."

"What's wrong?"

My insides churned. I'd never opened the message from Joseph, the guy I had looking into Samuel's whereabouts. I hadn't wanted to ruin my trip with Lee. A bitter laugh crawled into my throat. I'd ruined the trip all right. Spectacularly. But it'd had nothing to do with an email.

I ran my finger over the subject line. *You'll want to read this.*

Not true. I dreaded reading it, of having my hopes dashed yet again.

"Kadon?"

I looked up at my brother. "I've had a private detective searching for Samuel for over a year."

Blaize's eyes widened. "You have?"

"Yeah." I swallowed. "I have to get closure, and this is the only way I know how. I have to know he's okay."

"And is he?"

"No idea." I updated him on the many false starts, ending with the email from Joseph that I hadn't opened yet. "I'm afraid this is yet another disappointment, and I'm not sure I can take that right now. Not with my life in the shitter."

Blaize huffed. "Y'know, this woe-is-me bullshit wears thin after a while, and it isn't you. Not the real you. Not the annoying little shit I grew up with." He set down a plate of bacon and eggs. "I believe he's still in there somewhere. Maybe the answers are in that email. Open it."

I snapped off a piece of bacon. "You burned it."

"I'll burn you if you don't open the damn email." Sitting opposite, he shoved a forkful of eggs into his mouth, then jabbed the empty fork at me. "Do it."

Heart galloping, I tapped the screen. Blood pounding in my ears drowned out the sound of Blaize biting down on charred bacon. The words swam. I blinked a few times. No better.

"Here, you read it. They're all jumbled up."

"That's because you're in a panic." Blaize took the phone from me. His eyes darted from side to side. Time stopped. Blaize set down the phone, his gaze seeking mine, expression flat. I couldn't read him.

"Well?" I ran my tongue over dry lips. "What does it say?"

"He's found him."

My shoulders sagged. I caught my head in my hands. *He's found him.* Taking several deep breaths, I waited for my head to stop spinning.

"Is he alive?" I croaked.

"Very much so." Blaize broke into a smile.

"Where is he?"

"Lausanne."

Less than twenty miles from the school. "What's he doing in Lausanne?"

"He's a therapist. Has his own practice. He treats victims of sexual abuse."

God. *God.*

"According to this message, Samuel's parents changed their surname after what happened, and given the Swiss authorities' propensity to confidentiality, tracking him proved difficult."

"Do you think...?" My throat narrowed. I forced a swallow. "Do you think he'd see me?"

Blaize hitched a shoulder. "Do you want me to call?"

"Would you?"

"That's what older brothers are for."

Chapter 32

Kadon

**As one door closes,
another one hits you in the face.**

MONT BLANC ROSE MAJESTICALLY IN THE DISTANCE AS our car wound around Lake Geneva, the Jet d'Eau firing an impressive arc of water into the air. This was my first visit to Switzerland since the authorities had concluded their investigation into Henry's death and told me I was free to go.

Free. What a joke.

Henry's death had trapped me in this place ever since. With Lee, I'd had a few weeks of blissful peace, but since the car accident, the nightmares had returned, as traumatic as ever.

Except now, it wasn't only Henry's face I saw, a red stain pooling beneath his head, the distinctive smell of blood filling the air. It was Lee, that jagged piece of metal sticking out of her face, her incoherent mumblings, the blind panic that I couldn't find my phone to call for help.

The look on her face when she'd told me to go, that she didn't need me.

Didn't *want* me.

It was all I could see every time I closed my eyes. Not that I blamed her for feeling that way. If I had the choice to escape me, I would. In a heartbeat.

"How's the cruise ship coming along?"

Truth be told, I wasn't all that interested in that side of the business. Cruising was my idea of hell, no matter how much Blaize tried to convince me otherwise. My soul craved freedom. Give me a sandy beach and undulating waves every time.

Not that I'd surfed in weeks. I hadn't felt the urge. Lee had been my freedom.

Until she wasn't.

"Okay, I think." He heaved a sigh, plucking a piece of lint off his pants. "There's a lot to do, but we're on track."

"You'll make a success of it. Everything you touch turns to gold."

His wry smile gave me momentary pause. Blaize's confidence had always shone brighter than the sun at the height of summer. He had this intrinsic and unshakable belief in himself. Yet I could have sworn that smile carried a tinge of doubt in it.

"I can only try. It's the biggest thing I've ever worked on."

"I believe in you."

His lips curved up on one side. "That means a lot."

We fell into silence. I stared out the window as the mountains whizzed by. Switzerland was a stunning country, but I'd never voluntarily come here. If it weren't for Samuel, I wouldn't set foot on Swiss soil. The memories were too vivid, too laden with anxiety. I was only glad he'd agreed to see me. If his memories were as painful as mine, I wouldn't have blamed him if he'd point-blank refused.

I'll look forward to it, he'd said to Blaize when he'd made the call earlier this morning. Three hours later, here we were.

My palms were clammy, and my heart tripped over itself as we drove past the Mövenpick Hotel opposite the marina. The car swept to the right, stopping a few hundred yards from the shoreline.

Samuel's office building, where we'd agreed to meet, was nondescript. A beige façade, a shiny black door, a chrome bell. I took a breath, then another, each one having little effect on my nerves.

"Do you want me to come inside with you?"

I shook my head. This was a journey I had to walk alone. Only three people had experienced the full horror of that night, and one of them wasn't here to tell the tale. Because of me.

"I'll be right here. Take your time."

My lips lifted, then fell, the smile impossible to hold. I got out of the car and rang the bell.

"Bonjour." A woman's voice.

"Hi. Um, bonjour. I'm Kadon Kingcaid. I'm here to see Samuel."

"Ah, Monsieur Kingcaid. Please, come in."

A buzzer sounded and the door popped open. With a final glance back at Blaize, I went inside.

A brightly lit corridor greeted me, colorful artwork on the walls of Lausanne and the surrounding scenery. I'd expected muted lighting and stone floors, not plush carpeting and this dazzling brightness.

The corridor led me to what looked like a waiting area. Brown leather chairs, a TV in the corner, and a green-covered table with a steaming pot of coffee and dainty china cups sitting on a tray. Another door on the opposite side opened. A man came through, round glasses set above a hooked nose, dark hair swept off his face in a classic side part, and an unmistakable scar from a cleft lip.

My heart stopped.

"Samuel?"

His eyes lit up with the biggest smile. "Kadon Kingcaid. You've no idea how good it is to see you." He thrust out his hand, shaking mine with vigor. "You haven't changed a bit."

I shoved my fingers in my hair, still a few inches shorter than before Mom had interfered. "You look... great."

And he did. Better than great. He looked happy, at peace.

More than could be said for me.

"Come on through to my office. Would you like a coffee?"

"I'm good, thank you."

A woman sitting behind a desk, her fingers flying over a keyboard, paused as we entered. She must've been the voice I'd heard over the intercom. Her smile rivaled Samuel's.

"This is Melanie," Samuel said. "My wife."

Wife? So he was happily married, as I'd hoped.

"Pleased to meet you," I murmured.

"Not as pleased as I am to meet you." Her eyes flicked to Samuel, then back to me. "Can I get you anything at all?"

"We're fine, darling." Samuel opened another door and motioned to me. "After you."

I took a seat opposite his desk. He rounded it, relaxing into a high-backed leather chair, creased from heavy use.

"It took a while to find you," I said.

He nodded. "I thought about contacting you several times, but I couldn't pluck up the courage."

"Why not?"

He rubbed his lips together. "I thought you might blame me for what happened."

My eyes widened. "Blame *you?* Never. You weren't at fault for a single thing that happened."

"But I could have stopped it. If only I'd spoken up earlier, then that night in the library might not have happened."

So that time in the library wasn't a one-off. My hands curled into fists. I'd spent nine years regretting what I'd done that night, but right this second, if I could murder that bastard all over again, I would, and fuck the consequences.

"This is *not* your fault," I reiterated through gritted teeth.

"I know that. Hell, I tell my patients that all the time. I

was looking at it more from your point of view. It can't have been easy for you to reconcile what happened either."

"You mean because I killed him?"

"You didn't kill him. You hit him to stop him abusing me, and he fell. An accident. Pure and simple. But you always were so *good*, Kadon. I might have known you'd carry that burden." He leaned forward, forearms on the desk, fingers knitted together. "If it weren't for you, who knows where I'd have ended up? Henry would have never stopped abusing me, and at the time, I was too weak to fight him. You saved my life, Kadon. Sincerely, thank you. I'm only sorry I haven't found the courage to say it earlier."

The tension riding me slid off my shoulders like melted butter dripping off hot toast. That night had ended tragically for all of us, but coming here, talking to Samuel, seeing him so settled and happy, I finally accepted the truth.

It *was* an accident.

I'd never meant for Henry to die.

All along, my loved ones had told me this. Lee had told me this. Yet it took this conversation with Samuel for me to finally listen. Lee's words at Grange Manor came at me, hard and fast.

"You'll find him. And when you do, that's where you'll find your peace."

The question remained, if I could accept that what had happened to Henry was an accident, could I accept the same about the car accident that had injured Lee?

K

The plane landed in torrential rain, bumping several times along the runway before pulling onto the taxiway and stopping. Blaize and I tore down the steps and into the car waiting for us.

"I miss Miami," he moaned.

"Well, now that you've done your Mr. Fixit routine, you can go back to Miami."

"Are you? Fixed, that is?"

"I got my closure."

"Over Samuel, yes. But what about Leesa?"

I gnashed my teeth together. "I don't want to talk about Lee."

Blaize's deep sigh filled the cabin. "You are a fucking asshole, you know that?"

I ignored him. We moved off. Blaize plucked out his phone and started tapping, probably answering emails. I stared out the window. It was New Year's fucking Day, for Christ's sake. Work could wait. Then again, Blaize was, and always had been, a workaholic. Christmas Day, Easter, Thanksgiving. Didn't matter to him what day it was.

The rain had lessened to a miserable drizzle as the car pulled into my driveway. We trudged inside and hung our damp jackets over the banister. I switched on the heating and made a pot of coffee. The weight of Blaize's stare burned the back of my neck. I busied about for a few seconds, then turned.

"You clearly have something on your mind, so spit it out."

He slid onto a stool at the breakfast bar and tossed his phone on the counter. Several notifications appeared. He swiped the screen, clearing them.

"Has it occurred to you that walking out on Leesa at a time she needed you the most was a shitty thing to do?"

My teeth gnashing took on a whole new level of enamel erosion. "I didn't walk out on her. She told me to go."

"We all say lots of things during times of stress. Doesn't mean they're true, or that, in the cold light of day, we might see things differently."

"She knows where I live."

"Jesus Christ." Blaize shook his head. "*You* broke up with *her*. Therefore, *you're* the one who needs to grovel. On your fucking hands and knees if need be. It can't be easy for a woman like Leesa to come to terms with what's happened to her."

Can't be easy for a woman like Leesa... a woman like Leesa.

My heart stuttered, my mind running in circles. Could it be...?

No. Surely not.

Except...

I fisted my hair. God, I *was* a fucking asshole. A gigantic fucking asshole.

"Bro, you're a genius." I mashed my hands to both of his cheeks and kissed him. "I have to go."

His eyebrows squished together. "Go where?"

"To see Lee."

Blaize threw his hands in the air. "Finally he sees sense."

I grabbed my car keys and strode to the front door. I wrenched it open to a man, his hand in a fist, ready to knock.

"Monsieur Kingcaid?"

My eyes drifted past the unexpected visitor to the cop car parked behind my Aston. "Yes."

"I am Monsieur Lavigne, and this is my colleague, Madame LaRue. We are from the Police Municipale. May we come in?"

Goddammit. "I'm busy right now. Is it important?"

"Oui, monsieur."

Sighing, I stepped back and let them in. Blaize stood as the two cops followed me into the kitchen.

"What's going on?"

"They want to talk to me. No idea what about." I motioned to a seating area off the kitchen. "Can I get you anything to drink?"

"No, merci."

The four of us sat. I folded my hands in my lap and tried not to fidget. Now that I'd decided to talk to Lee and beg her forgiveness for being an absolute—to use her favorite word—twat, this unexpected interruption was grinding my gears.

"We've recovered your vehicle," the male cop said. I'd forgotten his name. "There wasn't any fluid in the system, which is why the brakes didn't work."

Fuck.

I side-eyed Blaize. A pulse thrummed in his cheek.

"A mechanical error?"

"No. The maintenance records show that the mechanic topped up the brake fluid six weeks before you hired the vehicle, during its annual service. Besides, if the brake lines were empty to begin with, you'd have discovered the issue far sooner." He breathed in. "The lines were cut."

A hiss of air whistled through Blaize's teeth. I gaped at the cops. "Cut? By whom?"

"We were hoping you could tell us." He flipped open a notebook, pen poised. Must be an old-fashioned cop who preferred tradition. "Do you have any enemies, Monsieur Kingcaid?"

I laughed. "My family has businesses all over the globe. Enemies come with the territory."

"This feels more personal, though," Blaize said, his expression thoughtful. "You don't think—"

"No. I don't." I glared. It wasn't Henry's family. Not after all this time. If they were going to exact revenge, they'd hardly have waited over nine years to do something about it.

The cop's eyes volleyed between me and Blaize, his jaw tight. "If there's someone we should talk to, then it's important you tell us."

I pondered his question, giving it careful consideration. The only person I'd pissed off recently was Lee's ex. Benedict wouldn't do something like this, though.

Would he?

"Monsieur Kingcaid," the cop prompted. "This is a criminal investigation. Withholding information is a serious offense."

I scratched my forehead, flicking strands of hair out of my eyes. "My girlfriend and I recently went to her ex's wedding. He made it clear to her that he wanted her back. But I don't see him doing something like this. He's spineless. Weak. He wouldn't have the guts to tamper with brakes on a car, nor deal with the consequences."

"Let us determine someone's capability to commit a crime, Monsieur Kingcaid. His full name, please."

Chapter 33

Leesa

Saved again by my beautiful, damaged, surfer-loving, billionaire beach-club owner.

My stitches itched, and although it took superhuman effort not to scratch, my doctor's stark warnings about scarring did their job.

If I absentmindedly clawed at my face, I'd put on a pair of mittens.

Or wear oven gloves.

Although, both would make everyday tasks like going to the loo or cooking a little tricky.

Then again, what did it matter if I scratched? A small, confrontational part of me celebrated the disfigurement, almost a "fuck you" to the world who dared to judge women solely on their looks.

Besides, I had more than enough to keep me occupied. When I'd told Papa about Ayesha and my idea to launch a body positivity modeling agency, he'd given me the phone numbers of a couple of contacts worth talking to. As determined as I was to do this by myself, I'd take all the contacts I could get.

Dash jumped up onto my lap and curled into a ball. I stroked his soft fur. "Just you and me, puss. We'll be okay. Bank on it."

He purred, then hopped down, heading for the kitchen. Ah, he wanted his dinner. I followed him, refilled his water, and opened a packet of his favorite tuna cat food.

Before I could squeeze the pouch into his food bowl, someone knocked on the door. Frowning, I wiped my hands on a towel, ignored Dash's outraged meowing at being kept waiting, and went to answer it.

Shock must've rippled across my face because my visitor, the one and only Fenella Oberon, gave me a wry smile, shrugged, and said, "Surprise!"

"What do you want?"

My question came out pinched and unfriendly. Good. I wasn't in the mood to entertain my ex's new wife, especially after the altercation at Val d'Isère. I hadn't slept well since I'd left the hospital, I couldn't do as much as I wanted to without wincing, and now I had a pissed-off cat weaving in and out of my legs. Any second, he'd take a swipe at me, claws extended.

"I heard what happened." Her eyes flicked to my cheek. "I wanted to stop by and see if you needed anything."

A strangled laugh burst out of me. "Stop by? Fenella,

you live in England. In case you hadn't noticed, this is the South of France."

"I'm visiting friends in the area. I know we're not exactly best buds, but what sort of person would I be if I was literally staying down the road and didn't come to see you?"

I heaved a sigh. She had a point. If the roles were reversed, I'd have done the same.

On a positive note, Benedict wasn't with her. I should be thankful for that.

Standing back, I motioned for her to come in. "Would you like something to drink?"

"White wine if you have it."

She stepped around me. I pointed to the kitchen. "That way."

I set a bottle of wine on the counter and passed her a glass before giving Dash his dinner. He purred his thanks, claws withdrawn.

"Little shit," I murmured.

"He's so cute."

"Looks can be deceiving." On reflex, I touched my face. Fenella's gaze went there.

"You're lucky to be alive."

My throat closed up. "Yeah." It came out strangled.

"I'm sorry." She downed half the glass of wine. "It must be hard for someone like you to look in the mirror every day and see that." Her gaze went to my cheek again.

My spine stiffened. I crossed my arms. "What do you mean, someone like me?"

"You know. A model."

"I'm not a model."

"Well, no, not now. And you won't ever be a model again with that scar. But I mean, what else can you do, really?"

My mouth popped open. "There are plenty of things I can do."

Outrage licked through my veins. I wasn't about to tell Fenella about my modeling agency idea, but I refused to let her drag me down and make me doubt myself. I'd had enough doubts running through my mind to last me a lifetime. I was moving on.

"Like what? You can't work for the Kingcaids anymore. Not now that Kadon has dumped you. Was it because he couldn't stand to look at you any longer?"

Blood pounded in my ears, white dots peppering my vision. How did she know Kadon and I had split up?

"I bet it was," she continued, appearing unaware of my growing rage. "Can't blame him. I mean, he's gorgeous and you're... well..." She screwed up her face. "Mutilated."

I moved toward her, my footsteps slow and deliberate. I stopped a couple of feet away, too afraid of what I might do if I let myself get much closer. I'd never hit a person in my life, but fuck it if Fenella wasn't pushing every button labeled "violence."

She backed away, but instead of a look of fear in her eyes, triumph shone back at me. I stayed where I was, assessing her play. Because checking on me was *not* it.

"Since our wedding, all I ever hear is your name. Annaleesa this, Annaleesa that. He never shuts up about you. I got so *sick* of it." She laughed, a touch of madness elevating the pitch. "Little Miss Perfect." Another laugh spilled out of her, shriller than the first. "You're everywhere. You're in here." She jabbed a finger at her temple. "When Kadon told me what Benedict had said to you on our wedding night, I had to do something. I know why Benedict married me. I'm not stupid. But for all his faults, I love him. He's mine. I couldn't let you take him from me."

"Take him?" I snorted. "I wouldn't take Benedict back if he crawled to me on broken glass. It took splitting up with him for me to realize I didn't love him. I never loved him. He's yours, Fenella. All yours."

"No." She shook her head so violently her brain must've rattled inside her skull. "No, he's not mine. Not as long as you're alive. Not as long as there's *hope*. That's why I did it, you see? If you weren't here, then he'd turn to me for comfort. Only then could he see that I'm the one he wants. I'm the one he should have been with all along."

My blood ran cold, the tips of my fingers and toes tingling. "What did you do, Fenella?" I whispered, moving toward her once more when I should probably move away. I kept waiting for fear to nail my feet to the floor, yet it never came. Strength flowed through me, courage. I wasn't afraid of her. I wasn't afraid of anyone or anything.

She reversed another few steps, stopping only when her back hit the kitchen counter. "No one will want you, Leesa. You're washed up. Useless. You're nothing without your looks."

Until the accident, a comment like that would've floored me. But in the last few days, something inside me had shifted. I'd spent so long worried that no one would take me seriously, that I'd never amount to anything outside of my looks. Yet my mind had lied to me all along.

I had so much to give, starting with my modeling agency. But it wouldn't end there. I had plans. Big plans.

And none of them relied on what I looked like for success.

"You're wrong. I pity you, Fenella. I have so much to look forward to, whereas you... all you have ahead is a life filled with bitterness and jealousy."

"I don't want your pity," she spat. "At least I ruined your face. Benedict won't be interested in you now. Not looking like that. My husband has many faults, and shallowness is one of his most prevalent." She flashed her teeth. "It was so easy. So easy. One little cut. Not all the way, of course. See? I told you I wasn't stupid. But enough that with every mile you traveled, the brake fluid would leak out until the reserves were empty. It's a shame you didn't smash into a wall, or plummet to the bottom of that mountain. But at least I got what I wanted. I got my husband back."

Oh my God.

She'd admitted it.

And, fucking hell, there wasn't a single witness to corroborate what she'd said.

Goddammit. She was a wily cow. Even if I called the police, she'd deny it. I should have been smarter; I should've recorded our conversation.

"Attempted murder must be fifteen to life, Fenella."

"But it's your word against mine. And who is going to believe a washed-up, ugly, airheaded former model over Sir Darren Grange's debutante daughter and wife of up-and-coming political heavyweight Benedict Oberon?"

"Me."

We both snapped our gazes in the direction of the voice. My knees sagged. I grabbed the back of the nearest chair for support. "Kadon."

He stood in the doorway, his imposing figure filling the space. Every cell in my body relaxed. Despite his rejection, I still loved him. I'd always love him. We'd both said things we didn't mean. And he'd come for me.

Hold on, Leesa.

Just because he was here didn't mean he'd changed his mind about us. In which case, what *was* he doing here? How did he get in? Had he heard it all, or only the last part?

Kadon held up his cell phone. "Well... me, and the police when I play them this recording."

Fenella's eyes darted between me and Kadon. She grabbed a knife from the wooden block to her right, brandishing it in the air. I gasped.

"Stay back. Don't come any closer."

"Fenella." Kadon spoke softly, as though trying to calm a frightened puppy. "You're in enough trouble already. Attempted assault with a deadly weapon will only lengthen your sentence."

He slipped the phone into the back pocket of his jeans and reached out his hands. "Put the knife down. Come on now. You don't want to do this."

She hesitated. Her fingers loosened around the hilt. The knife clattered to the floor, skittering across the tile.

Fenella collapsed to her knees, violent sobs racking her slim frame.

Kadon looked at me. "Call the police."

The gendarmerie led Fenella to the waiting police car in handcuffs. It began to drizzle again as the car drove away. My shoulders drooped, my neck spasming from holding myself stiff for so long. Kadon's muscular frame appeared at my back. He kneaded the tight muscles, his thumbs digging into the separate knots.

I groaned. "I'm mad at you."

"I'm mad at me, too."

"How did you know she was here?"

"I didn't."

I pivoted, tipping back my head to meet his warm gaze. I searched his eyes for signs of disgust or rejection. Love shone back at me, clear and wonderful, and all Kadon. My beautiful, damaged, surfer-loving, billionaire beach-club owner.

"I came here to apologize, to get on my knees and beg you to forgive me for walking out on you, and to tell you what's happened these last couple of days. It's been a *lot*."

He tucked my hair behind my ear, his fingertips lingering on the soft skin there. I shivered, my body already halfway to forgiveness.

More like three-quarters.

"The front door was ajar when I got here. I almost knocked, then I heard voices. I recognized Fenella's. No idea what made me turn on the voice-recording app on my phone. I crept inside and hovered in the hallway, listening." His lips twisted. "Fuck, the restraint it took not to burst in there when I heard the things she said to you."

He traced my bumpy scar with his thumb. I ducked my head.

"No. Don't you hide from me. Not from me." He clipped me under the chin. "She's wrong, Lee. So wrong. To me, you're as beautiful as you ever were. A beauty like yours is soul deep. It radiates from every cell in your body."

"It's horrible, though," I whispered. "Ugly."

"No. It's skin that's suffered trauma and needs to heal. My cousin Johannes has a scar across his neck where he was attacked a few years ago. He struggled to cope with it at first, but eventually, he found a way to deal with it. And you'll do the same. In time."

Kadon hadn't ever mentioned this to me before. "How did he overcome it?"

"With the help and love of a good woman." He cupped both my cheeks, his hands rough and warm and comforting. "It doesn't change a thing about the person you are, nor how I feel about you. I'm here for you. Always."

I wanted to believe him.

Damn it, I *did* believe him.

I refused to let something so superficial ruin my future with the man I loved.

I was stronger than that.

Better than that.

He bowed his head. "I'm so fucking sorry, Lee. Guilt ate me up for so many years, and the accident set off a trigger. I handled it badly. I made what happened all about me when it should have been all about you. For so long, I thought I was poison, a man to avoid, a man who didn't deserve to love and be loved. I let you in. I shared my poison with you, and you accepted me anyway. But I threw it all away because I'm a blind, stupid fool, as Blaize so articulately pointed out."

"He came to see me."

"Yeah, I know." He grimaced. "Something he said made me realize that I walked out on you at the exact time you needed me the most and that my actions would probably reaffirm your worries that people only wanted and liked you for your looks." He glanced away again, his tongue poking the side of his cheek. "Can you ever forgive me?"

I grazed a hand over his cheek. "We're both at fault, Kadon. As much as I've let my fears that I'm nothing without my looks rule me, your fears that you're better off alone so you can't hurt anyone else have ruled you. I pushed you away."

"And I let go too easily."

"You weren't the only one I pushed away."

"Oh?" He arched a brow.

"My parents came to see me in the hospital. I said some pretty mean things, yet, like you, they didn't give up. After I was discharged, they came here, and we talked. For the first time, I was able to tell Maman things I'd kept to myself, things I'd convinced myself she wouldn't want to hear. She shared things with me, too. I understand her a lot better now. We've cleared the air."

"I'm so glad." He hit me with a wry smile. "The private investigator found Samuel."

I sucked in a breath, covering my gaping mouth with my hand. "He did? Where?"

"Lausanne. Blaize and I flew there this morning to meet with him." He cupped my face, dropping a kiss on my lips. "He's good, Lee. He's *good*. Happy. Married. He's a therapist, helping victims of sexual abuse. He thanked me. *Thanked me* for saving his life. I can't even begin to explain how that felt."

"God bless Samuel," I murmured. "He gave you peace."

Chapter 34

Kadon

Changing the world, one step at a time.

ONE WEEK LATER...

"Snuggle closer." I tugged Lee into my body. "You're not close enough."

Ever since we'd gotten back together, I hadn't let her out of my sight. I missed her even when I slept, and while I hadn't told her this in case she accused me of being a creeper, I often woke in the middle of the night and lay there, watching her sleep.

"Any closer and I'll be inside you."

I waggled my eyebrows. "Soon, my little sex fiend, I'll be inside *you*."

She laughed. "Well, the hospital said two weeks, and I make it"—her eyes rose up and to the right—"twelve days."

"Which is not two weeks."

She stuck out her tongue.

"Mature."

"It's why you love me."

"One of many reasons." I kissed the top of her head, shifting my weight to stop my dick from rubbing against my zipper. It hadn't gotten the memo that Lee was recovering from surgery and therefore fucking was out of the question until the doctor gave her the all-clear.

"There are other things we can do, you know. Things that don't involve vigorous sex."

I raised an eyebrow. "Horny, are we?"

She put her hand on my dick. My solid-as-a-bat dick. "I can take care of this."

I groaned, pushing my hips up, thrusting into her hand. "I guess there are things we can—" Dash landed on my lap, sharp claws digging into my erection. I yelped, jerking my hips. All that did was make him dig in harder. "Jesus Christ!"

Lee gingerly lifted him off me, laughing far too hard for my liking.

"Fuck, that hurt. I swear, that cat has lived the last of his nine lives."

"Love me, love my cat." She set him down in the hallway and closed the door to the living room.

"You're lucky you're worth it," I grumbled, the sharp pain receding. "That cat is a fucking cockblocker."

"He's been the man of the house for months. It's hard for him to relinquish his place in the hierarchy. You have to earn it, and that's his way of telling you you're not there yet."

"Man? He's a cat."

"Not in his head."

Huffing, I tucked her into my side once again. I flicked through the TV channels, my dick—and my ego—a bit battered and bruised.

Lee walked her fingers up my thigh. "We're safe now. He's—"

She broke off, seeing the same thing I had at the same time. Sir Darren Grange's jowly face loomed large on the TV, a man that had to be his lawyer on his left-hand side, and a trembling and scared-looking Fenella on the other. Benedict stood off to one side, only half in the shot, almost as if he didn't want to be associated with any of this in case it affected his career. Fenella's father probably insisted that he be there to show a united front. Flashbulbs lit up the screen, popping as photographers all vied for the money shot.

He made a short statement that said practically nothing and had obviously been penned by his legal team.

"They let her go, then?" Lee murmured.

"On bail, most likely."

"I thought they'd have kept us informed."

"If we have to give evidence at any trial, I'm sure they will be in touch."

"Do you think her father has the power to make all this go away?"

I'd had the same thought myself but hadn't wanted to voice it. I hitched a shoulder. "Mine did."

"Kadon." One word spoken, steeped in castigation.

I forced a weak smile. "Powerful men can make anything disappear, Lee. Criminal charges. People. Money. It's the way of the world. I can hardly complain. I benefited from it."

"That's not the same."

"Isn't it?"

"No." She sat upright. An icy chill raced over me at the loss of her warmth. "You were a child, Kadon, and what happened was an accident. Fenella is a grown woman who cut the brake fluid lines, knowing her actions would cause serious injury at best. That's not the same thing at all."

"No, I guess you're right."

"Wow." She grinned at me. "That's progress."

"I'm trying."

"I actually feel sorry for her. I might have scars to remind me of what happened, but Fenella is the one who will have to live with the consequences, even if Daddy fixes it for her. Deep down, I don't think she's a bad person. I think she fell in love and discovered that the man she thought loved her, too, didn't. And not because he was in love with me, as she thought, but because Benedict is incapable of loving anyone but himself. In the end, living with the guilt will be Fenella's punishment."

I nodded. Yep. I knew what that felt like. Torture. And while I'd finally recognized that the cause of my guilt was an accident, Fenella wouldn't have the same luxury.

An idea I'd had for a few days, but quashed because Lee deserved all my attention, nudged me. Since meeting Samuel and discovering how he'd turned a dreadful situation into one where his experience benefited others, I had this idea that wouldn't go away. An urge to play my part, too. A bit like Lee wanted to with her body positivity modeling agency.

"Can I run something past you?"

"Always."

"I've been thinking about what happened to Samuel, and how sexual abuse happens in places that should be areas of safety, and men and women, boys and girls can become victims. It occurred to me that we might not change the world, but we could change things one tiny step at a time."

Her brow furrowed. "How so?"

"I want to work with other businesses in the area to set up a scheme where, if it was a venue that served alcohol, we could, oh, I don't know, have the drinks change color if someone drops a date-rape drug in it. Signs on the toilet doors to ask for "Julie" at the bar if you're in danger or think you might be in danger. Sharing of information on known predators in the area, although the latter one might have to be done on the QT. Can't see the gendarmerie being too pleased about that. It's all running around in my head, and the details are sketchy, but—"

"I think it's a *wonderful* idea."

"You do?"

"Yes. Such a worthwhile venture."

"And I was thinking of reaching out to the local schools and seeing if they'll let me talk to the kids about the importance of speaking to an adult about anything that feels wrong."

"Oh, Kadon." She canted her head. "Samuel would be proud."

My gut clenched. I smiled ruefully. "Might need to work on my French a bit before that."

Her eyes sparkled and she gripped my forearm. "I could teach you. We'd have so much fun."

I wrinkled my nose. "You have a warped idea of fun, Lee."

"Is that so?" Her gaze dropped to my mouth, then to my groin. "Sure about that, Kingcaid?"

"You're ill."

"No. I'm horny."

"Twelve days, Lee. Twelve days since you almost died."

"Since we *both* almost died. And isn't that even more of a reason to live for today, to wring the most out of every moment?"

"And you want to do that by having sex?"

"At this moment, yes. Tomorrow, I might want to ride a horse or pilot a hot-air balloon, or go surfing."

I laughed. "You, surf? As I recall, the last time I took you, some months ago now, you swallowed a bucketful of seawater and declared my beloved hobby a complete waste of time."

"Oh, yeah." She tucked a strand of hair behind her ear. "I'd kinda forgotten about that."

"I haven't." I held a fist to my chest and made my eyes doleful. "It hurts me to this day."

"You're such an over-actor."

She tugged down my zipper and freed my cock, gripping it firmly. I groaned, angling my pelvis and pushing further into her hand. "We aren't fucking, no matter how hard you pull on my dick. You're not fully healed."

She touched her tongue to her canine, a devilish sparkle in her eyes. When she let me go, I cursed my benevolence. Until she slithered out of her panties, swinging them around her forefinger.

"Sixty-nine?"

Fuck.

I'm dead.

Epilogue

Leesa

The perfect beginning.

Four Months Later...

"I appreciate that, thank you." I held up two fingers at Kadon, who'd appeared at the door to my office, or rather, the converted bedroom at my house. I hadn't seen the need to hire off-site premises. I could run my business as easily from here. He took a seat opposite my desk and crossed one leg over his other knee.

"Of course," I said into the phone. "I'll confirm our agreement in an email. Thanks, Jéan. Speak soon." I ended the call. "Another company wanting to hire Maman for their advertising campaign."

In line with my company's mission statement, I'd

opened my doors to all kinds of amazing, talented, beautiful women, including my gorgeous maman, who was my most in-demand middle-aged model. Being able to make her long-held dreams come true was one of my proudest achievements since I'd officially launched thirteen weeks ago. I still hit multiple brick walls with organizations that weren't ready, or willing, to change, but more and more were opening their eyes to the opportunities of diversity.

"She's a popular lady. As well as a beautiful one, just like her daughter."

I narrowed my eyes. Kadon had that look on his face, the one that said he was up to no good.

"What are you doing here?" I glanced at the clock. "Not far into the season and you're playing hooky already?"

"Leaving a business I own at five thirty is not playing hooky."

"It is when you haven't replaced me yet." If I had to guess, I'd put Kadon's fussiness with hiring a new VIP Operations Manager down to his doomed hope that I'd change my mind and return.

"Meh. You weren't that good anyway."

I thought I'd feigned nonchalance, until Kadon chuckled.

"You're so easy to tease."

I scratched my temple with my middle finger. "Shut up and tell me why you're interrupting me at work."

"Is that any way to talk to your beloved?" He got up and came around to my side of the desk. Taking my hands, he pulled me to my feet. "Work's over for the day."

"But—"

"But nothing. You're done. You've worked your ass off these last few months starting this business. It'll survive without you for a couple of hours."

"Aww, are you missing me?"

"Like a boil on the bum."

I laughed. "I knew my English side would rub off eventually."

"I prefer it when your French side rubs off." He explored me slowly, gaze heated. "Or rather, rubs *against*."

"Against what?" I batted my eyelids.

"Anything you want, Lee." He leaned in, brushing my lips with his. "But first things first."

He led me to his car. We drove for about thirty minutes. Every time I asked him where we were going—which I did at least once every ninety seconds—he'd wear this expression, a half smile, a little wink, eyes shining as if he held the world's best-kept secret and he only had a few minutes left to wait before he could blurt it out.

I lost track of time, falling silent when he refused to answer me, deciding instead to enjoy the beautiful scenery. The country of my birth, although not where I'd spent most of my childhood, was truly stunning, and I couldn't be happier that this was where I'd chosen to settle. I often wondered if Kadon might want to return to America at some point. Not that he'd ever mentioned it. He appeared as happy here as I was. Though if he did, I'd go with him. I'd follow him anywhere. The beauty of my work was that location didn't matter.

He eventually stopped the car on a narrow road with shrubbery on either side and yellowed grass starved of water. I couldn't see much in the way of civilization, other than a couple of houses dotted about the hillside. His lips pressed together as he cut the engine and climbed out. I did the same.

"Where are we?"

"France."

I rolled my eyes. "I'm sorry I ever put the effort into teaching you sarcasm."

"Why? Because I'm better at it than you?"

I snorted. "Dream on."

He laughed, taking my hand. "Come on. It's not much farther."

"Will the car be okay?" I glanced up and down the street. "It's pretty desolate."

"It'll be fine." We crossed the road and ducked through a gap in the hedge. The crystal-clear waters of the Mediterranean Sea twinkled in the evening sunlight, and below, a deserted golden beach stretched for miles. The path down to the shoreline was pretty steep, and I slipped a couple of times, held upright only by Kadon's tight grip on my hand. He picked his way down as easily as Dash would have, sure-footed and confident.

I kicked off my shoes at the bottom, digging my toes into the warm sand. We trekked along the beach for about five minutes in comfortable silence. The only sounds came from birds flying overhead and large, white-tipped waves crashing to shore.

"This is all rather mysterious." I side-eyed Kadon, who still wore that smug, secretive look. "I don't trust you."

"Charming." His grin stayed fixed in place, assurance oozing from every pore.

"If you're planning to murder me, I will come back

from the dead and tell Dash what you did, and he will rip your balls from your body with his huge talons."

Kadon threw back his head and laughed. "I adore your vivid imagination. Although, why it jumped to murder is a little alarming."

"I mean... take a look around. It's deserted. No one knows we're here. It's primed for nefarious activities."

"Damn." He hit his thigh with the flat of his palm. "You got me. Nefarious and me, we're like that." He crossed his fingers.

"I taught you too well," I grumbled.

"Quit complaining. We're almost there."

I trundled along beside him for a few more minutes, my mind spinning with what he could have planned. One thing the last few months with Kadon had taught me was to expect the unexpected. He'd taken to having at least every other Saturday off work, and he often organized something fun for us to do. Life wasn't boring. That was for sure.

In the mouth of a small cave, a wicker picnic basket caught my eye, sitting alongside a large, thick blanket. Something Kadon had said to me months ago sprang to mind. That time we'd practiced for the wedding and our fake relationship, and I'd asked him about the first time we'd had sex. He'd come out with this romantic story about a hidden cove on a beach, a comfortable blanket, and a picnic.

"Kadon." The cave before me blurred. I blinked to clear my vision. Hands down, this was the most romantic thing ever.

"Come, sit." He maneuvered me inside. Opening the

picnic basket, he produced a bottle of Dom Pérignon. Just like the tale he'd told months ago.

"Are there lobster rolls and caviar in there, too?"

His eyes softened. "You remembered."

"How could I forget?"

He poured two glasses of champagne and handed one to me. The cool liquid slipped down my throat, bubbles shooting up my nose. I didn't ask how he'd done all this, including serving chilled champagne. That would ruin the illusion, and he wouldn't like that.

Sure enough, the picnic basket contained lobster rolls and caviar, as well as tuna sandwiches with the crusts cut off and the most melt-in-your-mouth strawberry mousse I'd ever tasted. As the sun dipped lower in the sky, I finished my glass of champagne and fluttered my eyelashes at Kadon.

"Are you going to kiss me and undress me and make love to me, and then hold me in your arms under a starlit sky until we fall asleep?" He'd promised the same thing all those months ago, and although this wouldn't be our first time, it'd be no less special.

"No." He took my empty glass and turned his back to me, putting it in the picnic basket along with his own.

"Oh." Disappointment did not taste anywhere near as good as Dom Pérignon. "Right. Fine. Whatever."

He ignored my petulant outburst, although I was sure I spied his shoulders shaking with suppressed laughter.

"What *are* you planning to do, then?"

"This."

He pivoted slowly, and in his hand was a diamond as big as my fist. Okay, not quite that big, but big nonetheless.

Fifteen carats at least. Maybe more. My heart stuttered, then stopped beating altogether.

Omigod omigod omigod.

Kadon rose up on one knee, holding the ring out to me. "If you say yes, then I'll kiss you and undress you and make love to you. I'll hold you in my arms all night, unable to look away, unable to sleep in case you were a dream and I wake in the morning alone and bereft. And if you are real, I'll make love to you all over again, and from that moment on, we'll know that in each other, we've found the other half of us."

It was the second time I'd heard him say those words, and they had the same effect on me, rendering me breathless, needy, wanting. "And if I say no?" I whispered.

"If you say no, I'll spend the rest of my life proving to you that yes is the right answer."

"That's a long time."

"It is."

"I'm not sure I'm worth it."

"Oh, you're definitely worth it, Lee." He picked up my left hand, holding the ring an inch from my fingertip. "So, what's it going to be?"

Only one possible answer existed.

"Yes."

He pushed the ring onto my finger, his smile lighting up the dusky cove. "I love you, Lee. From the moment I found you crying on that beach, I knew I'd found my soul mate. You saved me. You showed me I deserved love, and I'll always be thankful that it was your love I earned."

I slipped my fingertips underneath the hem of his black T-shirt, exploring ridged abs, firm pecs, warm skin.

Tracie Delaney

"It's time to make good on your promise to kiss me, undress me, and make love to me."

He didn't need a second invitation. He eased me onto the blanket, and as the sun dipped beyond the horizon and stars peppered the sky, our bodies and souls merged into one.

THE END

A Thank You from Kadon

Thank you so much for reading! I know, I know, I probably shouldn't have tricked Lee into the whole fake boyfriend thing, but it worked! And sometimes, when we want something, we have to... think outside the box.

If I had to make the same decision again, I would. She was worth the risk, and then some. Finding inner peace for myself in the process was just the icing on the cake.

Next up is *Devoured By You*. My older brother, Blaize, has his panties in a twist over this new cruise ship he's launching. What he doesn't know is that's the least of his problems. Enter Jillian Rowe, a successful novelist with a crippling case of self-doubt and imposter syndrome who is about to blow his life wide open and make him question his usual no-second-date rule.

Can't wait until then for more billionaires? Then have you read the ROGUES series yet? Pick up your copy of the first book, *Entranced* today.

Or, if you'd like a free prequel to the ROGUES series, all you have to do is join Tracie's newsletter and your copy of Entwined will magically arrive on your device of choice. Go to her website at www.authortraciedelaney.com and click on "Claim My Free Book" on the home page.

Devoured By You

Life's full of surprises.
Some I could live without.

Things I'd hoped for on this vacation:

- Have a wonderful, relaxing time with some of the best friends a girl could wish for.
- Overcome the crippling doubt that had taken hold since I achieved Number One New York Times Bestseller status.
- Send my editor *something* to stop her from messaging me seventeen times per day.
- Get a tan.

Things I didn't expect to happen:

- Joining the mile-high club.

- Engaging in an altercation with a Hugh Hefner wannabe.
- Finding myself in a life-and-death situation.
- Falling in love.

Nor did I expect to have my happily ever after torn from my grasp by a cruel twist of fate.

But one thing that clawing myself to the top has taught me; I'm a fighter.

And this is one battle I will win.

Coming Soon on Amazon!

Books by Tracie Delaney

BILLIONAIRE ROMANCE

The ROGUES Series

The Irresistibly Mine Series

The Kingcaid Billionaire Series

PROTECTOR/MILITARY ROMANCE

The Intrepid Bodyguard Series

SPORTS ROMANCE

The Winning Ace Series

The Full Velocity Series

CONTEMPORARY ROMANCE

The Brook Brothers Series

BOXSETS

Winning Ace

Brook Brothers

Full Velocity

ROGUES Books 1-3

SPINOFFS/STANDALONES

Mismatch (A Winning Ace Spin Off Novel)

Break Point (A Winning Ace Novella)

Control (A Driven World/Full Velocity Novel)

My Gift To You

Acknowledgments

As I said in the reader note at the beginning of this book, I had a tough time writing this one, not because of my characters, but because I've had a few difficult things going on in my personal life that made writing a real challenge. There were times I didn't think I'd get to the point of releasing this book, but somehow, I made it work.

But that was not without help.

To my incredible husband who has propped me up more times in the last few months than I can count. Just knowing I have a soft place to fall is priceless. I never forget how fortunate I am. Never.

To my wonderful PA, Loulou. There isn't much more I can say other than thank you for being there. You're right at the center of the small group of people I know I can trust. It's a select group, but goodness me, we're mighty. Love you to bits.

Lasairiona, my wonderful Woo friend. You know how close I came to being unable to finish this book, yet you steadfastly remained by my side and pushed me onwards and upwards. And you gave me regular slaps (metaphorically) when needed. And boy, at times, I needed them. I know you won't agree, but I truly don't think this book would be in readers hands if it weren't for you. Thank you for everything, not least of loving Kadon. But he's still mine!

Clare. It's funny to think it wasn't all that long ago that we didn't know each other. And now I can't imagine a day going by without talking to you. In fact, when those days do pass, it just feels weird! Thank you for your support which I've needed recently more than ever. I appreciate and adore you. Also thanks for loaning me Dash, and for the invaluable cat info for this dog owner!

Bethany - thank you so much for your brilliant editing as always.

Katie - My heartfelt gratitude for reading my words, unearthing my Britishisms (and sometimes learning a thing or two along the way), and for your friendship. It means everything to me.

Jacqueline - Whoa. Four typos. I truly thought there'd be a raft in this book because of how much I struggled. If the last few months hadn't been so awful, I might consider shifting to a new process LOL. Thank you, as always, for your keen eyes and endless support, and the coffee house meetups.

To my ARC readers. You guys are amazing! You're my

final eyes and ears before my baby is released into the world and I appreciate each and every one of you for giving up your time to read.

And last but most certainly not least, to you, the readers. Thank you for being on this journey with me and taking a chance on a new series. I'm damned lucky to do this for a job, but without you, I wouldn't be able to. I hope you carry on and devour the rest of the Kingcaid series. There is plenty more to come.

If you have any time to spare, I'd be ever so grateful if you'd leave a short review on Amazon, Goodreads, or Bookbub. Reviews not only help readers discover new books, but they also help authors reach new readers. You'd be doing a massive favor for this wonderful bookish community we're all a part of.

About the Author

Tracie Delaney is a Kindle Unlimited All Star author of more than twenty-five contemporary romance novels which she writes from her office in the freezing cold North West of England. The office used to be a garage, but she needed somewhere quiet to write and so she stole it from her poor, long-suffering husband who is still in mourning that he's been driven out to the shed!

An avid reader for as long as she can remember, Tracie was also a bit of a tomboy back in the day and used to climb trees with her trusty Enid Blyton's and read for hours, returning home when it was almost dark with a numb bottom and more than a few splinters!

Tracie's books have a common theme of women who show that true strength comes in all forms, and alpha males who put up a great fight (which they ultimately lose!)

At night she likes to curl up on the sofa with her two Westies, Murphy & Cooper, and binge-watch shows on Netflix. There may be wine involved.

Visit her website for contact information and more www.authortraciedelaney.com

Printed in Great Britain
by Amazon

34765548R00233